Clare Curzon began writing in the 1960s and has published about forty novels under a variety of pseudonyms. She studied French and Psychology at King's College, London, and much of her work is concerned with the dynamics within closely-knit communities. A grandmother to seven, in her free time she also enjoys painting. *Body of a Woman* is the ninth book in the series set in the Thames Valley area.

BODY OF A WOMAN

Called to investigate the death of a young woman found dumped in woodland, Superintendant Mike Yeadings and his Thames Valley CID team find the body in exotic evening dress, her face covered by a feathered, bird-featured mask. Yeadings realises he had once briefly encountered her, in quite normal circumstances. This was Leila, the dutiful if undervalued wife of Professor Aidan Knightley; owner of a little gift shop in a quiet Buckinghamshire town; devoted to her two teenage step-children; on good terms with her neighbours. The circumstances of her death seem totally alien to all who knew her.

Books by Clare Curzon
Published by The House of Ulverscroft:

THE FACE IN THE STONE '
THE BLUE-EYED BOY
DEATH PRONE
COLD HANDS

CLARE CURZON

BODY OF A WOMAN

Complete and Unabridged

ULVERSCROFT
Leicester

First published in Great Britain in 2002 by
Allison & Busby Limited
London

First Large Print Edition
published 2004
by arrangement with
Allison & Busby Limited
London

British Library CIP Data

Curzon, Clare
    Body of a woman.—Large print ed.—
Ulverscroft large print series: mystery
1. Yeadings, Mike (Fictitious character)—Fiction
2. Poice—England—Thames Valley—Fiction
3. Detective and mystery stories
4. Large type books
I. Title
823.9'14 [F]

ISBN 1–84395–344–7

Published by
F. A. Thorpe (Publishing)
Anstey, Leicestershire

Set by Words & Graphics Ltd.
Anstey, Leicestershire
Printed and bound in Great Britain by
T. J. International Ltd., Padstow, Cornwall

This book is printed on acid-free paper

The Body

1

Friday, 2 July

'Beautiful,' he whispered, watching himself slit-eyed in the tilted cheval glass. With one long forefinger he traced the wingspan of an eyebrow, then followed down the line of his nose from bridge to chiselled nostril. He knew whose features his own copied. She had been beautiful too. Before the accident.

He moaned and his image lurched at a surrealist angle, foreshortened, kneecaps enormous, chalky face elongated and planed like a Lucian Freud nude's.

The woman, face uppermost, curved limply over his splayed thighs. The pair of them made a pietà in white marble. Her eyes were shut now. He must have overdone it, but he couldn't remember how. Or quite when.

He'd left her for only a moment, bound. Bound to be bound — he smiled — because she was a wild thing, spitting like a llama at the zoo. So he'd taped her mouth, like her wrists, with the sticky-backed plastic used for sealing parcels.

When he got back, so few minutes later,

the gag was torn off. She was different, older somehow. He wasn't even sure it was the same doll. Her unpinned hair seemed longer. He saw now it was tinted with henna. How could she have changed so much while he was gone for the stuff; more for himself and something for her. But she'd no longer need it; not like this.

He passed one hand over his eyes. Time was treacherous. Days passed in a moment, or were lost entirely. Things could happen twice over, making you think time had stopped and you were in a forever-now. Or in a dream dreaming you were waking from a dream, but instead you went on asleep dreaming you were waking, over and over again.

He leaned across, shifting his feet so that one thigh was accommodated by the hollow above her buttocks; the other nudging in between her scapulae. Admiring in the mirror his fine, long-fingered hands, he touched one pointed breast. There was no response.

She was no use this way, beautiful but spoiled. He frowned, peering closer. Her face — it seemed there were two faces, one (from memory) hovering like a transparency over this other which he did not care to stare at long. The wide rictus was an animal snarl, the purple tongue extruded. Her eyes — dear

4

God! He closed them with his hand.

Anger roared through him like a fireball. That she should make herself so hideous! It was indecent. Cover her, cover her quickly. He groped about his feet for the dress, forced it over her head, laid her on the carpet to pull her arms through the fine shoulder straps.

He peered at her again. Suspicion hardened in him that there had been two dolls, one now and another some time ago. This was the false one. He was flooded with fury.

She did not deserve that lovely hair. It was wasted on her. He wound its ends around his left wrist. The kitchen knife he'd used to free her ankles slashed close against the scalp as he sheared. Bright blood like little scarlet beads sprang from her flesh but she made no protest. He did not want her.

If she comes again, he told himself, I shall know her that way. She cannot pretend then to be the other one. Chloë's hair will be loose about her shoulders. This one's, the imposter's, I shall keep. She must come begging for it back.

He had to conceal that face. Her party mask had fallen between the legs of the mirror stand. He crouched to reach through and met his own face aggressively thrust at him. Retrieving the mask, he bunched his other fist and beat at the glass. Shards fell tinkling from the frame and were silenced in the thick carpet.

It didn't hurt at first. He had fitted the bird-mask over her shaggy skull before he was aware of the ripped flesh on his knuckles. From its black frame of cock's tail-feathers the cruel beak curved towards him as his own blood spurted. He whimpered.

'*Plus becquetez d'oiseaulx que dez à couldre!*' The words sang in his ears. That was François Villon's 'Ballade for the Hanged.' He closed his eyes to savour the sweet decadence and saw a body suspended from a gibbet. The birds' tearing beaks were pecking and pocking the dead flesh like any half-coconut hanging from a string in the garden.

First-year Uni French Lit returning to give him the shakes. But this black raven here was incapable of pecking. And people weren't hanged any more, whatever their crimes.

A burst of loud voices and party music signalled a door opening somewhere deep inside the house. There was a shout of wild laughter. A girl squealed with glee. People coming this way. He heard steps in the passage outside.

He couldn't be found like this. Nursing the hurt hand against his chest, he nudged the body aside with one foot, thrust the curtains apart and swung himself over the windowsill,

6

dropping sixteen feet to the shrubbery below. A twiggy bush rasped painfully against his quivering flesh.

Cowering, he recalled that he was naked.

2

Nan Yeadings stood back by the theatre's closed entrance, distancing herself from the boisterous hallooing at taxis. The crowd began to disperse with a slamming of car doors. Couples broke away, walking off into the scented summer night, silently linked or babbling enthusiasm. One of the older men she'd glimpsed in the crush bar wobbled across and peered into her face. 'Coma longa us,' he invited. 'Cram in together, eh? Much more fun.'

'Thank you,' she said, 'but my husband's fetching the car.'

Owlishly the man considered this, slowly shook his head and staggered off as Mike drew up at the kerbside and leaned across to open her door.

'I think I was just propositioned,' she claimed happily, belting herself in.

'M'm. The streetlighting's not too good just here.'

'Thanks, but I refuse to be deflated. It was a great play and it's a lovely night. Just see that wonderful velvet sky.'

He looked admiringly across at her still

8

sparkling with excitement from the final curtain, at the uplifted chin, the bright eyes and hint of a smile. 'You're lovely too. That was a cheap crack of mine.' He leaned across and kissed her lightly on the cheek.

They stayed silent as he steered free of the dispersing crowd, threading through Windsor's narrow streets under the Castle's humped shadow. She had lowered her window and was drinking in the night air as they headed for the motorway.

'I love being out in the dark,' she said suddenly. 'Everything comes so vibrantly alive. I feel a kid again. There's a thrill in all those lighted windows reaching out from the blackness. I can imagine the hundreds and thousands of unknown people behind them, all busy with their secret lives.'

Well, she was right there, about secret lives. Not that he was so enchanted himself by those unknown thousands. It was part of his ever-present problem: penetrating too many of those same secrets, worming out the truth about unpalatable activities. In the best of all possible worlds, which Nan would dearly love to believe in, there would be no need for his job.

Not that his steady, pragmatic Nan permanently wore rose-coloured spectacles. No one who'd been a casualty nurse and theatre sister at the old Westminster Hospital kept her illusions long. He remembered from his years as a young copper in the Met the sort of scenes she'd faced in A&E on a Friday night, threatened with flick knives and broken bottles by crazed junkies desperate for a fix. Nor had dealing with the shattered bodies of IRA bomb victims been a petalled path.

At present her life provided what she claimed she most wanted, with a husband, children and a home to run. Yet he doubted it could really be enough for anyone so vital — the restraints of dull domesticity plus the demands of a riotous toddler and an older Downs' Syndrome daughter. His Nan fitted the role so well that he was accustomed to seeing her that way. It took an evening such as this to remind him she was so much more than an efficient home-maker.

Nan didn't often expose her inner emotions. It was perhaps the play that made her put so much into words, having agonised for almost three hours over the intimate problems of invented characters, taking them on as her own, as was the way with women.

The Rover took the next motorway exit and almost instantly they were in real country, their headlights slicing through avenues of arching trees, picking out a single golden group of beeches leaning to the road, and the tiny rounded shapes of rabbits bunking off to the safety of long grass. Nan was sitting forward, drinking it all in like a child.

'We must do this more often,' he offered. He reached forward to the radio and smooch music filled the car, good old fifties stuff from before the world got so cynical; a remake of Nat King Cole.

'We really were kids then,' he allowed.

'Mike, we were barely born!' A gurgling laugh escaped her.

'They try to tell me I'm too young,' he crooned. Then the song changed to 'Some Enchanted Evening' which he'd nostalgically hoarded in vinyl. It recalled sad memories finally chased away by their finding one another. For a brief moment they were separate again, each knowing the other vulnerable.

Home soon, Yeadings thought. Drive the child-minder back; a drop of The Macallan for nightcap, a look-in on Sally and Luke, then bed, with Nan warmly yielding in his arms. Not perhaps a showbiz Enchanted Evening, but certainly the satisfactory end of a tender and comfortable one. He was a very lucky man.

Then, just short of Shotters Wood, blue lights flickered ahead. 'An accident?' Nan queried as they cruised close.

'That's Mott's Saab.' Yeadings passed to draw up beside a marked police car. A constable shone a flashlight towards them.

'I must ask you to move on, sir. There's been — oh sorry, Mr Yeadings. I didn't see you. DI Mott's attending, sir. There's room to park further down.'

'I'd better show my face,' Mike told Nan, pulling in on the opposite verge. 'The constable's a chatty sort and Angus might wonder if we breezed past. I'll take a quick look and be straight back. Do you mind waiting?'

So much for his aroused romantic feelings, he thought wryly, fetching his wellies from the car boot and stuffing in his trouser legs. There was starlight enough to follow the blue and white plastic tape that marked out a path to the incident.

It was, as he'd guessed, a body.

No more than fifty yards in among the trees he came upon it. Little effort had been made to conceal it under the edge of a scratchy hawthorn. The dry earth had been roughly hollowed out by hand and a thin layer of leaf mould scattered around.

'Just passing by,' Yeadings greeted his DI who looked at him curiously, standing up to make room.

He took Mott's proffered flashlight and hunkered alongside. At first sight his breath escaped in an audible whoosh. He had half expected an old vagrant worn out from a hard life on the road and gut rot from meths. But this was bizarre; at the other extreme.

The body lay curled on one side in the shallow dip, knees to chin, with the neck twisted to make it seem to gaze skyward. Except that there was no face.

Instead he met the head of a huge bird of prey. Behind the cruelly curved beak eagle features glittered with black sequins, surrounded by a sable burst of cock's tailfeathers.

From its clothes the body appeared to be female, but Yeadings wouldn't assume as much. The extravagantly exotic outfit posed a question, and at one point where the long feathers were crushed he glimpsed dark hair razored close, almost non-existent, with skin showing through bone-white in patches.

He lifted aside a thorny branch to get a clearer view and observed dried blood beading the scalp where the blade used had left savage gashes. Never a haircut of the victim's choosing.

This mutilation reminded him of ritual punishment to women traitors after World War II. Such hair as showed seemed almost black, but with the metallic red glint of henna.

The bloody gouging suggested the victim had struggled against being sheared. Had this resistance pushed the attacker further, into killing? Or was death intended in any case to follow the mutilation? Murder in a frenzy of retaliation, or cold-blooded sadism? And was there a sex angle here?

'What have we got?' Yeadings asked his DI.

Mott straightened. 'No ID. No handbag found so far, and I haven't uncovered the face because I know Littlejohn would want to see her untouched in situ. He's on his way.

'Duty police surgeon has come and gone. He just confirmed death and took preliminary readings of rectal and air temperatures. Minimal interference with limbs or clothing. Got instantly called off to an RTA on the M4. Gave no hint of cause or time of death, but he did admit she hadn't started to stiffen.'

She, Yeadings noted: something the medic wouldn't have missed. It eliminated his most dreaded kind of case. All violence affected him despite the many years he'd had to view its outcome, but self-destruction through sexual experiment plagued him with an extra sense of tragic futility. Seekers after the ultimate in sensation were the sorriest of

14

human kind, creating a terrible legacy for those surviving.

But this was no cross-dresser who'd chased orgasm too far and been dumped in panic by his fellows. It was a woman able to enrage another human being into taking her life. Or else, in the classic phrase, one who was simply in the wrong place at the wrong time. In this case he felt there must surely be more to it than that.

He looked for the marks of ligatures. They were present in abrasions on the crossed, bare ankles. Her wrists, hidden by the way she lay tucked half under the bush, were pulled back behind her, possibly still bound.

He rose to his feet, returned the flashlight to Mott and thrust his hands back in his jacket pockets. He had no wish to uncover the face obscured by the feathers and spangles. He had already seen too much, risking his own traces being left on the murder scene. Best leave the body to Mott and the sterile-suited SOCO team in their white paper overalls.

Yeadings moved back beside his DI. 'Who found the body?'

'Two boys cycling through the wood. Larking about after escaping from their bedroom windows. It scared them stiff and they shot off home. One was caught climbing back in and he spilled the beans. His father came out to check and then rang in. He claims they're both in shock.

'Two patrolmen from Area took a look. Fifteen minutes later Dr Lamont and myself; so the ground's already trodden.'

This was nothing new. Yeadings nodded. 'I want a lid kept on all description of the scene. Warn everyone concerned. Simply 'the body of a woman has been found in Shotters Wood. The death is thought to be recent.' See to it yourself that the boys and their contacts stay stumm about the rest. Also warn whoever they've already talked to. I've a gut feeling this one is going to prove a stinker.'

He stared back towards the hidden face, again resisting the impulse to uncover it, then nodded to his DI. 'You don't need me here. My regards to Littlejohn when he turns up. He'll be ringing me with time of the post mortem. I know tomorrow's Saturday, but my guess is he'll want to get on to it straight away.

'Meanwhile see that SOCO get all they can from approach routes before they start in on the close stuff. The soil's very dried out round here, but they might get something from it.'

Keeping again to the route which Mott had had marked out with police tapes, he returned to where the strobing blue lights had attracted a little knot of residents dog-walking or out for a late-night stroll.

He let himself out under the plastic tape and nodded to the uniformed sergeant on guard there. 'Is the site secured from the far end?'

'Yessir. I sent two constables round there with flashlights. They're setting up bollards.'

'And the children who found the body?'

'At home, sir. Your DI's got their addresses.'

'Right. We can leave them to him and a WPC. Goodnight then.'

He stood a moment in the dark before approaching his own car, intent on fixing the murder scene in his mind.

There had been three known visits to the site before the police presence: a pity, but some trace of who placed the body there might yet remain. He considered the body itself, extravagantly clothed and lying barely hidden, as though asleep except that the arms were restrained behind and the neck unnaturally twisted to make her seem gazing up through the feathered eye-slits.

Despite evidence of duress the precise cause of death wasn't immediately obvious. That was often par for the course in the initial stage of a murder investigation, but the rest was unreal — fantastically theatrical, with a Gothic, Hammer Horror mark of evil.

The woman's long evening gown had been of clinging chiffon printed with lurid swirls of purple and poison green overshot with a sort of spider's web design in silver thread. Surely no ordinary, off-the-peg label.

Returning now in even more vivid detail as he concentrated with closed eyes, was the bizarre bird-face covering the human one: an elaborate sequin-spangled confection of black papier maché with cut-out eyeholes and wide-swept wings fashioned from the shiny, black tail-feathers of a cockerel.

The mask was uniquely striking. And he recognised it. He heard again a whisper of bamboo chimes as the door opened and he stepped into the little gift shop in Mardham village about three weeks back. He saw the black, sharp-beaked, feathered mask displayed with others strung against the bull's-eye glass of the door. The shop was called PARTY FUN.

Tonight the carnival bird-face had been worn by a woman going out exquisitely dressed for a very sophisticated occasion. Of all the party junk in that little village shop she had selected the most eye-catching. If she'd intended making an impact, he'd accept she'd done that.

Now she was grotesque, her hair savagely shorn like a traitor's. Then her killer had replaced the bird-mask over the dead human face and dumped her contemptuously in a public place, to be discovered by children or any sniffing dog let loose in the woodland.

What kind of perverted mind would do that?

And what kind of life would be uncovered once they started digging into the dead woman's past? A sensation-seeker certainly; not short of money; possibly a drug user? That last would be for Littlejohn to discover when he performed the post mortem.

Despite the warm midsummer evening Yeadings shivered, turned up the collar of his dinner jacket and stomped back to his car. He didn't trouble to remove his wellies as he rejoined Nan. Tightlipped he put the car in gear and steered off the grass verge.

'A bad one?' she assumed.

He nodded. Any magic that the evening had had was gone. Tomorrow could be unpleasant.

3

Shaving next morning, Yeadings froze half-lathered and stared at his own reflection. For a moment his nose, protruding from downy foam, had seemed beak-like under the dark brows and slitted eyes. Momentarily, he saw himself as a bird of prey.

The connection was automatic, bypassing last night's incident and cueing an instant replay of that June Saturday morning when, on a sudden impulse, he'd seized a way out of a personal dilemma. He had braked and drawn into the kerb as he drove home through Mardham.

The little gift shop had an olde worlde frontage, with PARTY FUN scrawled in loopy script over the fascia. In the bulging bay window bobbed heart-shaped silver balloons with cartoon-face stickers and brightly coloured messages: 'It's a Boy!', 'Happy Eighteenth', 'Welcome Home Darling'.

As he opened the door a hanging mobile set off a set of bamboo chimes. Inside, quivering against the glass panes, were strung clusters of fantastic masks, spangled, sequinned and feathered; some exquisite, some comic, others malevolently scowling; all ghosts of a Venetian Carnival.

Immediately ahead he saw enticing trays of hand-made chocolates displayed in a chilled, triple-shelved glass cabinet.

Mike Yeadings had gazed down the shop's narrow interior, his mind far from partying, having — for the second time within a fortnight — slept in his suit and shaved roughly in his office. It had been a night of sporadic emergencies involving an armed man holed up with two women hostages in a housing estate. Not until dawn had the man thrown his shotgun from an upstairs window and allowed the women to run out.

With that little excitement over, what the superintendent pursued now was no dangerous criminal but a suitable gift to sweeten his delayed arrival home. Something rather special because last night's kerfuffle had made him fail young Sally, whose birthday it had been.

There were no 'Sorry I Stood You Up' balloons, much less any with excuses for the policeman's lot. There was a rich choice of furry toy animals; covens of plastic witches and trolls; Batman, fairies', ballerinas' and wizards' costumes; crystal balls; dangling spiders; hovering bats; comic hats; strings of tinsel and wads of glitzy gift wrapping; also acres of greeting cards to cover every imaginable occasion except his present one. None would guarantee delight on the morning after he'd missed a special daughter's birthday party.

Yesterday there had been balloons and gifts enough at home, including his own offering presented solo by Nan. Now had dawned the morning of the juvenile hangover. Not that Sally was spoilt and demanding, but she had asked for a conjuror and he had rashly agreed to stand in as the magician's apprentice. Moreover he had promised to be there. By now he should certainly have known better.

He made a solemn circuit of the shop, aware of the two women assistants keeping a surveillant eye on his progress (non-progress so far as inspiration went) while the younger, winding a blonde curl round one finger, continued to consider aloud the romantic potential of someone called Josh despite the other's warning glances.

Beside himself, the only other customer on this early Saturday morning was a dumpy middle-aged woman muttering over the greetings cards.

'They're all so sloppy,' she confided as he passed her. 'The verses inside.'

Yeadings paused, an eyebrow raised warily.

'What would you like them to say?'

The woman shrugged. 'Well, it's for my 'usband's birthday.' Then she let out an eldritch cackle. 'Cor, they'd never dare print what I reely wish 'im.' And, so cheered, she seized on a florid garden scene, matched it to its envelope and waddled off to pay.

Arriving back at the entrance Yeadings made up his mind as promptly. Luxury chocolates were a dietetic no-no in his household, but could flatter a little girl in ankle socks. No harm in just a dozen specially selected and wrapped in one of those gilt boxes tied in blue streamers and with a little silk rosebud tucked in. The cost would, of course, be exorbitant.

The darker-haired of the two assistants opened the glass cabinet with ritual reverence, covered one hand with a latex glove and fastidiously lifted out each chocolate as he made his selection. Yeadings left the shop with the casket inside a dinky carrier bag proclaiming (untimely in his case) PARTY FUN in elegant gilt script.

★　★　★

From the landing window Nan Yeadings had glimpsed her husband's return. 'Daddy's back!' she called, watching him slither

23

shamefacedly out of the car. Despite a perfect June morning his face as he walked up the path showed left-out-in-the-rain dejection.

Their eyes locked through the glass and he grimaced in mock penitence. Not entirely an act, she thought: Mike took his fathering earnestly, assuming it rather later in life than most. On occasions when police children met, their two gravitated towards the youngsters of junior ranks. Mike's own team were short on offspring, both DI Mott and Sergeant Rosemary Zyczynski being single, and DS Beaumont's quirky teenage son already facing serious school exams with hopes of an eventual career in medicine.

Nan kissed her husband at the front door. 'Sally is making you a special breakfast,' she warned him.

'Cremated toast and soggy cereal.'

'That could well be, but not intentionally.'

'Good. My absence wasn't intentional either.'

'Actually we discussed that last night. You'll find you're already forgiven.'

Again their eyes met and she almost giggled, bringing on his rueful grin. He shed his jacket.

'Where's my birthday girl then?' he shouted joyfully, and Sally promptly appeared in the kitchen doorway, her puppyish Down's

Syndrome features earnestly puckered over the task in hand. Her voice was cheerful enough. 'Daddy, I'm making your breakfast!'

He bent to kiss her. Case dismissed; he was grateful for the acquittal.

★ ★ ★

Now, weeks later, he grinned at his reflection, completed the lathering and cut the first swathe through with his safety razor. There was nothing like the finish of the old-fashioned method, he considered, rubbing a hand over the smooth surface produced. He even kept an old cut-throat for special occasions.

Littlejohn's assistant rang through while he was still at breakfast. The post mortem was set for 10.30am.

'On a Saturday,' Nan grumbled. 'He must be keen.'

'It suits me. Ample time to see the team beforehand. I'd like to get it over.'

'You're attending, yourself?' She didn't sound surprised, having wormed some of the story out of him before bed last night. 'It's that mask, isn't it? You feel it involves you.'

'I guess so. I should have mentioned to Angus last night that I'd seen it before. The truth is it gave me a bit of a . . . ' He shrugged. 'I'd better arrange with him now to meet up beforehand.'

★　★　★

Entering his office the Superintendent nodded to his two sergeants. Beaumont was leaning forward in his seat with a star-pupil intensity, or perhaps more like a terrier poised to leap for the flung bone. Rosemary Zyczynski smiled, casually brushing an invisible speck from her tan linen skirt.

'I'll be attending the pm with Angus,' Yeadings informed them, 'and since the body's female, I think we'll have Z along.'

'Sir,' she acknowledged, gratified.

'I'd not mind a look-see,' Beaumont put in quickly, unwilling to miss out.

Yeadings considered. Everything of importance would have been recorded by the SOCO photographer on site. Shots of the body would show detail, but there was still the obscured face. Beaumont was as entitled as anyone to see it revealed in the flesh. He was getting pretty uptight these days about even-pegging his woman rival, and competition would keep him on his toes.

'All four of us then, with the coroner's officer,' Yeadings allowed, his face sardonic as he noted that, appropriately, they would make quite a little party themselves. It was fortunate that Prof Littlejohn thrived on pulling an audience.

'Any new Misper reported locally?' Yeadings enquired of his DI as they walked to the lab.

'Nothing as yet, sir. She looked to be heading for a really wild night out. Likely its survivors won't be stirring yet, let alone sobered up enough to count heads and find her missing.'

Survivors, Yeadings considered. Like himself Mott had assumed she was bound for some mega-rave. Recall of her outlandish appearance struck him as even more bizarre by the light of day. She'd dressed for a decidedly exotic brand of nightlife. So where could such have been provided?

Obviously at some distance from where she was found, because no one would choose to dump a corpse in their own back yard.

But if the body was discovered without noticeable rigor in Shotters Wood at 11.28pm, she'd not had time to deck herself out and travel far. Bizarre parties of the kind he suspected were unlikely to get going much before midnight. Maybe these 'survivors' — ravers, musicians, smack merchants, whatever — would at most have noticed that she hadn't turned up. Which meant they'd be in the clear, with nothing more to survive as yet than the usual after-effects of alcohol and amphetamines.

So, in mentioning fellow revellers, was Mott already considering collusion in a ritual killing? Even black magic — an arcane satanic ceremony requiring a sacrificial victim? Certainly the corpse's masking brought to mind some kind of Comus rout. But in that case the ceremonies would surely have been more protracted and the corpse not released until dawn.

⋆   ⋆   ⋆

Professor Littlejohn was prompt on the job. When the team arrived they found the body naked under a partly turned-back sheet, toe-tagged and spotlit, ready waiting. Either refrigeration had been minimal or thawing had been started early.

Yeadings had a word with the pathologist as he stood shaking talc into his latex gloves to ease them over his bony fingers. Then he went over to where the merciless lights shone brightest. The team's other three shuffled aside, making room for him to stare down on the dead face.

That should have been his first sight of it, but, even distorted by a hideous death and shorn of its dark, hennaed hair, it was one that, with sudden shock, Yeadings realised he knew.

He couldn't put a name to her, but he had watched her, alive, for several minutes; spoken with her. She wasn't any chance customer of PARTY FUN but the older saleswoman there. She was the dark-haired one who had served him, fastidiously, with Sally's chocolates; was possibly the shop's manager.

He moved the sheet to expose the hands. Any jewellery had been removed and bagged, together with the clothing, but on the left-hand fourth finger a paler indentation showed where she had previously worn a ring. Somewhere there could be a husband who had woken up a widower this morning.

Yeadings stared at the scratched black enamel on the fingernails. He remembered the earlier butterscotch shade glinting through the translucent gloves as the manicured hands lifted each chocolate singly and nestled it into tissue paper in the little gilt casket. Now the slender wrists were rubbed almost raw by the chafing of bonds.

It shook him, the pathos of it. Alive she had seemed so elegantly in charge: a breathing, likeable person reduced now to the official police description — 'the body of a woman'.

He turned to Mott. 'Have we a name yet?'

Apparently they hadn't. He let Littlejohn drone out her physical particulars into the mike clipped on his rubber apron: 'Body, female, between twenty-five and thirty-two years of age; height five feet six inches; weight one hundred and thirty-three pounds; well-nourished but slender; in apparent good health — apart, as DS Beaumont might say, from being dead.'

Perhaps the killer had done well to replace the mask because, whatever else Littlejohn was to find, she had died from garrotting with a sharp ligature. The features were cyanosed and distorted, eyes staring, purple tongue obscenely extended. Petechiae present on the scalp were barely distinguishable from scars caused by the shearing.

In places the cord or wire used had cut into her flesh, marking it like a finely strung necklace of unmatched garnets. The ligature had been removed after death, then the bird-mask added. Or replaced.

Nothing resembling the murder instrument had yet been discovered in the locality of Shotters Wood.

★ ★ ★

'Are you sure, sir?' Mott ventured to ask when Yeadings later explained where he'd encountered the dead woman. 'If you only saw her the once? I mean, there was a lot of facial distortion.'

'I remember her all right. It was at the shop that sold the mask. There was that small black mole high on the left cheekbone. She'd darkened it with mascara to look like an eighteenth century beauty spot. It added a certain piquancy.'

He recalled how she had paused at one point in the wrapping as if she might start up a conversation, then quickly glanced sideways at the younger woman and thought better of it. It might have been some small help to him now if she'd actually opened up. At least he'd have a shred more knowledge of the person she was.

Accustomed to taking quick stock of strangers, he'd put her down as normally a reserved woman, educated and conventional, perhaps a little lacking in self-assertiveness but meticulous within her own sphere of activity; quite beautiful in a smooth-featured way, yet not trading on the fact.

With Yeadings apparently lost in reverie, Mott avoided Beaumont's meaningful stare. So what, if the Boss had picked up on such details in a single brief sighting on a drive home through Mardham? He was famously observant.

All the same — when a sobersides like Mike Yeadings got to close-studying racy women . . .

Zyczinski read through a list of the dead woman's clothing, comparing it with what she could see of the plastic bags' contents. 'No shoes then?'

Mott nodded. 'Bare feet when found. And nothing of the sort has turned up yet. Uniform are doing a daylight search of the wood now. Someone transported her there, so let's hope the shoes are eventually found where they shouldn't be, to give us a connection.'

'Without a description how shall we know they're hers?' Z grumbled.

'Feminine intuition?' Beaumont suggested snidely. 'Can't you match them to the rest of her gear?'

'Only roughly. You'd hardly expect galoshes or trainers. But then, under a full-length skirt she might have preferred comfort to high fashion. I know a violinist who wears fur-lined boots under her evening dress. Chilly places, concert platforms.'

'What about it, Boss?' Beaumont pursued. 'You're the one who knew the dead woman.'

Yeadings considered this. 'Saw her once,'

he corrected. 'So — given the fancy dress and her earlier appearance — my money would be on fashionable high heels and a collection of straps. But bear in mind what Z says. From the state of her soles we know she didn't walk the woods barefoot, but she just might have gone there prepared for the terrain. So keep an open mind.'

Now the team were aware of him moving off; apparently he'd seen enough. Was he letting the dead woman get to him? His face gave nothing away.

'Rather touching, innit?' Beaumont said in a hoarse stage whisper. 'Reminds me of that ancient film with Celia Johnson: Brief One over the Counter, or sommat.'

'The shop should give us a name for her,' Z said coolly. Of late she'd a convenient way of not hearing Beaumont's questionable wit. 'The assistants will know who she is.'

'Was,' Beaumont corrected her woodenly. He was back in Pinocchio mode, puppet-faced policeman, totally impersonal.

'You go,' Mott ordered him. 'Slope off now and get her particulars.' He knew that Littlejohn's sharp ears could pick up their asides. Anything jokey over the mortuary slab had to be of the pathologist's own sardonic honing.

Littlejohn looked up now, electric saw in

hand. 'Splendid idea,' he said lightly. 'Get me a Saturday *Telegraph* while you're at it, there's a good lad. And have them put it in a carrier bag for you, otherwise all the supplementary bits drop out.'

He swung the magnifying spotlight closer over the chest aperture.

'Which brings me — if you others are quite ready for it — to the innards.'

The Woman

4

Yeadings might not know her name, but she had known his. He was widely remembered in Mardham because of the murder inquiry two years before when briefly the dozy little Buckinghamshire town hit page one of the tabloid press. The invasive police presence had been at the same time vaguely unnerving and yet a reassurance. She had been reminded of a nature film where a school of sharks swam with silent menace through a shivering mesh of smaller fish: immediate danger suspended but the threat ever present.

By sight the main four members of CID had become familiar to her, three continually darting into crevices after titbits while their chief finned blandly around soaking up the atmosphere. She had watched him one morning gazing wide-eyed, into the pastry cook's window, savouring the smell of fresh-baked bread like any hungry schoolboy; and again leaning chummily with the old codgers on the river wall, wreathed in a communal blue haze as they puffed out pipe smoke against the midges. He had seemed the sort of big, slow-smiling man you could too easily find yourself opening up to.

The morning he had appeared in the shop he was still driving the same green Rover and had parked it by the kerb to come in for chocolates. Briefly she'd wondered who the lucky lady they were intended for was, but mainly, while she made up his order, she had questioned whether she dared speak to him of a personal worry which nagged at her.

★　★　★

What decided her against it was Rita's being present, with her sharp ears and her even sharper taste for fabricating scandal out of nothing. And perhaps not exactly nothing in this case.

But anyway the opportunity was lost because the instant he had paid for the chocolates her customer was off. Later that was something Leila would regret.

She stayed on at the shop a further half-hour until Maggie arrived to relieve her. That was a drawback in running a small-town business, this reliance on part-timers for staff. Housewives were dependable up to a point but their families came first; which meant she was never entirely free herself. As well as retaining a financial interest and keeping the books, she was obliged to stand in as dogsbody to cover gaps caused by ailments, music lessons and the dentists' appointments of other women's children. Which stung her the more because she was childless herself.

She was fond of her teenage stepson and stepdaughter. In a curiously detached way they, she believed, returned their own, but inadequate, kind of fondness. There was a time when she had hoped that the arrival of a baby would bring new warmth and closeness to weld them all into a real family; but in that she'd failed, never becoming pregnant despite various efforts at medical intervention.

It hadn't seemed to trouble Aidan. But then why should it? He had proved himself twice over, had already done with breeding and moved on to alternative interests almost totally scientific and academic, leaving her shamed as infertile and deficient. It didn't help one's self-esteem.

Within her husband's professional circle she sensed herself regarded as a social accoutrement and little else, hardly a person in her own right and certainly an intellectual lightweight: almost like something inadvertently picked up on a shoe.

Once, she sadly thought, I counted: I had a future, if not precisely mapped out, at least roughly sketched. Studying for a degree in Modern History, barely eighteen years old and inexperienced, she had happened on the very campus where Aidan was the indisputable Big Shot currently in demand by the scholastic press and already making guest appearances on TV's scientific programmes.

She was flattered to have gained his notice. They had danced together twice at the Freshers' Ball, and a week later, passing in the quad, he had impulsively stopped in his tracks, his black gown billowing heroically in the wind, and asked her out to dinner.

There had been student gossip about him but she had taken it with quite a deal of salt. Apart from following his open lectures she had never encountered him in action, not being in the Faculty of Science. She quickly picked up that Arts undergraduates were by implication inferiors, and she accepted what seemed the common devaluation, seeing herself in every way many rungs down, while he, made of finer stuff, breathed a more rarefied air.

She was young and untried. He delighted in her coltish beauty, in watching her opening perception, her ready enthusiasms, even sometimes her unforeseeable reactions. He felt it incumbent on him to seduce her, which he did with a deal of practised skill and an unaccustomed persistence.

Halfway through her second year, when he was drinking overmuch, being between books and tetchily impatient for fresh inspiration, he uneasily discovered that he had actually proposed marriage and been happily accepted.

Scarcely four months earlier Marjorie, his longtime ailing wife, had departed this life taking with her his sole irrefutable excuse for withdrawal from entanglements. Partly through the mischief of colleagues, but mainly from the romantic imagination of genuinely interested onlookers, it became accepted that a wedding was planned for the Easter vacation. With preparations increasingly made on their behalf, he had found it more onerous to block than to accept the apparently inevitable.

So, on April 8, just over nine years back, Professor and Mrs Aidan Knightley had shaken the confetti out of their new, matching suitcases in an Athens hotel. They settled to conduct their honeymoon, in the sticky atmosphere of an unseasonal heatwave, while attending the International Conference of Physical Chemists and Allied Scientists.

Sex as a single girl, Leila then discovered, had been better.

＊　＊　＊

The Saturday morning of Yeadings' appearance, once Maggie had shown up, Leila retrieved her car from the shop's rear courtyard and made posthaste homewards. Today was to be another of Aidan's public occasions, so her place at his side was obligatory. Uncomfortably so, she knew in advance, because again she'd prove quite hopeless at sustaining his high level of discourse and would be passed on as intellectually inadequate to new acquaintances who would fail to find common ground. Finally she would be relegated to the dolly-bird role by any greybeards inclined to take the easy line of sexual badinage and unsuitably adolescent innuendo.

At home she found Aidan ready dressed and huffing with impatience. He was wearing a light summer suit in a milky tea shade, with beneath it a figured satin waistcoat which she considered utterly naff. Instead, either the waistcoat with open neck and shirtsleeves — quite mod — or the suit over a conservative cream shirt and plain silk tie: but never the mix.

It was his decision however and, equally stubborn, she let him wait while she took time over dressing.

She wasn't totally downcast about the engagement. It was a glorious day and, however daunting the company, there was a lot to be said for lunch at Carlton House Terrace and drinking Pimms or champagne in the Royal Society's upper salon overlooking the Mall. This was the second year they were to be grandstand guests as the Queen reviewed her Guards at Trooping the Colour. Aidan clearly saw the invitation as the prelude to his being proposed as an RS Fellow himself. His upward move from a provincial university to the new London appointment must surely serve towards that ambition.

They travelled up by chauffeured limousine, Aidan preferring the expense of hiring, rather than losing face searching for parking space on such a grand occasion. Dropped at the door, they entered the lofty hall, aquarium-cool and shady after brilliant sunshine. There was a babble of striving voices; perhaps more querulous than in the year before? Certainly the gathering by the stairs appeared to have aged by at least a decade since then.

Leila looked towards Aidan for a lead. He stood wirily erect, chest expanded, making the most of his five feet five inches, his ginger goatee outthrust (and clashing badly, she thought, with the rosy pattern of the deplorable waistcoat.)

He was waiting for recognition and acclaim. He could wait a long time here: everyone was so full of him- or herself, all volubly chattering while nobody listened. 'Shall we go up?' Leila suggested.

He began to acknowledge acquaintances. There were congratulations on the new appointment and compliments on his most recent publication. Leila listened for the tone rather than the words, wise enough by now to pick up on professional jealousies and false good wishes. Some faces were familiar through photographs in scientific journals or television appearances. One or two of the older Fellows smiled at her vaguely, remembering introductions last year. There were a number of desiccated ladies with authoritative voices but few younger men and those Aidan seemed not to know.

Across the terrace she recognized a bushy, dark moustache and caught Lord Winston's eye. Kindly and charming as ever, he smiled, too discreet to let it show they were professionally known to each other. Not presuming on his successes in human fertility and gene research, he would leave it to his subjects to approach if they wished.

Leila turned aside as a long flute of champagne was pushed into her hand. From far away she heard a brass band strike up a military march but few craned at the windows to watch. Upper branches from the Mall's trees had been clipped for the occasion but still provided a hefty screen.

Unseen from Leila's viewpoint, Queen Elizabeth distantly alighted from an open carriage at Horse Guards and took her stand on the parade ground's dais.

'She's wearing bright yellow,' shouted an elderly woman farther along who was using field glasses. She was one of the few who took much interest in the ceremony, or even in personal appearance. Not a smart lot, the Royal Society ladies. But then, with brains who needed fashion? Style without content was more the politicians' line, Leila supposed.

Aidan was deep in conversation with their host, a geophysicist at Imperial College, and between them the technical terms were rolling like the credits for a Spielberg film. Leila felt herself an alien among this assembly of the country's best, or most recognized, scientific brains.

'Mrs Knightley,' breathed a voice above her head. She recalled the man's name: Sir Arthur Waites, a wizened bean-pole with a few sparse hairs grown long to smear across his pale, bald peak in the vain hope of deception; but which any shaming breeze would float like filmy seaweed about his face. Last year he had been kind to her, so she owed him an effort.

Someone had told her that his wife, badly injured a year back in a car crash, was in a permanent vegetative state. Probably wiser in that case not to ask after her. She let him steer her by the elbow to an open window where there was a view of the military ritual.

Down on Horse Guards Parade the mass movement of red tunics and bulky black bearskins froze into stillness. On foot two solitaries advanced on each other with swords drawn, saluted, remained motionless, then retreated to their former positions. From one flank a group of riders approached centre front, jingling and jogging, with standards flying, dark uniforms bobbing under rather more merciful hats — busbies, weren't they? She imagined they were Hussars but, viewed from so far away, they remained faceless toy soldiers.

By any standard the horses were magnificent. They performed some elaborate wheeling motion and presented a new pattern. Except for when the standards passed, the Queen had remained seated. In earlier times she would have saluted them from on horseback, gracefully seated side-saddle. This year she was dressed as a civilian but the Press had announced that as a Colonel-in-Chief, Princess Anne would be mounted astride.

Meaningless to Leila, the troops' geometric combinations and permutations would continue for half an hour yet. While sections circled and wove, the sun bore down on serried, unmoving lines where only fear of their RSM's blistering threats kept the sweltering ranks from dropping with heat-stroke.

'I suppose,' she suggested to the maths-man beside her, 'that you admire all this geometric precision.'

'Not really,' he admitted, sipping slowly at his Bollinger. 'My principal interest is in the chaos theory. I get high on cause and effect.'

She looked again at Waites. Perhaps he was more interesting than she'd assumed. He had been talking Oceanology with a stout woman to Leila's left and without actually eavesdropping she'd picked up an intriguing term foreign to her.

'What is an algorithm?' she asked suddenly. 'Logarithms I've a vague memory of from school. So is algorithm just a mathematician's joke anagram of the same?'

Waites came suddenly alive. 'It might well be. You'd have to ask the Ancient Greeks.' He considered for a moment. 'To give you the broad definition, it's a procedure to solve a well-defined problem in a routine manner. We use it to deal with equations; perform calculations and construct geometrical figures; sort our data.'

He was becoming quite pink with enthusiasm, waving his empty champagne flute perilously close to her hat brim. 'To take a simple example: when a computer arranges a list — of, say, your party guests — into alphabetical order, that is performed by an algorithmic procedure of moving upwards initial letters according to pre-imposed pattern; then the second letters in the same way; and so on through each word until the required order is achieved.

'Euclid himself contrived a mathematical algorithm to find the highest common factor, or divisor. Take for instance the numbers 35 and 150. Divide the greater by the smaller and the remainder is 10. Now divide the original 35 by that remainder and the new remainder is 5. Next divide your 10 by that 5 and the remainder is nought. Arriving at zero remainder proves that both original numbers are divisible by the last number you have reached. And that, being the first to obtain zero, is the greatest.'

'Which was 5,' she said faintly, accepting

but still not seeing why. She had always imagined a parallel between mathematics and religion: that reasoning in either was beyond her. Which left only a choice of blind faith or disbelief.

He was beaming at her delightedly through thick lenses which made his eyes into huge, dark beetles, his wire-rimmed spectacles askew on the beaky nose.

Well, she had brought that on herself. To escape sinking further out of her depth, she glanced past him, seemed to recognise an acquaintance and gave a little social wave. 'It was lovely meeting you again,' she lied, smiled and moved on.

'Gorgeous hat,' intervened an old goat breathing brandy fumes over her. She kept her gaze ahead, content in the knowledge that a wide brim ensured a certain degree of privacy. Few dared plunge under to kiss since the exercise required some co-operation from the wearer.

Perhaps the best part was the luncheon itself, although she sat in a group of Aidan's choosing. Happily the vein of high-flown technicalities appeared to have dried up, but their pettish talk was mainly of research underfunding, grumbles at the government and (from the more elderly) unpleasant details of ill health.

Leila refused the offer of liqueurs with the coffee, hoping that Aidan might do the same, but he was set on going the whole hog, by now flushed and self-important. Not that there and then it would be noticeably unique.

Returning from the ladies' room she found him alone, strutting about the hall, waving his mobile phone and loudly complaining that he'd sent for the car ten minutes back and the bloody chauffeur hadn't turned up. When he did, Aidan gave him the Ozymandias brush-off.

'God,' he said, leaning back against the cushions, 'what a lot of boring old farts they are. I'll be glad to get home.'

Not more, Leila thought, than she would. There was plenty to do there; at least six tea chests remained to be unpacked from the old house, and family guests were expected tomorrow for lunch.

5

Leila's Uncle Charles was a big man in several ways, but wherever he was invited and took along his middle-aged mistress, he invariably introduced her as his housekeeper. Leila, feminist rebel over this if nothing else, had once questioned what she considered a slight. Janey, subject of the disagreement, was forthright about it. 'Housekeep is what I do. Wife I'm not. And what we get up to in the bedroom is between him and me.'

She was a totally honest woman, or as near as dammit. She had a flat, rectangular face, with a straight nose and high, straight brows set precisely at right angles to it. The parchment-pale flesh over her cheeks fitted tightly to the bony infrastructure so that her lips often drew apart, making her look slightly aghast; which she never was. Her manner was always calmly pragmatic, and Leila was very fond of her.

They arrived for lunch half an hour early which irritated Aidan although, knowing Charles, he should have expected it. 'Tell me what I can do to help,' Janey offered.

'Sit down, relax and stop fussing, woman,'

Charles growled. 'Where are your kids, Aidan? Backpacking to Taiwan or prostrate over exams?'

'Edward's in the States, fixing himself up with some research into Artificial Intelligence. Chloe's staying with her grandmother in Nice.'

If Aidan had hoped to dazzle the older man he was disappointed.

'So Eddie's into robotics, eh? Great future in that. Especially in astronavigation. Gone to Houston, I suppose.'

Leila darted him a glance. His response was too instant and informed. She guessed Eddie had been writing to Charles. Which could indicate he was short of money again. (And Charles not even a blood relative, although both children preferred to ignore that shortcoming.)

'We thought you might like to look over the house,' she suggested, 'while I finish getting lunch.'

Charles sat on over his drink, digging himself out for the guided tour with Aidan just minutes before the hot meal was ready for serving.

'And the wicked old thing knows exactly what he's doing,' Janey remarked confidently, sitting on the kitchen table and swinging her legs like a teenager. 'As in Alice, 'He only

52

does it to annoy / Because he knows it teases.'
I do think you've got yourself a lovely house
here, Leila.'

'It will be, I think, but there's a lot to be
done. I'm glad Aidan decided against living in
London. I just hope the commuting doesn't
get him down.'

'A grand new job, a grand new house, with
both the kids growing up and away. This will
be a quite different lifestyle for you both. So
what are your plans?'

Leila straightened after transferring the
roast beef from cooker shelf to cork mat and
paused a moment, hands in oven gloves on
her hips. 'Do you know, Jancy, I've no idea.
Aidan will be pretty involved with the
university, of course.'

'Damn Aidan's plans; what about your
own? You must get yourself a life, Leila. It's
more than time.'

'Well, I have the shop. I'm really grateful to
Uncle Charles for setting me up with that.'

Janey grimaced. 'It wasn't what I'd hoped
he would pick on, but you know Charles: two
years ago the lease was up for grabs and
property hereabouts gets more valuable every
year. He felt it was too good to pass up. But
running a shop doesn't exactly stretch you,
does it?'

Leila smiled. 'It's a bit like that fully-stocked

doll's-house he gave me when I was ten.'

'And you should have been five. It wouldn't have happened if I'd been around then, my dear.'

Leila laughed. 'You certainly know how to work on him.'

'I don't manipulate, Leila. I simply tell him what I'd prefer. Like that dress account he opened for me. I really didn't need it, so once I'd explained he cancelled it and gave me carte blanche at the bookshop instead. Much more sensible. I'm sorry I can't take you for a new swish outfit again, but do let me have a list of what you fancy reading.'

By now Janey had slid off the table, seized some tongs and was arranging roast potatoes for her in a ceramic dish. 'These are crisped perfectly, Leila. Oh, I do enjoy eating what someone else has cooked.'

Leila reached out and hugged her. This plain-faced little woman dressed as a middle-aged flowerchild was one of the most comfortable people she knew.

At lunch Janey left the men to do the talking, only piping up during the dessert with a question to Leila about picking up her studies again. It had the effect of halting the others' conversation.

'I should hardly think she'd want to do that,' Aidan decided.

'She needn't do it at your college. Why not the Open University?'

'Yes,' Charles agreed wickedly. 'If she keeps it dark you won't lose face, old man. How about it, Leila? I was sorry you never went on to get your degree. Whatever happened to your early thirst for history?'

The truth was it had got crowded out. Her special fascination was with pre-colonial Africa, and she'd hoped to spend a few years out there in research. Aidan and marriage had put paid to that.

'Maybe it wasn't all that pressing,' she offered. 'I hadn't actually fixed my options for if I graduated.'

'Not if: when,' her uncle said staunchly.

'A piece of paper!' Aidan cried scornfully. 'One advantage of passing through the entire academic process is learning that degrees and diplomas aren't worth the paper they're printed on. But of course you must acquire them to dare point out the fact.'

As Janey mumbled into her plate Leila thought she caught ' . . . pissing from a great height.'

When they had consigned the china and cutlery to the dishwasher the two women rejoined the men who had decided on a local stroll. 'We'll see what your new neighbourhood's like,' said Charles benignly.

'Beech woods and farmland in that direction,' Aidan offered at the foot of the drive, squire-like and waving a fancy walking-stick. 'The village is over to your right. Though village or town, we haven't quite decided yet. Anyway there are shops and dwellings, pubs and churches, bus and train stations. That sort of thing. Leila tells me there's even a Tuesday market.'

By common consent they turned left where the road began to twist and narrow, descending between over-arching beech trees.

'Deer? You really get wild deer?' Janey cried in delight, pointing to the roadside warning.

Leila nodded. 'Now and again. They don't gallop about as the sign shows. A lone one will just stalk across the road, very dignified and snooty. That's why motorists need to cut speed. Let's go through that gate and strike off into the woods, then we can work back in a circle.'

The roundabout route took a good hour and a half, including a twenty-minute lounge on the sunbaked grass of a large clearing. Then they climbed steeply between silver birches and oaks to a wicket gate in a barbed wire fence. Beyond it were signs of a community presence. An asphalt path, shaded to one side by an avenue of tall lime trees, opened on the other to a sports field where a cricket match was in progress.

'Bless my soul!' declared Charles as a fielder came streaking towards their boundary, hands cupped for a catch. 'Surely that's a . . .'

'A woman,' Janey completed. 'They've picked a mixed team. I wonder how well she bats.'

'We'll never know. According to the scoreboard this is the second side in.'

They strolled around two sides of the field to bring them close to a tiny pavilion. About twenty relatives and friends were sprawled in deck chairs or on the grass to cheer on what were clearly scratch teams kitted out in a wide variety of whites. On folding tables among the spectators were scattered the remains of a picnic lunch.

The scoreboard, a clumsy, wheeled affair with slots for figured cards was being managed by a plump girl rising on tiptoes to record the runs. 'Nineteen required to win,' she shouted and the little crowd ad libbed with cheers or groans.

'Theess,' said a tall, rangy young man in a battered panama, carefully placing tongue between teeth to achieve the unnatural Anglo-Saxon double consonant, 'ees a crehzy ghem.'

Leila smiled at him. He had a long, droll,

sad-clown face with a hint of crescent-moon to the profile. When he was older, she imagined, nose-tip and chin would grow closer, with the wide, loopy grin trapped in between. A humorous Mr Punch with an Inspector Clouseau accent, almost too Gallic to be true.

He rolled his eyes at the newcomers, waving an arm towards the field. 'Can sohmwohn explehn to me pleess ow it works? I think per'aps there are some roools about the weather. But today it as not rhenned and so the ghem goes on forever.'

'It just feels like that, Pascal,' said the plump girl briskly, and as a shout went up from the field, 'Oh Lord, was that a four or a six?'

Flat-bellied, in baggy cream flannels of ancient vintage stopping two inches short of his ankles, and topped by an immaculate white silk shirt, the Frenchman must surely be dressed for play. 'How many did you make?' Leila enquired of him.

'Do not ask. I just 'it at the ball when I see eet and I nearly knock out the uhmpire.'

'He got forty-seven,' said the plump girl kindly. 'He went in as number five and he may have saved their day.'

But he hadn't. As they watched, his team's score rose bravely by singles and a couple of fours until with a howl from the watchers the heroic schoolboy batsman was run out.

Their last man stomped in. He must have been eighty but he squared his shoulders, hit out low and took a single, leaving the other batsman to lose the match with an easy catch to square leg.

'So who is playing?' Charles demanded amid the applause and cheerful commiserations.

'Acrefield Way,' said the plump girl. 'We have this match every year in June, and a return one in September. One side of the road plays the other; the odds against the evens.'

'And which has won?'

'We did,' she said, total partisan. 'Evens, of course.'

Stumps were being drawn as batsmen and fielders came streaming back to surround them.

Charles was grinning as he poked Aidan in the ribs. 'Go on, admit to everyone that Acrefield's where you live. Next year we'll see you out there with your pads strapped on, showing what a Blue can do.'

'You know I detest all sports,' Aidan muttered. 'And anyway our house has a name, not a number.'

'You really are — ' the plump girl asked, 'the new folks at Knollhurst?'

'Yes,' Leila admitted happily. 'And now we

can meet our neighbours.'

'Wohnderfoool,' said Pascal, savouring the word. 'You leeve on the sehm side of the road as myself. Welcohm to the loozairs.'

They were toasted with flat lager, plied with leftover sausage rolls and the offer of sandwiches drily curling under the scorching sun.

'A true village community,' boomed Charles, enjoying Aidan's embarrassment at being surrounded by locals he'd had every intention of staying aloof from.

'Look, we have to get back. I've things to do,' Aidan reminded Leila tetchily.

Charles beamed back at him. 'If you must. I think I'll stay on for a bit; circulate and get to meet folks, don't y'know. So thanks for a great lunch, and we'll pick you both up Tuesday at eleven on the dot. Best bibs and tuckers, eh? Cheerio then.'

'Tuesday,' Leila agreed, kissed them both warmly and followed in her husband's wake. Tuesday would be fun. Tuesday meant the thrill of Ascot, and forecasts promised that the good weather would continue unbroken.

⋆   ⋆   ⋆

'Swish' was what the fashion-blind Janey had called the expensive suit. Three years old now, it was still Leila's favourite, folded away

60

in tissue paper between the rare special occasions when she graced it. And now, with the invitation to Ascot, already she'd be wearing it twice in four days.

Its pale shade was the same 'apricot creme' that filled the hand-made Belgian chocolates at the shop. The jacket was long and beneath it the short, floaty skirt's handkerchief points drew attention to slim legs and delicate matching sandals.

The fine straw hat, however, was new this year, wide-brimmed and translucent. A classic: nothing idiotic or eye-catching.

Anyway it was Janey who would turn heads, with her strange assembly of charity shop cast-offs. One sure bet was that she and her outfit would later feature in some glossy colour magazine, falsely attributed to one of the famous wayout designers.

Owning one leg of a horse that was running in the three o'clock, Charles was persona grata in the saddling enclosure, chatting almost knowledgeably with jockey and trainer. Although the syndicate's newest member he was the only one present that day. The chestnut gelding, satin-coated and inclined to prance, was drawn number four.

'It won't win,' Charles forecast breezily, 'but we should back it as encouragement. Good lad, that jockey. He'll give it what it takes. Meanwhile let's get back to our box for some strawberries and bubbly.'

On the way they encountered a knot of Charles's City friends, then the crowd opened as the royal party came through.

'Ello,' said a voice above Leila's hat and she looked up to recognize Pascal of the cricket field. Today, elegance personified, he was escorting two exquisite young women, one on each arm. He detached them and reached for Leila's hand.

'Oh, hello. We were admiring my uncle's horse. Number four,' she gabbled, for some reason feeling shy at the encounter.

'Then we mohst certainly back eet.'

'No, I didn't mean that.' She felt her face flushing, caught at a loss among these sophisticates. Now they would imagine Charles owned the whole horse.

'Yoor ohncle?'

'Yes, he — ' She looked around, discovered his party had moved on and that she was stranded alone. 'Look, I'm so sorry. I have to catch them up.'

His eyes were laughing at her. 'We shall meet again.'

'I hope so.' Now why did she say that? A smile would have sufficed. She nodded to the women, turned and fled.

The rest of the day was enthralling.

Quincunx, their number 4, appropriately came in fourth, to Charles's great delight.

'Why Quincunx?' she asked him as their car slowed, manoeuvring through the home-going throng. 'What does it mean?'

'It's a pattern,' he explained. 'Five dots: four arranged in a square with one at the centre. Like a five in dice or dominoes. But he's called that because he was by White Domino out of Queen Mab. Quin for queen: sort of pun, d'you see?'

'He should have drawn number 5 then,' Janey suggested airily. 'Maybe the 4 confused him.'

'If he's that numerate,' Charles said damningly, 'he'd've likely seen fit to come in fifth. As it is, I'm well pleased for a start.'

But Pascal won't be, Leila thought. I wonder how much he lost? Why on earth did I allow him to bet on Charles's latest fad?

6

Two days later Leila was expecting a grocery delivery, but when she opened the back door it was to Pascal nonchalantly leaning there, a bone-china teacup held out like a begging bowl. 'I do not recall,' he said, his brow furrowed, 'eef eet ees flour or sugar I am supposed to run short of. These British social nuances are a leetle difficult to pick ohp.'

She found herself responding to the laughter dancing in his eyes.

'According to the TV commercials you're hoping to share my instant coffee. Anyway, do come in.'

She was aware of Hetty Chadwick's vigorous vacuuming upstairs suddenly hushed and suspected that the twice-weekly cleaner was leaning over the banisters to listen. It was unfortunate that he had chosen one of her days to call, but at least his arrival offered Leila the chance to apologise for her gauche retreat at Ascot.

He heard her out and nodded. 'I could forgeeve your horry on one condition,' he told her sombrely. 'Eef you will please accept a spare ticket for Wimbledohn next week,

Friday on Centre Court. I know it ees ard on the neck, but the strawberry cream teas mehk up for eet.'

She couldn't accept, of course. One spare ticket meant that he didn't pretend to invite Aidan too. 'Why me?' she asked. 'I'm sure you have lots of friends who would love to take you up on it.'

'But I wish to know you better, Leila. I may call you that, I ope? We could share my big ohmbrella when it rehns.'

'It's going to be fine and sunny all next week.'

'But Wimbledohn, sooner or lehter, eet alwehs rehns.'

'It's a very kind offer, but I really don't know. There's still so much to be done here, unpacking. Come through and see what a mess we're in.'

He followed her into the drawing-room from which open patio doors led to the large conservatory and a panorama of half-emptied crates. A trestle table held several trays piled with china, linen and kitchen equipment.

'Isn't it grim? I didn't know we'd accumulated so much junk.'

Pascal surveyed the scene. 'You must ave been a collector from birth.'

'Most of it's from Aidan's old home. He was married before I came along. I've two stepchildren and they're pretty acquisitive too. But once they'd sorted their best stuff into their rooms they went off for the summer, leaving me to dispose of the rest.'

She knew she was talking too much because his presence challenged her: he so urbane, while she, the housewife, had never been anywhere, never made anything of her life. He didn't want to hear all this trivia. He'd think her a fool.

'Theess eez your stepdaughter weeth you?' He had picked the photograph off a side table and regarded it with interest. 'She could be your own. You are so alike, particularly since you ave changed your air colour since theess.'

Leila touched her head nervously. 'Mine's really dark brown. It was Chloe's suggestion I should try tinting it like hers. In this photo she was only eight; it was taken seven years ago and she's not so ginger now. Really dark red.'

'And you ave been married to the Professor ow long?'

'Just over nine years.'

Pascal smiled: a melon-slice of white teeth. 'The child bride.'

'I was a student,' she said shortly, remembering. Aidan, though she hadn't guessed it then, had an ongoing predilection for nubile eighteen-year-olds. But that was information she had no intention of sharing with this stranger.

Perhaps by accepting the chair at the University of London Aidan really would change and cut free from his current entanglement at Reading. It seemed a vain hope, but he had managed to imply something like that, without actually admitting he was still in the throes of an amorous adventure.

Not that amorous was quite the right word. Sexual, she supposed; love and romance being foreign to his nature. But in extramural sexual research the Professor was well qualified. It made her own situation the more hollow. She sometimes thought that if it hadn't been for Eddie and Chloe . . .

If. How bitterly ironic that she was reduced to a life of recurrent 'If Onlys'.

'Leila,' Pascal cooed. 'Cohm back. You are miles a-weh.'

'I'm sorry.' She waved towards the carrier's crates. 'There's such a lot to be done.'

'But by a week tomorrow all will be streht and you will be looking for an escape from duty. See, I will leave my card. Ring me at any time before then and say you accept. Oo knows, we may even see the admirable Mr 'enman in action.'

He gave her a jaunty salute with the empty

teacup. 'Coffee another time per'aps. I will see myself out.'

She knew she wouldn't take him up on the offer, because it wasn't the sort of thing she did. Quite outside one's wifely remit, she told herself.

But why not accept? There'd be no harm in it. God knows, Aidan was never slow in picking up on an invitation to something he fancied. And if anyone else had invited her she'd probably have accepted like a shot. So was it because of Pascal himself that she hesitated?

He was personable, amusingly eccentric, and she'd admit she found his easy familiarity attractive. Not handsome. Handsome men always left her rather uneasy. They had such an opinion of themselves, and since childhood she'd had this fear of being looked down on.

She went back to unwrapping and washing the surplus china.

So — Wimbledon. She would be glued to the television for the entire fortnight if she had the chance. But to be actually there, feeling the atmosphere, being a part of that involved crowd — that was something she'd never had the chance to aspire to.

So it was a great pity — she told herself as she tore tissue paper off a quite hideous dinner service — that she had to turn down the offer.

She had prepared a fricassé of chicken in a sauce of liquidised pineapple, red pepper and mango for dinner, but twenty minutes after Aidan was due back he rang in to say he was tied up with some finals students. They were panicking over a paper they'd already taken and wanted to conduct an inquest. It could go on quite late. If so he'd stay there overnight, be back tomorrow evening.

Leila stood with the phone cradled in her hands listening to the dialling tone purr after he'd rung off. She supposed there'd be a smidgen of truth in what he said. Probably one finals student, female, had gone weepy over the likelihood of getting a low grade. He'd find a way of consoling her. As he'd done to others before.

He knew she knew the truth, and still he handed out these fictions. So why hadn't she the courage to snarl, 'Tell me another!' and slam the phone down on him?

Would it come to that some day? Or if she let the years drag on without real protest could she believe that with age he'd finally come to his senses? But suppose someone special came on the scene, very attractive and more determined than most; he might want to move on permanently — or think that he did. Then where would she stand?

She'd be free to pick up where she'd left off her real life. But it might be too late by then to resume as a student. And with divorce it stood to reason she'd lose Eddie and Chloë, because his was the blood link with them.

She wasn't as daring as she'd once been. It would take courage to stand alone, stripped of the daily domesticity she'd used as her armour.

She'd become a coward by habit. She had to stop the process, make a decision, opt for something she wanted to do for itself. Dammit, for a start she'd accept Pascal's invitation to Wimbledon. It would be a gesture of defiance, and no harm to anyone in it.

It even seemed a kind of joke. While she felt the warm blood of rebellion coursing in her veins she would strike her midget blow for freedom. She propped Pascal's card against the phone and dialled his number.

★　★　★

Aidan was away for two days. Then he came back mid-morning on the Sunday in a bustle of organization, showered, changed, packed an overnight bag, collected his mail and read three messages off his answering machine.

'There's a lot of clearing up to be done before I'm finished there,' he said shortly, 'and I can't waste time or energy commuting.'

Leila served him a cold lunch and no warmer a reception. After an hour's nap on his study couch he left at 4.30pm.

He hadn't asked about the children. Out of sight they might be, but Leila was left feeling doubly responsible. There was that suspicion that Eddie had again been touching Uncle Charles for money.

And Chloë — where was she? Supposedly with Granny at Nice, but old Mrs Knightley's last letter had as ever been full of complaints that she never saw the children and none of the family had time for her. So Leila had rung her twice since then and discovered that the old lady's grumble was just the same. Clearly Chloë had never arrived, nor even informed Granny she intended to come.

Arthritis might reasonably have prevented her meeting her granddaughter at the airport, but Chloë had been insistent that Granny's hired chauffeur was to be there instead. The girl claimed to have arranged it all by phone. None of which could be true.

When Leila drove her to Heathrow for the flight Chloë had brusquely ordered her to drop her and go: such a hoohah with parking

71

there and anyway she loathed sloppy leavetakings.

Her phone call on arrival said that all was well, but it could have been made from anywhere. So far as Leila knew with hindsight, she might still be in England, or indeed anywhere within four hours' travel of Heathrow.

There were reasons for not having shared her unease with Aidan. If he cared at all he would blame Leila herself for Chloë's being out of control. And there would be terrible recriminations when the girl did return. Chloë wasn't a bad person, just wilful as fifteen-year-olds felt was their right.

The truth would be that she'd planned a more interesting alternative which she didn't care to share with her stepmother: some venture involving schoolfriends. Leila understood the bid for independence, hurtful though it was, and basically she trusted her. Aidan wouldn't.

And yet shouldn't she do something? Although what could be done without alarming Granny and causing Chloë awful embarrassment by raising a hue and cry? She wished there was someone she could share her concern with. She had missed the opportunity when Janey was here with Charles, just as earlier she'd bottled out of approaching that comfortable senior detective who came into the shop. Not that she'd expect anything of him but an outsider's suggestion of how she might discreetly trace Chloë.

Tomorrow, she decided, she would again ring her mother-in-law for a general chat. If she learned that Chloë had finally arrived there, all well and good. If not — she didn't know what she could do.

She still hadn't decided after making the call, during which Mrs Knightley senior had asked after Aidan and both children.

★ ★ ★

Pascal was to pick her up at twenty to twelve on the Friday of Wimbledon. They would have lunch en route: much better, he promised, than in one of those corporate hospitality tents at the All England Club. And it was superb, because he made a détour to Marlow and they ate at the Compleat Angler with the dazzling Thames streaming slowly past, festive with little boats and graced by swans.

Although curious she didn't enquire which company lunch he'd opted out of, and Pascal didn't inform her.

At Wimbledon the men's singles had

breathtaking moments, running to five deuces in the final game of the fifth set. Their seats were in shade until mid-afternoon when Pascal produced a tube of sun barrier cream and offered it for her bare arms. She was aware of him watching and smiling as she spread the cream on.

Their shared excitement as the match approached climax had created a new familiarity. 'Have I missed a bit?' she challenged him, and it seemed quite natural that he should take the tube from her and cover what he chose to see as bare patches.

Keen to stay watching play, they couldn't spare time for the celebrated Wimbledon tea. Instead they broke their journey home at a country pub where Leila refused anything to eat. 'My eyes have been devouring all day,' she protested. 'I have really enjoyed myself so much, Pascal. Thank you.'

She thanked him again as they stood at her front porch before she let herself into the darkened house. For a moment there had recurred that long-forgotten teenage uncertainty about asking him in. But he solved it for her.

Pascal simply took her face in both hands, bent and kissed her on the forehead. 'I've had a wonderful time too. Goodnight, Leila. Take care.' He left without looking back.

It was only as she undressed by the shower that it struck her how he had spoken. With an English Oxbridge voice. And without a hint of the Inspector Clouseau accent.

The following day, after she had worked a shift at the Mardham shop, and since there had been no message from Aidan about the weekend, she rang to invite Pascal to lunch. They spent the afternoon together, talking and lazing in hammocks in her garden. When Leila thought to listen for the way he spoke it seemed that sometimes he still sounded French. At others she couldn't be sure. Perhaps she was becoming more accustomed to his voice.

She learned that he had a serious side, loved classical music, had once studied art and exhibited in London and New York. His age made him only four years her senior, but there were decades of experience separating his life and hers.

It was on their third outing together that he drove her to Henley-on-Thames and they boarded a small cruiser to sail upriver. While she took over the helm he performed masterly moves in the galley, producing omelettes stuffed with creamed ham, and a dressed salad of mangetout, spring onions, olives, cucumber and mixed peppers.

When they'd moored she went below to

where he'd set the square table and opened wine from the miniature fridge. He'd known where everything was kept and hadn't hesitated over the basic cooking facilities. So if it wasn't his own boat, at least he'd had use of it before.

'There is no sweet,' he announced, carrying off the used dishes. 'Except you.'

He came back from the galley carrying two globes of cognac and sat beside her on the padded bench. 'To us,' he said, put down his glass and kissed her. Kissed her properly this time, deliberately, drawing away once to challenge her eyes.

'No,' she said weakly.

'Oh, but I think yes. You think so too, don't you? It is time you took a chance with me. I know you want to.'

They made love tenderly and exploratively, and talked until the sky darkened from primrose to purple. Then he let her steer the boat back to where they had found it, relocked the cabin and led her back to the car. When they neared home she knew she would be staying with him, whether there were lights in her own windows or not.

It was the first time she had seen where he lived. Unlike the trim little river craft the cottage was old and almost tumble-down, one of the two original flint and red brick labourer's dwellings from before the village was gentrified. Since it was built there had been infilling for the full stretch of the long lane, with a mixture of Victorian villas, thirties' semis and postwar detached four-bedroomed houses. Amongst them this pair of ancient cottages was as eccentric as Pascal's own appearance when they first met, with his battered panama hat and cream flannels stopping two inches above his ankles.

She found it endearing. Indoors she ran her hand along the uneven whitewashed brick, smiling as Pascal bent to avoid the beam before the narrow doorway and showed her the minuscule kitchen and bathroom beyond. Colourful daubs covered the living-room walls, some mounted and framed, others curling with heat and casually attached by blu-tack. Perhaps there was no electricity, because he lit an oil lamp, turned up the wick and said, 'Behind that curtain you'll find a crooked staircase. At the top is the bedroom.'

She held the lamp high and went up in front of him, stumbling a little at the steepness of the irregular wooden steps. She found the bed already turned down, and the linen was fresh. Pascal had put a bottle of chilled Sancerre and glasses to hand.

'You knew I would come,' she accused him.

'Of course. Welcome, Leila, to my country retreat.'

★ ★ ★

Next morning he showed her how to operate the shower from an overhead tank with a hand-held release chain. She dressed again in the pyjamas he had lent her, waiting in the sitting-room while Pascal fried bacon over the kitchen's wood-burning stove. The dream quality of the previous day continued. She had no thought for a possible awakening. As she finished towelling her hair there came a rattling outside and the sound of steps receding over flagstones.

'That will be the post,' Pascal called. 'Would you mind fetching it in?'

She found a handful of letters thrust into a horizontal drain-pipe fixed at waist height just outside the front door. It was junk mail mostly; also a wrapped newspaper; three business envelopes and one duke size, hand-written, with a foreign stamp.

Her heart lurched at sight of the writing. She must be mistaken, but there was that curious capital G for his surname Gregory. There was only one person she knew who slashed the letter through with that extravagant curlicue. And there below was her ornate capital B that began the county.

How on earth did Chloë come to know Pascal? And be writing to him from abroad?

Leila held up the envelope to the window's light to make out the postmark. The stamp was a Swiss one franked in Montreux.

And Chloë had done her vanishing trick almost two weeks back, on a supposed trip to southern France.

7

She should have remained there and faced him out. It was too late by the time she knew that.

So much had already happened in the last twenty-four hours, such an emotional upheaval in her drab life, forcing passion from her, shaking her concept of what she stood for, that she couldn't take in this new shock. It had struck alien into a warm experience of being awakened after coma. Her mind seemed to fall about inside like one of those equilibrist dolls which you push one way and it keeps swinging back at you. Totally overcome, like a hunted beast she had instinctively run for home.

All her misgivings now revolved about Chloë. At least the girl had been able to write and post that letter, so at least she was in control of her own actions. This was something to hold on to. But the connection with Pascal remained inexplicable.

Leila blamed herself bitterly that she'd allowed her fascination for him to smother her unease over Chloë. Since the last negative phone call to Mrs Knightley she'd taken no steps to discover where her stepdaughter might have gone. Now, in view of the letter, she was little wiser, except to know from which town and country Chloë had written. If the girl was bent on travelling through Europe she could well have moved on by now.

She'd had Chloë's letter in her hands and left it behind. Why? From scruples because it was addressed to Pascal? That was stupid. She should have hung on to it and insisted that he explain. Or concealed it, taken it away to open in private. Which could have given her time to think before she faced him over it.

And Pascal — surely a stranger — clearly more in the child's confidence than she was herself! Where did he stand in this? When she fled from his cottage he hadn't run after her.

So what had he thought when she suddenly vanished? He had been preoccupied in the kitchen, cooking breakfast, still talking to her through the open doorway. Eventually he would have come out to see why she didn't answer.

Then he'd have picked up the mail which she'd dropped. He'd have seen Chloë's writing on the envelope and surely he'd know she'd recognised it.

So now he would realise her shock, would

surely follow her here and offer some explanation.

She thought of the morning she'd found him on her doorstep with the empty teacup. It seemed months ago. Amused at his fake excuse, she'd invited him into her home, where he'd picked up the photograph. He'd remarked how alike they were, stepmother and stepdaughter.

All this time he had known Chloë and he hadn't let on. That was deliberate deceit. What need had there been to keep their association secret? The deception was scary.

As for herself, this — this tenderness she'd thought she felt for him, and his pretence of interest in her — she could see now he'd been playing her along for some ulterior reason. To what purpose? How would he expect to use her? Was he intimate enough with Chloë ever to confide to her that her father's wife had slept with him? Was that his intention? — to shame Leila in the child's eyes, widening the gulf between her parents?

Deliberate entrapment. That much was clear now. Even at their first meeting, out on the cricket field, he must have known who she was, and on some whim he'd set out to charm her. Why her? It hadn't been for her brains or beauty: she couldn't fool herself she was something special.

What she'd taken for interest — fondness even — was deliberate mischief-making. The reason had to be that she was Chloë's guardian. In some way he hoped to get at the child through her.

And Chloë only fifteen!

If Leila herself, supposedly adult, could be so easily hoodwinked, what chance against him had a schoolgirl with even less experience?

I have to keep a cool head, she warned herself. Whatever else, I've put myself in a position to be blackmailed. But I won't cover up for him. I'd rather it all came out and Aidan blew his top, than allow that fiend to get anywhere near my daughter. Anyway, why should I be afraid of what my husband thinks, with him the pathetic womaniser he is?

She went through to the kitchen and put her face under the cold tap, letting water dribble over her hair. Her underlying fear was that she was too late. Perhaps the Frenchman already had the child submissive to him. Chloë seduced? But if so he would surely have been abroad with her now. No, maybe she was sent on ahead and he would be joining her later. There might be a chance yet to keep them apart.

Certainly Chloë concealed secrets Leila had never suspected. It was vital she find out more. Perhaps upstairs Chloë had left behind a diary or an address book. There must surely be some way to get in touch and warn her off the man.

Normally scatterbrain with her belongings, the girl had taken some pride in her new room. It was twice the size of the one in Caversham and she had chosen the decoration herself. One wall was painted bright yellow, one dark blue and the other two terracotta. Leila had gone with her to choose the bedcover and curtains of wildly patterned indigo.

As a parent she had never invaded Chloë's privacy and it shamed her to be reduced to it, but as she cautiously went through her stepdaughter's clothes and papers she told herself it was for protection rather than invasive.

The room's tidiness seemed unnatural, although Leila knew the girl was almost obsessively meticulous when it came to her schoolwork. She'd be an academic perfectionist like her father, although still a scatty teenager.

The written exercises, stacked and tied in subject bundles, were stored on the floor of her wardrobe behind the four mirror-fronted sliding doors. There was no private correspondence there.

She wasn't on the internet but the work station for her word processor had been set up in the window's bay so that she could sun herself over her revision. Floppy disks, all neatly docketed, were boxed on a lower shelf. Leila helped herself to the one labelled Personal. A quick skim through revealed no more than girlish correspondence with her friends.

Chloë at only fifteen was bright enough to have tackled several GCSE subjects a year in advance, but these letters revealed a childish innocence only thinly masked by a pose of sophistication. Young and silly, her mild adventures would have been recounted with a superior smirk and read with giggles: childish opinions on adult eccentricities; the occasional snide poke at someone who'd briefly offended. But no passion; no angst; no real duplicity.

Finally Leila went through the drawers of the tallboy. Again nothing unexpected, except that the lowest drawer jammed as she shut it. The runners were slightly warped and she had to force it back in place. That was perhaps why the drawer contained only leftover Christmas wrappings, glitzy paper, gift tags and satin ribbons provided by Leila herself from PARTY FUN stock.

Slamming the drawer finally shut made the

whole piece shake. The triptych mirror on top wobbled, threatening to fall. She reached out instinctively to save it and her fingertips closed on a lump behind one edge of the frame.

She laid the mirror flat and peeled off the sticky tape which secured a small flat package wrapped in a white tissue. The contents yielded like granules of coffee sweetener.

She held her breath and gently eased off the tape seal. The tissue tore but she could always replace it. No, of course she'd never replace it; not if inside there was what she suspected.

In her hand lay a small plastic envelope containing white powder. One corner had been snipped off and a little eased out as she held it. Dear God, no!

Pointless to try it on her tongue. What should it taste of? Shouldn't taste of? And in any case she knew: she'd seen it so often on television, in films; little packages like this, and the knowing glance exchanged between investigating police. She knew the contents because she knew the cliché.

But what had this to do with Chloë? It made her present disappearance more alarming. Supposedly visiting her grandmother, she was deep into deceit, concealing her whereabouts from her family; perhaps planning her flight to Montreux with a grown-up lover. Or waiting there alone, and writing back to demand why he hadn't caught up with her?

It had to be Pascal she was involved with. And now this new discovery must surely mean that he was her supplier.

Everything had suddenly changed, yet again lurched into a Kafkaesque distortion. She saw now that searching she'd been looking for something different, proof that Chloë's link with the man was less serious; some innocent reason for her writing. It would have been disturbing enough because unsuspected, but hurtful on a personal level only because Leila herself had been attracted, and deceived, by him. She'd not have needed to see Chloë and herself in the same predicament.

Now that she knew for certain that the child was in moral danger she must search more thoroughly. She began again, desperately.

Nothing new in the drawers, which yielded only underclothes, with school uniform strictly segregated. The sliding doors of her wardrobe re-opened on to the same hanging garments; on the floor the same games gear and files of school notes, lacrosse and hockey sticks; a box with microscope and slides; shoes neatly lined up in pairs; stationery for personal correspondence and for printer.

Nothing. Leila sat back on her heels. If Chloë had anything relating to her secret life she would have taken it away with her. So what had she actually packed in her single suitcase? Which of her clothes were missing?

As Leila's hands brushed along them a hanger clattered and some filmy material cascaded down. She bent to pick it up and saw that at the top it was still attached to the hanger. A full-length evening dress.

She lifted it out. It was of semi-transparent silk chiffon and low cut, panelled on the bias. Weird purples, black and poison green merged into each other under a glittering tracery of silver thread. Quite fabulous.

She laid the dress on the bed and stared at it; imagined Chloë spellbound by its fantasy. And she had never spoken of it, kept to herself what must have been a very thrilling, personal gift, because no way would her pocket money ever have stretched to this.

Leila felt sick at how easily the girl had been bought: with drugs and a fabulous dress.

But she was a greater fool herself, when it took no more than a Centre Court ticket and a river trip to have her convinced that Pascal was in love with her! And herself with him. That had been enough to destroy a lifetime's belief in a wife's due loyalty. Something inside seemed to shrivel at the thought. 'God,' she moaned, 'what a pathetic fool!'

She heard the squeal of the garden gate. Someone was approaching the house by the front path. From behind the curtain she looked down and saw Pascal loping towards the front porch. So at last he had thought up some scheme of damage limitation.

She wasn't ready for him. He shouldn't find her here.

He rang three times with long pauses between. Even when his footfalls had died away she stayed crouched beside Chloë's bed, the fabric of the abominable dress crumpled in one fist. She let time pass before standing up, and found she had stiffened.

She straightened and took stock. One thing about the dress now puzzled her: that it was still here. That and the powder, whatever it was.

If Chloë had special plans for Montreux, why hadn't she taken these things with her? It was unaccountable, on a level with Pascal himself having stayed behind.

She had thought she knew her stepdaughter. Was it just possible that the extravagant gift of the dress had embarrassed her and she'd sense enough to see through the motive behind it? Handing it back might have been awkward, involving seeing the man again. The letter from abroad could be her way of explaining how she felt.

No, it was a wilful stretching of imagination to think that Chloë had repudiated him and that, rejected, he'd then meant to use her stepmother to regain access. And yet why else such deliberate pursuit? — and it had been deliberate, she saw now; from the first, with that self-guying, stage-Gallic role he'd played to catch her attention at the cricket match.

Holding the dress close Leila now became aware of its perfume. The whole wardrobe had smelled faintly of Chloë's favourite Je Reviens — one of Uncle Charles's unsuitable gifts last Christmas. The scent certainly didn't come off her laundered school uniform. It was this filmy material that had perfumed the rest.

Which suggested that Chloë had already worn it.

Now that Leila examined it more closely she found a drawn thread puckering the fabric of one slim shoulder strap. And the hem had been amateurishly turned up to make it two inches shorter. Not even hemmed, but secured at distances of four or five inches with stationery staples.

At some time Chloë must have gone out dressed in this seductive outfit and her parents had known nothing of it. Nor that she was experimenting with what could be cocaine.

There seemed no end to the disasters that threatened to submerge her. For a short while Leila's reason deserted her. In febrile shock she went round the house double-locking outer doors and closing windows, as if preparing for a high gale. She felt the house under siege, and herself gone to earth like a hunted beast.

Shaking, she fetched a decanter and a tumbler from the dining room and went back upstairs. In her own room she slid beneath the duvet. One outstretched arm encountered Aidan's folded pyjamas and she recoiled, dragged herself from the bed and fled to the ochre and terracotta stage-set of Chloë's room. Nothing, herself included, was normal any more. She was become part of the surreal.

There she closed Chloë's dark curtains and turned on the overhead light — at eleven o'clock on a bright summer morning. It was insane and she dimly acknowledged it. She shed all her clothes and slid between the cool sheets, poured brandy into the chattering glass, then lay shivering, despite a temperature already in the eighties.

★　★　★

It was the doorbell's shrilling that half-woke her. Still confused by the brandy she stumbled downstairs. The brain inside her skull felt swollen, pressing hotly behind her eyes. It beat at each step and her balance was uncertain. In the hall she clung to the newel post to steady herself, gasping as she bruised her naked breasts.

She was aware enough to seize a raincoat from the lobby and cover herself before opening the front door. It was then she recalled the danger: that Pascal could have come after her.

Someone she didn't know was standing there — a young man in shirtsleeves and chinos. He was trying not to notice her dishevelled appearance. 'What is it?' she demanded.

He had to explain twice over because she didn't grasp his connection with the library. Then it appeared that he worked there and he'd called here on his way home.

So it was evening now. And yes, she did remember him after all. He had been the serious one usually date-stamping or working at the computer keyboard.

It seemed the book was for her daughter. Chloë must have left it behind: one from her list for exam work. By mistake it had been put back on the shelves where a helpful browser had reported something of Chloë's inside. Then a librarian remembered a student laying it down to riffle through her tote bag. She could have gone off without it.

The young man hoped it wasn't too late to be helpful with her work. It must be the end of term soon.

'Yes, yes. Thank you.' It was too complicated to explain that Chloë was away, having been allowed, like other pupils, to slope off early once her own exams were over.

The young man wanted to linger and chat but she shut the door firmly on him and relocked it.

The book was a novel by Martin Amis. Leila hadn't known it was on the Eng Lit syllabus. If she left it in Chloë's room she would find it when she returned. Not that it was clear when that would be, or if at all.

Drowsily she went back and sat on the side of the bed, opening the book at the first page. She read a paragraph through and it made no sense. Well that was probably intentional. There were people who read Joyce's *Ulysses* for the fun of its obfuscation. Amis appeared rather the same, only simpler. *Time's Arrow*. Chloë might enjoy it. Not herself.

Reaching out to the bedside table she miscalculated and the book fell, exploding on its face. A square white envelope had detached itself from the pages.

This was what the young man had mentioned: something of Chloë's which another reader had found. The envelope, printed with the girl's name but no address, showed no sign of having been opened.

Until today Leila had respected her stepchildren's privacy. But no longer. Opening this was no more taboo than searching Chloë's room had been. She inserted a fingernail in the envelope and tore the flap back.

The deckle-edged card it contained was a formal invitation requesting the pleasure of the company of . . . Chloë's name was written in by hand, with the word 'over' after place and time.

On the reverse side the same script offered a personal message: 'A few very select friends look forward to meeting you. Come precisely at ten and you shall have what you asked for.'

Come where? Leila turned back to the card's die-stamped heading. Carnaval Masqué. The address was a house near Henley. The date two days ahead.

Whatever it meant Leila felt a cold shiver of premonition. On the surface the invitation was formal and proper, yet she was aware of menace in the wording. The written sentence was ambiguous, but for Chloë it must hold a specific message.

Would she have known who they were, these few very select friends eager to meet a young schoolgirl? And given a precise time at which to appear — like a servant or some kind of performer. And what was promised that she had asked for?

Had she really made some demand, or should the phrase be taken in the other sense, as a bully's threat that she would 'get what she'd been asking for'?

The envelope was unstamped, so delivered by hand. As the book had been just now. It could mean that the young man from the library was involved. She would see him and demand to know.

But no: anyone could have left that for her at the library, where her name and face would be familiar. If the young librarian hadn't brought it Chloë would have been handed it next time she went in. Which meant the sender had no idea Chloë was away and untraceable. Had she disappeared for just that reason, being afraid of what might happen? Scared for the results of some action of her own?

And where in this was the link with Pascal revealed by today's letter to him? 'Carnaval Masqué': because of the use of French, Leila felt this had to be more of his doing.

There was also the recurrence of Henley in

the address, close to where he had taken her yesterday! She mistrusted coincidence. She wished she had a clearer head, because it was up to her now to find out what these 'few special friends' expected of Chloë. She had been a weak fool to befuddle herself with drink.

Leila went through to the kitchen and poured a tumbler of water. It made her retch and she recalled she'd run out on breakfast and had only brandy since. She must force something down.

With a slice of wholemeal toast inside her she felt more normal. Thank God Chloë was away and hadn't received the invitation. It was up to her, Leila, to follow up the card, drive over to Henley while it was still daylight to hunt out the house where the masquerade was to be held.

Quickly she tidied both beds and dressed to go out, but as she opened the front door she saw Aidan's car turn into the driveway, blocking the way out for her own.

He'd said he'd be gone for two days, hadn't he? And that must have been three or four days ago. She seemed to have lost all account of time.

Whatever, he wasn't in the sweetest of tempers. As he passed her in the hall he stopped and stared suspiciously. He sniffed.

'You've been drinking. I hope you let someone else drive you home.'

It was easier to let him think she'd just come in. 'Of course,' she said, dumped her shoulder-bag and made again for the kitchen. The smell of toast there was less conspicuous than the brandy but she opened a window straight away. A few minutes later he followed her in and demanded, 'What's for dinner?'

'Breasts of lamb,' she invented quickly. It seemed to have almost Freudian aptness but her womanising husband missed it.

'You're earlier than I expected,' she told him, 'so they're not marinaded yet. We'll be eating at eight.'

He hardly seemed to hear what she said, and certainly hadn't picked up on her uncustomary sharpness. 'I'll be in the lounge,' he said shortly. 'You can bring me some coffee through.'

Drawing-room, she corrected him silently: you're in the wrong house. You aren't at your little bimbo's semi now.

It amazed her how strong her distaste for him had suddenly become, and what pleasure surged up from such petty rebellion. It seemed she had passed over an invisible line, and instead of the expected guilt at adultery it brought her a kind of angry release.

At least for that she could thank Pascal.

She wondered how far rebellion could take her; whether she would become like one of those vengeful wives who cut up their husbands' suits, poured away their vintage claret and slashed their car tyres. Perhaps, some day; but for the present there were more serious worries to occupy her. And in comparison Aidan's affaires seemed of little importance.

What most rankled was his utter inability to understand or help with whatever fix his young daughter had landed herself in. She could never even suggest to him that anything was amiss in Chloë's life. It would only send him berserk, raging at Leila herself.

She continued to play the distant housewife, allowing rancour to build silently inside throughout their meal, fortifying her. When the hall phone shrilled she was on her way to the kitchen with her hands full of dishes and all her tension flooded back.

He beat her to it, anxious to prevent her taking the call. His body language gave him away, hunched with his back towards where he guessed she must be standing. Then the loosening up, the turning to include her: 'It's Chloë; she's calling from Granny's.'

After a few meaningless words he handed the receiver across. 'Mum,' her stepdaughter greeted her, 'how're things? Is the heatwave still on? It's terrific here. I've been swimming in the sea with the boy from the apartment opposite, name of Roger but pronounced Ro-zhay; a bit of a prune actually.' She was talking fast to prevent her stepmother squeezing a word in.

Leila attempted to hold her voice steady. 'Hello, love. Yes, it's been baking. Someone dropped by to see you this evening. Remember that serious young man from the library? He brought a book you left behind there.'

There was silence at the far end of the line and she tried to picture the girl's face. 'He seemed disappointed you weren't here.'

'Yeah; think I know the one you mean. Rather sweet really. What book was it?'

'A Martin Amis. I didn't know you were into that gloomy stuff.'

'Nor did I. I guess he made it up for an excuse. Philip, I mean. If so, that's quite enterprising. For him, that is.'

Aidan was hanging about in the hall and it wasn't possible for Leila to probe what she needed to know. 'Could I have a word with Granny now?' she asked, falsely casual.

'Sure. She's right here. Wait a minute while she plugs her ear-thingy in.'

Leila's mother-in-law came on, gushing about how wonderful to have little Chloë turn up. They were going to visit all sorts of places together. And she would take really good care of her. They weren't to worry at all about her darling granddaughter.

'I'm sure you'll have a great time together,' Leila assured her, shaky with relief. 'Make her stay as long as you can.'

She chatted on about airy nothings and hung up after another fruitless little session with Chloë.

In the kitchen, preparing after-dinner coffee, she heard the phone ring again and Aidan rush to take his expected call. This silly affair of his didn't matter so much, now that Chloë was where she should be — safe, at least for the present. Perhaps Aidan could be persuaded to pay his mother a long-promised visit and act as a damper on Chloë's flitting again. But not bring her back until the mysterious business of the Henley invitation was sorted.

The girl's phone call had settled some doubts but raised a fresh suspicion. It had come too opportunely on Leila's intercepting her letter from Montreux. So had Pascal, realising what her running off signified, immediately rung Chloë in Montreux and advised her to beat it to Granny's fast? It would have taken her the best part of the day to get there and settle in.

That could be the reason Pascal hadn't come back here with excuses after his first fruitless call. He'd expected that whatever had been going on between himself and Chloë could now be swept under the carpet.

But then he didn't know what Leila had turned up during her search of Chloë's bedroom. Nor that she held the sinister-sounding invitation with the Henley address.

8

Aidan's return had stopped any chance of her getting out to Henley that evening. She must leave it until daylight tomorrow. He should be flitting off again then. She was aware of him rooting about for fresh clothes and furtively sliding a suitcase under the bed.

They'd had a chance to achieve separate sleeping arrangements in this new house. Leila had funked broaching the subject of twin beds, but her mind was made up now. In fact with so much more space there was no need even to share a room. However, for tonight anyway she would let it ride. She undressed in the bathroom and slid in beside him, turning her back and moving to the mattress edge.

Aidan, half-asleep, gave a deep sigh and promptly rolled back to take over the centre. Stiff with anger, Leila lay hunched, feeling herself all bones pressing into each other, imagined herself a skeleton; and when at last she fell fitfully asleep it was to enter a zombie-life of Halloween horrors.

★   ★   ★

Dawn brought a haze that promised further heat. It hung silvery-blue across distant trees and the sky shimmered with a dusty Saharan colour that must indicate pollution from the city.

Uncle Charles claimed that London air rose on a thermal, spread into a doughnut ring and produced fallout over the Home Counties. Which was his excuse for still living among all that traffic chaos instead of taking a peaceful country estate. Well, even he had tired of cities for the present and gone up to Scotland for a whiff of heather and malt. Hard luck on poor Janey, who said it was a country of cowpats, drizzle and gnats.

'I'm off then,' Aidan announced brusquely, clattering his cup into a saucer ringed with spilt coffee. It cut into her breakfast musings, signalling the moment for action.

And she was ready for it. Today, even stiff from her uncomfortable night, she felt strangely competent. As soon as Aidan's car had pulled away she filled a thermos flask with the rest of the coffee, collected sandwiches from the fridge, and fetched her own car round from the garage. Finally she rang her PARTY FUN assistant manager to ask her to open up.

The scale of the road atlas on the seat beside her, pressed open at page 22, was 3 miles to the inch; probably useless because she knew the route well enough as far as Henley-on-Thames and really needed an Ordnance Survey map from there. She drove by the way she'd been taken only two days before, tasting bile as she passed through Marlow, remembering how at lunch there she'd already been in thrall to the charmer Pascal.

In thrall: that was an archaic description. Weird, how it had come to her mind. Perhaps it was due to the country she had just passed through, historically soaked in occultism and sexual fantasy: the decadent Medmenham revels of the Dashwood coven and the almost Black Forest mysticism of the snaking valley sunk between tiers of densely packed conifers. It must be due to the shaken state of her mind that she felt at the same time menaced yet tempted beyond her normal limits.

Henley had a more wholesome air. The narrow streets with their tiny shops crammed with bright touristic kitsch; sun-drugged visitors spilling from crowded pavements into the roadway; ice cream cornets dripping in toddlers' hands; the scent of freshly roasted coffee beans wafted from open cafe doorways; and then the horizontal vista opening out to the steady-flowing Thames with white-painted boathouses, and scullers floating past in their fragile shells. It brought back normality, making her waver for a moment and question whether she'd been imagining non-existent dangers.

But the house she sought wasn't here. She parked at the far end of town where the small cruisers' moorings were and enquired about the address. No one seemed to have heard of it. Finally a shopkeeper thought it was out Stonor way so she drove back into town and and turned left away from the river.

It was a road she remembered from visits to Grays Court and Stonor as a girl, when the governess, inflicted on her by Uncle Charles as holiday guardian, took her to stay with her mother at Fawley. The two countrywomen were ardent admirers of stately homes, making pilgrimages to both houses two or three times each season. She could still feel the magic of walking under a ceiling of ornamental white cherry blossom at the one, and watching the proud-antlered stags at the other, with a tantalising glimpse of the Judas-deer's white rump flickering between distant trees to betray where the herd merged into tawny undergrowth.

The road rose quickly from the river valley, dipping and rising between rolling hills where for centuries the ruling classes had built their mini-palaces either on crests to dominate the panorama or in folded valleys, hoping to stay discreetly safe from the persecutions of their day.

Somewhere out here lived the party-giver who had sent that enigmatic message to young Chloë. Leila guessed he would have opted for a valley.

A network of narrow lanes led her in circles and figures of eight, passing and repassing the same landmarks before she espied a stony track through a shallow ford and, fifty yards farther on, saw a pair of old stone pillars with the name chiselled in. On one was the word Havelock and on the other House. By some irony of fate, ivy trailing from the gryphon-mounted finial obscured parts of the initial word so that at first she read it as Hav . . . oc . . .

There was a pair of tall wrought iron gates in quite good repair and painted a rusty black with gilt ornamentation of vine leaves and grape clusters. Through their intricacies she could make out a curving, macadamed drive. There appeared to be some kind of lake and the house wasn't far beyond because the trellised brickwork of its red Jacobean chimneys showed above mixed woodland planted to guarantee privacy. Leila counted the chimneypots and visualized a house of considerable size on a single building line.

Any additional wings could have been removed in a more frugal period to leave something the size of an average private hotel. Or perhaps a discreet country club. Certainly Havelock House hadn't featured on the list of stately homes open to the public when she was a child.

The recent fine weather had left no marks on the macadam drive, but the stony track that led to it was deeply rutted where cars had swung in at speed. So sometimes the gates were left open. If guests were expected for the Carnaval Masqué in two days' time that could well be the case again.

For the moment, however, there seemed no chance of penetrating further because the metallic box affixed to one pillar suggested electronic surveillance. Leila had no intention of advertising her interest. She put the car into gear and continued on her way to find a point for turning.

After a hundred yards or so the track broadened to become a made-up lane and subsequently met a recognisable road at a T-junction. A signpost pointing right offered High Wycombe; the left indicated Henley. There was no finger for the direction she'd come from. But certainly she was now on the recognised route to Havelock House and she'd arrived at it in reverse. If she came back in darkness it would be much easier to find from here.

And would she? she asked herself. Was it more than a hare-brained fancy to consider taking up the invitation to Chloë and finding out for herself what the girl had become involved in?

Engrossed in this question she rounded a sharp corner to face a large silver car speeding towards her on the crown of the road. She jerked the wheel wildly and braked. The Volvo spun and ended at a crazed angle on the grass verge, its front left wheel in some kind of ditch. Through the rearview mirror she watched the other car, a Mercedes, continue unchecked until braking to turn into the lane she'd come out of.

A few minutes earlier and she could have been caught spying on the house. That was alarming enough, but what really shook her was the glimpse she'd caught of the Mercedes' driver.

She didn't think he'd recognized her, being fully taken up with controlling his own speed. But she knew him. Less than three weeks back they had chatted together at the Royal Society lunch. He had seemed a reasonably friendly person, even if his appearance was a little eccentric.

Could he be bound for Havelock House?

That track led nowhere else apart from a network of other narrow lanes. What connection could the place have with Sir Arthur Waites, the celebrated mathematician who'd amusingly claimed that chaos was his obsession?

Could that wizened beanpole with his wispy hair actually live there? If so — it suddenly struck her — then it could be no accident that its name was partly obscured, reading as Havoc. Havoc was a good old mediæval word, and one of its meanings was chaos. Wouldn't that just suit the man's quirky humour?

There was no reason, she told herself driving home, why he shouldn't at some time have come across Chloë in Aidan's company. And then a follow-up invitation to his house, although unconventional, wouldn't necessarily be sinister. And the message promising to provide what she had asked for could have a quite innocent meaning — perhaps some mathematical shortcut that would help with her examination work?

Except that Aidan didn't take his daughter with him on his social rounds. There were few professional occasions when he thought fit to have even his wife tagging along. Besides — before she dismissed her earlier alarm as paranoia triggered by Pascal's duplicity

— what was a man of Waites's age doing setting up a rendezvous with a teenager at ten o'clock at night? How on earth would he have supposed she could get herself to it?

No, it just wasn't on. In her right mind Chloë would never have encouraged anyone like that, however much she might chuck her adolescent chest at a personable male of her own age.

In her right mind. The words echoed in Leila's head.

So suppose Chloë sometimes wasn't in her right mind. Suppose she'd become dependent on that white powder hidden at the back of her mirror.

Dear God, don't let that old monster be dealing the stuff to her!

There was only one way to be quite certain, and that was to accept the invitation in her place. With a domino mask and in the dress Chloë must have worn before, she might not be instantly recognisable. If the entire party was kept in period, maybe by candles or torchlight, she could perhaps pass as her stepdaughter.

It was a risk she had to take. She'd arrive early, say at nine, park the car at some distance and walk to the house through its surrounding woodland.

And if she was discovered? She would have

to appeal to Sir Arthur, always supposing he was present. And if not, then she could claim he'd sent her along by way of a joke: part of the chaos that gave him his highs. Havoc House after all.

Investigation

9

After Littlejohn's conducting of the post mortem, DI Mott and Rosemary Zyczynski joined their chief in Yeadings' office for coffee, having declined the less appealing offer of a brew-up at the morgue. The Superintendent was passing out mugs from a desk drawer when Beaumont sauntered in.

'Gotta name,' he announced, 'assuming you're right, Boss, about her being the one in the novelties shop. One Leila Knightley, married to a prof at Reading University — some kind of scientist. They used to live at Caversham but moved here four weeks back when he got himself a new job at a London college. I've just run their names through records but there's nothing on either of them. Not so much as a parking ticket.

'In Mardham she was quite well liked, if considered a tad highfalutin' by the girls she employs. She half-owned the shop and worked there part-time three days a week. Drove a red Volvo but nobody knew its number. I had a word too with the newsagent

115

three doors down. He lives over his shop and holds her spare set of keys against emergencies. He's an awkward git; won't hand them over until her partner gives permission. Said partner's a sleeping one, name not generally known.'

'Her address?' Mott demanded.

Beaumont produced a folded page headed PARTY FUN from his inner pocket. 'Right close here. Knollhurst, Acrefield Way. And guess what: it's no more than half a mile from Shotters Wood.'

'Let's hope we find the husband at home,' said Yeadings sombrely. 'If he was partying with her, why hasn't he been in touch to report her missing?'

'Think he did it? Could be, though my money's on a lover,' Beaumont asserted. 'A sexy-looking wench, going out dressed to kill; it could be that her target had the same idea, in spades, and she got done instead.'

Mott gave him a stony stare. 'We'll be looking for the party-thrower, checking the Knightleys' acquaintances. There can't be all that number of flashy entertainments in this neck of the woods. I want you to run a check on hotels and nightclubs within a thirty-mile area. See what gala affairs were billed for last night.'

Yeadings grunted. 'There's also a chance

116

she was dumped by car from farther afield; and we don't know yet how long she was held while tied up. The party or whatever could have been earlier than Friday.'

Mott nodded impatiently. 'Right. I want photographs of the dress circulated to fashion shops as soon as Forensics have finished with it. It's striking enough for someone to remember.'

'Z?' Yeadings invited, 'can you suggest any other line of inquiry?'

The woman DS nodded. 'The victim's hair was sheared off before death. Either the killer's a fetishist and it may turn up as evidence when we eventually get to him; or else he'll have tried to dispose of it. So we should organize a search of refuse bins locally and sniff round bonfires; though burning's a less likely option because of the giveaway stench.'

'Yes,' Yeadings agreed. 'Hair is difficult to dispose of totally. Even if he mainly succeeded there could be the telltale wisp left behind. So — where would you start your scavenging?'

'At the dead woman's home; then discreetly at her acquaintances'. As Angus says, our priority is to find the party-thrower, who could be a neighbour or colleague.'

'So, first interview the husband,' Mott said

decisively, 'and any other family. Saturday's a good time to catch people at home. I'll cover breaking the news myself, with Z along in case there are womenfolk.'

He turned to the other sergeant. 'Beaumont, in addition to the hotels angle I want a report on the clothing asap. Get on Forensics' tail. No excuses about weekend leave.'

Beaumont grunted. Twice already Z had pulled the plums on this inquiry. Political over-correctness dealt the mere male a bum card. Some principle, sexual equality!

His shoe nudged the plastic carrier bag he'd dumped on the floor. 'Any bids for a quantity of processed rain forest? I lugged all this to the morgue for Littlejohn and he'd scarpered. It's no use to a higgorant tabloid-skimmer like me.'

'Don't look my way,' growled Yeadings. 'I already have Saturday's armful of newsprint and it lasts me all week. That's if I get to tackle it at all. Read it to broaden your outlook. And don't let me see it on your expense sheet.'

'Bloody hell,' the DS complained as the team trooped along the corridor; 'what's soured the Boss? Anyone'd think the body was family.'

★ ★ ★

They found that Acrefield Way was a straggling lane with Tudor cottages huddling matily between Georgian elegance and prim Victorian villas. Knollhurst, at the far end before woodland and hedged fields took over, was one of two elegant Edwardian houses standing back from the road within their own grounds. The panelled front door was newly painted a glossy black and the rest of the woodwork white. On this hot June afternoon all the windows appeared to be shut.

'They're away,' Z guessed. The brass knocker produced only a hollow echo, so after waiting a short while Mott took off for the rear of the building. He found side windows similarly closed, also the glass-panelled back door where cream-coloured holland blinds obscured any view of the interior. Farther on, a large domed conservatory with double doors giving on to the terrace offered a view of plumply cushioned rattan chairs and sofas punctuated by two potted palms and an oversized fatsedera. Glaringly out of place among their stylish arrangement stood a large trestle table covered with trays of domestic junk, and beneath it half a dozen removals cartons spilling polystyrene packaging. Mott recalled then that the family had only recently moved here. So maybe everyone had gone back to the earlier home for a final clearout.

Doors to the double garage at the back of the house were locked, but by hauling himself up to the rear windows Mott discovered it was empty. It appeared likely, then, that the woman had driven herself to wherever she met her death, and any recent sighting of the car might lead them there. As the other space was also vacant Mott assumed the husband was separately absent with his own car.

'Get hold of her licence number,' he ordered Z as he returned to the front garden. 'The computer might still have her old address on it. Then get what you can from the nextdoor neighbours.'

★ ★ ★

Jeffrey and Madeleine Piggott were an irascibly separated couple who occasionally threatened each other with divorce, but so far neither had had sufficient persistence to set it in motion. Their two boys, living with the exasperated mother, were tetchily claimed on occasional weekends by the father, a turf accountant whose shop was considered by many local residents to be a blot on the village's good name.

In summer, when the weather permitted, he would invariably discharge his paternal duty by driving his sons on Saturdays to the coast where, loaded with coins, they conveniently disappeared into amusement arcades. On the Sunday the brothers, one eleven, one nine, and constantly at loggerheads, would spend most of their time locked in a near-lethal grapple on the hearthrug in his decidedly poky flat in Aylesbury. The only remedy for which, Piggott père had discovered, was to pay them to sit in a cinema until he was disposed to transfer them to the nearest McDonalds and feed them to the point of semi-stupor before delivery home.

The older, Dunkie (for Duncan), was a good-natured dreamer, slow but not stupid. Patrick — bright and a tease, with a short temper and an even shorter concentration span — was the more vicious thumper, irritated by competition unless assured he'd come out on top. Jeffrey took some pride in recognising him as a chip off his own worthy block.

On this particular Saturday, due to a glitch in distant planning, each parent had understood that care of the boys fell to him- or herself.

'You've got the wrong week, silly cow!' Jeffrey stormed, snatching at his wife's diary. 'Look! there's jam or something sticking two pages together.'

'Well, I'm all dressed up now,' Madeleine

retorted. 'And I'd turned down a chance to have my sister across. Besides, you should've got here sooner. There's barely time for a jaunt to the seaside now.'

'So what? Whose fault is that? Not mine. You're the one wasting time arguing.' He glared at the boys. 'Out in the car you two. We're going down to Brighton.'

'She said we could take grub to the Zoo,' Patrick protested, scenting the occasion for an unholy row. 'We've got pork pies and chocolate gateau ready waiting in the fridge.'

'Brighton,' his father threatened darkly.

'Boys, you know you'd rather see the animals,' their mother pleaded.

Dunkie hesitated. Patrick jumped in. 'Why can't we go to Brighton today, stop here overnight and all do the Zoo picnic tomorrow? Dad can drive us.'

'I don't do picnics,' Jeffrey said with scorn.

Madeleine considered. 'They do have restaurants there.' If Jeffrey joined them she'd not have to pay. Flashing a bulging wallet was one of her husband's less offensive habits. And the spare room had a bed made up if he needed it.

Jeffrey hesitated. He was damned if he'd trail back home and admit to a wasted weekend. This way he could still use the new car, so he'd be seen to have won, sort of; and admittedly brats shared were brats halved in a manner of speaking. He could leave their management to their mother and tomorrow take a dander on his own, see what new tricks the blue-arsed monkeys were up to. He hadn't been to the Zoo for donkeys' years. Not since spending a weekend with that blondie who lived in a narrowboat on Regent's Canal. 'Right,' he said. 'But Brighton today, like I said, and we'll eat properly both days, so you can bin the junk food.'

The family was jockeying for seats in Jeffrey's Mercedes as DS Rosemary Zyczynski turned into their drive on foot and made purposefully towards them.

Madeleine squared her jaw, prepared to repel Seventh Day Adventists. 'We're just going out,' she declared aggressively.

Rosemary flourished her ID. 'Sergeant Zyczynski, Thames Valley CID. If you live here I'd like a word, please, before you leave.'

'She does,' Jeffrey claimed harshly, scowling towards his wife. It was a cause of some rancour that over accommodation she'd come off better than himself because she had the boys to house.

'We already belong to Neighbourhood Watch,' Madeleine claimed primly. 'And we don't need any more Crime Prevention lectures.'

'No lecture,' Z promised. 'Just one or two questions about your nextdoor neighbours. Do you know where I could get in touch with Professor Knightley? Nobody seems to be at home there just now.'

'She's usually there at weekends,' Madeleine offered. 'Don't see much of him though. Tell you what: ask their cleaner. She lives in one of those tumbledown cottages towards the far end. Hetty Chadwick she's called.'

'Right,' Zyczynski said. 'Thanks. I don't suppose you've really got to know them yet anyway.'

'Dunkie has,' Patrick said sneakily. 'He's got the hots for the girl there. Been inside the house too.'

'You never told me,' his mother accused.

'I fixed her bike chain,' Duncan admitted. 'So she asked me in for a Pepsi. That's all.'

'Ah. So the Knightleys have children?' Z probed.

'Seems so,' Madeleine sniffed. 'I heard there's an older boy too, but I've not set eyes on either of them yet. Hetty said he's gone to America.'

It sounded as though the cleaner was just the chatty sort needed. Z thanked them again and stood back for Piggott to sweep magnificently out of the drive.

She extracted her own car from nextdoor

and cruised down Acrefield Way. About two thirds along she saw a pair of flint and brick cottages tilting louchely towards each other in seventeenth century intimacy. On the grass strip in front of one and backed by a line of pink hollyhocks, a fleshy middle-aged woman was making the weekend peace hideous with an ancient hand-operated mower.

'Mrs Chadwick?' Z called.

'Aye. That's me.' She halted, resting muscular forearms on the machine's cross-handle and surveyed the young woman smiling from the car's open window. She looked a good prospect; with any luck they'd be a double-salaried couple, both out all day: little wear and tear on the house. Hetty's slow gaze belied her mental cogs' activity as she calculated what price she'd name for her services. Not that she'd finalise until she'd had a dekko at how the place was kept. Polished wood floors and priceless rugs would be a quid an hour more than wall-to-wall carpets.

'I believe you know the Knightleys who've recently moved in along the road?'

'I do for them, Tuesdays and Thursdays, right?' Cautiously.

'Ah.' The girl was getting out and coming round the car towards her, holding out a badge or something.

'Who?' she demanded suspiciously, and made Z repeat her ID.

'Oh, perlice. Can't think what you'd want with me, chuck, but you'd best come inside.'

Z followed her into a small, brick-floored sitting-room crowded with oversized furniture. After the brilliant sunshine outside, the room seemed in almost total darkness. Mrs Chadwick steered her guest towards a cretonne-covered sofa that smelled faintly of scented washing powder. She was torn between disappointed hopes of fresh employment and a flutter of excitement at the promise of gossip. Police didn't feature hugely in the village; certainly not the plain-clothes variety.

'Them Knightleys,' she prompted. 'There's nowt wrong wi' them, is there?'

'I couldn't say,' Rosemary hedged. 'I've been trying to contact them but no one seems to be at home'

'Well, I'm sure I don't know where'd they'd be, miss. It's Saturday after all.'

'I wondered if they'd gone back to their old home to clear up. Do you know the address?'

'No. Oh, wait a bit though. She did write me fro' there before she moved in. Let's see if I can put me hand on it.'

Mrs Chadwick bustled into a back room where her solid heels rang out on stone flags.

There followed a brisk pulling out of wooden drawers, clanging of enamel pans and a rustling of paper.

'There, I knew I'd kept it.' She came back in triumph. 'Caversham, that's where they were before. D'you‚wanta copy it down?'

Z took her time transferring the address to her notebook. Then she looked up at the north-countrywoman, smiling. 'I wouldn't mind moving here myself. It's a lovely village. I expect the Knightleys are delighted they've come.'

'Well, it's a nice house. I'll grant them that much. Not that they're ever in it. The professor, he's barely spent a coupla nights there at a time, and the young people were off away almost as soon as they moved in. Of course Mrs K's got a shop in Mardham so mostly she's at home just evenings. All the same it seems a bit lonely like. For a youngish woman, I mean. Get to my time of life, you're glad enough for some peace and quiet.'

'I expect she'll soon make new friends here.'

A tremor animated the cleaner's pudgy face and was gone in an instant. Her opening mouth snapped shut like a rat trap. Z waited but nothing was forthcoming. A pity, because she was sure the woman had almost let slip an indiscretion. Well, let it pass. It was a point to come back to on a later visit. Once the family had been informed of the death and the news spread, Hetty Chadwick might be more eager to volunteer information and claim some local fame.

'Thanks for your help,' Z said, sliding her notebook into a shirt pocket. 'I'm sorry to have interrupted your gardening.'

As she belted herself into the car she heard the horrendous clatter and shake of the old hand-mower restarting.

Back at the Knightleys' house she found Angus Mott talking into his mobile phone. 'Right, sir,' he said shortly and switched off.

'The Boss has authorised a break-in. There's a patrol car on its way.'

He had picked on the glass-panelled kitchen door, expecting that, as with so many incautious householders, the key would be left inside in the lock.

'The lock's clear,' Z warned, bending to peer through.

He checked, and saw they were out of luck. 'Right then, it'll be the lavatory window for you.'

Goody: so I can plunge into the open loo pan, Z reckoned. However, the two uniformed constables who drove up five minutes later were provided with an electric ram and proceeded to demolish the kitchen door's lock.

'Stay outside,' Mott ordered them. 'One of you go round to the front. Z, you're to cover the ground floor. I'll look upstairs.'

On the threshold they listened for the noises of the house, identifying the refrigerator's hum and the more distant dragging tick of a longcase clock. There was a smell of newness and freshly painted woodwork. Despite the anti-burglar device on the house's outer wall no alarm had shrieked out at them. Mott made for the cupboard under the staircase and confirmed that the system had not been turned on. So was someone waiting inside, monitoring their movements?

Z acted on Mott's nod as he stood ready by the stairs. She moved through the empty kitchen into the square hall and slid into the first open doorway. There was no one in the large, green and gold dining-room. Two long windows overlooked the side garden and the drive. White-painted wooden shutters framed them both, matching smaller ones that covered the serving hatch to the kitchen. The inner wall between was covered with shelving and glazed cupboards stacked with an immense amount of good china and glassware. The long mahogany dining-table had eight chairs set close, leaving little space for anyone to hide underneath, even a child.

The next door off the hall was closed but

not locked. Z turned the cut-glass knob and eased the door open. There was a lingering scent of stale tobacco. Whether it came partly from the well-worn leather furniture or the stacks of books that lined three of the walls she couldn't tell, but it struck her as old-fashioned, a man's room belonging to an age that had been strictly a male world. The wallpaper, where it was revealed, was a peppery colour patterned with pictures of game birds, and clearly hadn't been changed for decades. Perhaps the books, together with their oak shelving, some of it glass-fronted, had been installed first before any part of the house was redecorated.

There would be time later, she promised herself, to see what the books were about. Between the windows stood an old roll-top desk with a key-ring hanging from the lock. This should contain correspondence and banking details. Z left that for Mott to go through and moved back into the hall.

Unlike the other rooms which sported pale, polished floor-boards, the hall was chequer-tiled in ivory and black marble. The front vestibule door was glass-panelled with an art deco design of pink water lilies and long-legged birds. When the outer south-facing door was left open sunshine would stream through and stain the floor with the warm colours of the glass.

Z stole across and stood in the last doorway, on the far side of the curving staircase. The drawing-room was immense, stretching the full depth of the house. And was unoccupied, as elsewhere. Fluted, cream-painted columns framed an impressive fireplace and overmantel. Another matching pair framed each of the four tall windows opposite, and she guessed they served to support dividing walls of the rooms above.

At the far end glass doors stood open and led to the domed conservatory into which they had peered from outside. Only in there was there any sign of interrupted domestic life, with the trestle table covered in household junk and a tray with an empty mug that appeared to have held coffee. Beside it a blue checked apron was thrown down. Under the table stood a bucket half full of soapy water, now cold, with a pair of yellow rubber gloves balanced on the rim.

A 'nice house' Hetty Chadwick had called it. It was all of that, once home to an Edwardian family of some substance. And the Knightleys couldn't be short of cash either, with the way house prices had soared of late in Thames Valley.

She heard Mott's footsteps on the stairs and went out to meet him in the hall.

'Nothing,' he said.

'No sign of anyone here either. Hetty Chadwick comes Tuesdays and Thursdays. Someone seems to have abandoned washing china and gewgaws in the conservatory though. She could probably tell us who that would be, and when.'

'If Knightley doesn't put in an appearance I'll be ordering a full search,' Mott said. 'What we need is a diary or address book.' He was scowling. 'It begins to look bad for the professor.'

'I guess so,' Zyczynski agreed sombrely. 'One way or the other.'

10

When the team met up again to compare notes Beaumont flourished the Caversham address already obtained from the computer via the Volvo's registration. Z had little fresh to offer the team beyond her suspicion that short though the Knightleys' stay in the village, there could already be a whiff of gossip. She described the cleaner's suddenly buttoned lips at mention of Leila making new friends. 'Not that she didn't need some,' Z granted, 'seeing that the rest of the family appears to be missing.'

'Missing since when though?' Beaumont demanded. 'And who drove who away?'

'Who, whom,' Yeadings corrected as if to himself. He rubbed his temples ruefully. 'I'd never deny village gossip has its uses, but a lot of it can be pure supposition. Facts often get a colourful twist. However, you'd do well, Z, to keep in touch with this Hetty Chadwick.'

Getting in touch with the dead woman's husband was another matter. A phone call to the old address was answered by the new owner. He had never, he assured Mott stiffly, so much as set eyes on Mr Knightley, all business over the house purchase having been conducted through their respective agents and solicitors.

'Another try with the University?' Beaumont suggested.

His phone enquiry — having been passed along a chain of porters, groundsmen and indoor domestic staff to an overworked and underpaid Reader in Biochemistry who was working there weekends on a paper he hoped to publish — drew an equal blank. It began to look as though the husband could be pencilled in as their prime suspect. Unless he'd shared a similar fate to Leila's.

'If he blew his lid and did his missus in, he's likely by now to have topped himself too. A familiar pattern for domestic murders,' Beaumont reminded them smugly. 'All we need do is wait, and body number two will turn up of itself.'

'So where are the children?' Yeadings asked heavily. 'Did he ensure they were both out of harm's way first? If so, that implies premeditation. How far ahead do you think this murder was planned?'

'A matter of days, perhaps weeks,' Z suggested. 'The party or whatever would take some arranging; invitations to be sent out, or tickets printed if it was open to the public.'

'You're assuming the occasion was vital to

the planning,' Beaumont complained. 'It didn't have to be that way. Something the woman said or did that evening could have been the last straw that broke the camel's back. Sudden rage on the way, say, and hubby whips a cord round her neck, bingo! Then he panics, dumps her in the wood, returns home to collect his clothes, money and passport. Exit panicky academic. He could be any-where on the continent by now, thanks to Eurostar.'

'In which case we'll trace him through his car,' Yeadings assured them. 'I've pulled its licence number out of the computer. It's being circulated, ports and airports informed. But your sudden-attack scenario doesn't account for Leila Knightley's hands and ankles being bound. She wouldn't have sat quietly in the car while he got out and came round to do that. However, whether the husband's our suspect or not we have to find him. Until then the body's not officially identified.'

'Except by yourself,' Beaumont said barely audibly. Into the ensuing silence he dropped a subdued, 'Sir.'

'That was bloody unnecessary,' Mott snapped when they were again outside Yeadings' office.

'But you'll admit the Boss feels personally involved?'

'No more than anyone would be who'd met the victim earlier.'

'You saw the body as found, Guv. I only saw shots of it. She looked a pretty hot number in that getup. Even if . . . '

'Oh, stow it, Beaumont,' Z cut in sharply. 'We're none of us icicles. We might even feel sorry to see you on the slab.'

'Go home you two,' Mott sighed. 'Nothing'll drop in our laps today, so get some rest. I'll see you at nine tomorrow to discuss Littlejohn's report. And you can thank your stars that he's seen fit to work through the weekend.'

In their empty office Mott found a message from Reading Area on his desk. Enquiries among ex-neighbours in Caversham had come up with the addresses of the Knightleys' lawyer and of an uncle of the dead woman, a Londoner who lived in Pimlico.

The former was an Edgar Gross, traced through particulars of the house sale. When interviewed by a Reading DC he had been quite shocked but was unable to suggest the professor's current whereabouts.

A message concerning the uncle, Charles Hadfield, was passed to the Met. The reply, received two hours later, informed Mott that Mr Hadfield was away on holiday. Neighbours who were keyholders for his London

136

home could say nothing more specific than that he was touring in Scotland with his housekeeper. When (or if) he phoned in he would be told to contact DI Mott at a Thames Valley Police number.

'Meanwhile we don't sit on our butts,' Mott muttered to himself. There was another Knightley listed in the address book he had turned up in the study desk at Knollhurst. She lived in France: a Mrs G. Knightley with an address in Nice. Z could pick up on that tomorrow.

He switched off the lights, collected his car and was more than halfway home when he was buzzed by Area. A Charles Hadfield had just contacted his neighbour and been advised to get in touch with DI Mott. He had immediately rung in demanding to speak to him, and had sounded more than a little upset at having to leave his number.

Mott sighed, tossed in his mind whether to continue, but decided to return. The call to Scotland was long distance, and he'd rather it went direct on to Thames Valley's bill. The expected conversation could be a lengthy one.

Hadfield was awaiting his call with impatience and while Mott briefly outlined what had happened the man had difficulty keeping himself from shouting. The DI visualized him: tall, spare, tweedy and redfaced. He'd be the sort to ride roughshod over the police once he got within galloping distance.

He too claimed to have no idea of Professor Knightley's whereabouts, but quoted the son's address in the US without hesitation. Then, 'Chloë? She'll still be at her Granny's, won't she?'

'Would that be Mrs G. Knightley, sir?'

'Are you being funny, young man?'

Mott was at a loss why he should think that. 'We have a Mrs G. Knightley in the family address book. An address in France, sir.'

There was an apoplectic snort. 'Thought you meant G for Granny. Yes, she lives in Nice. Invalid of some sort. Arthritis, I believe. Now I come to think of it her name is Gladys.'

His mistake had made him slightly more amenable. On a quieter note he explained he would be travelling south by inter-city rail, leaving next morning. 'We shall pick up my car in London and come direct to the house. I expect to meet you there. I'll phone you on arrival at King's Cross.'

Mott consulted his watch and decided that even with the hour's time difference he should contact the daughter in France at once. If he'd been in Nice on a balmy summer evening himself he wouldn't have retired to bed yet.

An elderly woman's voice answered his ring and she spoke in passable French. Nevertheless there was no hiding the authoritarian sharpness of an upper-class Englishwoman.

'*Qui donc?*' she insisted loudly. Possibly the sharpness came from apprehension over deafness.

'Detective-Inspector Angus Mott of Thames Valley Police, madam. I understand your granddaughter Chloë Knightley is staying with you at present?'

'What's that about Chloë?'

'Is she there? I'd like to speak to her.'

'How do I know you're a policeman?'

Dear, oh dear. Mott moaned silently, matching his mental expletives to present company, for all that she couldn't hear them.

He explained that she could ring Thames Valley Headquarters at Kidlington and they would verify his identity and present phone number. Then she could call him back and they could begin a proper conversation.

'But what would Chloë have to do with a policeman?' the old dear quavered. 'You must realise, young man, that I am responsible for her while she is under my roof. The child is only fifteen, you know.'

But I've no intention of seducing her, he wanted to bite back. However, in consideration of Chloë's tender years perhaps it would be better to hold off, leaving it to Granny to break the news, or a sanitised version of it. If only she hadn't chosen to retire abroad he could simply have off-loaded the chore by sending a sympathetic WPC round to see her.

'Anyway, my granddaughter is not at home at present.'

That was precisely his problem. But now, of course, Granny meant her own home.

'When she returns,' Mott said slowly and distinctly, 'would you kindly tell her that her stepmother has been involved in an accident. If she will return my call giving her flight number I will arrange for someone to meet her plane at Heathrow or Gatwick tomorrow and drive her home.'

Shock had apparently done much for the old lady's deafness or obduracy. This time she got the message in one, and Mott firmly detached himself from further babbled questions without divulging more precise details.

He wasn't happy about having understated the situation, but breaking news of a death wasn't something to be done lightly over the wires, especially to strangers. The incident left him strangely aware of the old lady waiting alone for the unsuspecting child to return late from an evening out with friends.

He wished he knew how Chloë had regarded her stepmother. If there was antagonism she might not respond by coming back. It was likely she would ring home and expect to speak with her father. Finding there was no reply she could assume he was at Leila's bedside in some hospital casualty unit. Even then she might well wonder why the only contact made with her was through the police.

Mott supposed he'd have to hang around indefinitely for some message from the girl.

No, dammit. He'd done enough. He'd arrange for the reply to be held over for him until the next morning. And Scotland was nearer than the Riviera, wasn't it? By the time the child arrived it could be left to the uncle — step-greatuncle, or whatever — to tell her the full story of Leila Knightley's killing and the professor's disappearance. Much better for it to come from someone she knew.

With that settled, Mott felt in need of tender loving care himself and dialled Paula's London flat. But his fiancée too, it seemed, was out on the tiles and not expected back until the early hours. 'Some kind of party?' he asked with a twitch of envy.

'I'll say!' her flatmate laughed. 'It's a hen night. One of her colleagues is getting hitched next Saturday. That's allowing a whole week for them to recover before the big day, so I guess tonight's going to get wild.'

'You're not going yourself?'

'No; they're all lawyers and I don't really fit in. Still, I have grabbed the contract for catering and floral decorations on the big day. We intend giving them the works.'

'Lucky you,' he said lamely. 'Tell Paula I called, will you? Her turn to ring next.'

He wished now he hadn't bothered, but he had needed to hear Paula's voice. He'd have treated her to a comic version of the Granny conversation and been rewarded with that low, throaty chuckle that was only one of the wonderful things about her.

What wasn't wonderful was that she still hung on in London. That and the way their own wedding plans had twice been put on hold already, without renewing a date; all because of her bloody work at those bloody moneymaking Chambers.

* * *

Saturday had not proved entirely satisfactory for the Piggott family either. While the parents bickered and quibbled in the front

142

seats, the boys had curled up in the rear, in their sock soles for comfort.

Duncan was endeavouring to track their route with an out-of-date map which utterly failed to recognise motorways, while Patrick systematically fired at him from close quarters with a spud gun until all the ammunition was exhausted. Tiny plugs of slightly mildewed King Edward potatoes littered the dove grey carpet or adhered to the other boy's clothes and hair, contributing an odour of musty rottenness to the air-conditioned interior.

When Madeleine rebelled and demanded a rear window opened it struck Patrick as mildly amusing to drop one of his brother's white trainers out on the passing roadway. Its absence was only noticed as they drew up on Brighton seafront and the family was evicted by Piggott père, his patience already sorely tried by Madeleine's vacuous prattle.

'That would account for the pong,' Patrick observed brightly. 'Dunkie's feet, I mean.'

'I had both on when I started out,' Duncan maintained doggedly.

'He just wouldn't know. He's a dope!' Patrick jeered.

'Well you can't hobble along on a sock,' snapped his mother. 'It'll be all holes before you've gone a couple of yards.'

So Duncan sat down on the kerb to remove the remaining trainer and both socks, wriggling his toes contentedly at the unexpected freedom.

Doubtless because of his bare feet Madeleine decided that she and the boys should repair to the beach and paddle; which wouldn't have been so bad if there had been a good stretch of sand and plenty of slimy rock pools for Patrick to ensure his brother fell into. The tide, however, was high and the pebbles extremely hard to sit on. They could all have had deck chairs but Madeleine was convinced that the scruffy young people who hired them out were bent on a rip-off. Rather than risk that and an enforced shouting match, she opted to suffer, but not in silence.

Patrick and Duncan, themselves suffering withdrawal symptoms from their addictive slot-machine games, made a nuisance of themselves until she suggested they find their father. Which they did to his annoyance while chatting up two bright-eyed young women who had braved his favourite pub in their bikinis. Their presence caused him to overplay the role of indulgent father when Patrick whistled from the doorway with his hand held out for subsistence.

The family met up for a lunch of fish and chips in a crowded restaurant where Madeleine smugly reckoned that Jeffrey paid six times what it would have cost her to provide it fresh at home. After double portions of banana split and knicker-bocker glory respectively Duncan and Patrick were persuaded that the tide was now far enough out for them to sample the sands.

But Brighton could offer none of the Beach Boy element they were accustomed to on TV. There wasn't a surfboard in sight, the waves being pathetic little ripples and all the sunworshippers wrinklies or toddlers.

Sun and air, however, wrought their customary effect and by the time Madeleine decreed it was time to go home everyone was sluggish and bad-tempered. The three slept for the best part of the journey back. Jeffrey, sitting on an uncomfortable quantity of canned beer, suffered alone the barely moving queue of traffic on the motorway, which came to a dead halt for a mile each side of Heathrow.

On finally reaching Acrefield Way they dispersed to all corners of the house, made separate raids on the fridge and went early to bed. With a minimum of surliness Jeffrey accepted the single bed in the spare room and, although she had rather wondered, Madeleine's night was undisturbed.

Taken all round, Saturday's experience did not augur well for a second day of family togetherness.

11

On Sunday Yeadings' team gathered outside his office at a little before 9am. They could tell he had arrived early by the established aroma of Mocha coffee in the corridor.

'Did the prelim path report come?' Z asked Mott.

'Yes. I hear he's got copies for us. We'd better give him a few minutes for a read-through.'

But Yeadings was aware of them waiting and opened the door. 'Get seated and let's tackle this together. As you know, death was by strangulation with a ligature.'

He nodded towards the coffeemaker. 'There's enough there for a first round. Fill your mugs. Then let's consider what Little-john's discovered.'

They all studied the sheets provided.

'No sexual interference with the body before or after death,' Beaumont commented, skimming through quickly.

'Not 'the body',' Yeadings murmured with distaste. 'From now on we'll use the name Leila Knightley, accepting the evidence of family photographs found at the house. You'll see there's also positive identification through dental records. We're lucky that Littlejohn has already accessed them on his old-boy network. It being a country practice the dentist lives in the flat over the surgery and didn't mind paper-shuffling on a Saturday night.'

'Right.' Mott was scanning the report. 'She was in good health prior to the incident, and not pregnant. It's pretty detailed about chafing of skin at wrists and ankles, but he's being chary about any length of time for her being tied up.'

'The marks must depend on how much she struggled,' Z said. 'There appears to have been an early attempt to break free, then a period while the skin lesions dried. Then a second burst of struggling, more frenzied than the first, which burst them open again.'

'Only at the wrists,' Beaumont pointed out. 'After that first stage the ankles seem to have been released. Does that mean rape was intended, even if not carried out?'

'Or she was made to walk somewhere,' Mott warned. 'Like the fingernails, we don't know much yet about the scrapings taken from under her toenails and between the toes. They have to be further analysed. But, although there were no obvious traces of woodland floor, this report does mention microscopic threads of fibre. They could have come from struggling against a blanket thrown over her in a car, but I think it's more likely she picked them up from walking barefoot indoors on a carpet.'

'Her ankles were still loose when she was discovered,' Yeadings reminded them, 'and we're assuming she was carried into Shotters Wood. If so, why not elsewhere? What reason can you see for making her walk on carpet?'

'She was too heavy for the first person involved, but someone stronger disposed of the body when they'd got it to the wood?' Beaumont suggested.

'She was alive at one point and dead at the other,' Z said sombrely.

Eyes closed, Yeadings was visualising aloud. 'She is indoors somewhere. Her mouth is taped so she can't cry out. Her hands are secured behind her back, and she is being led, not carried.'

He was clearly seeing her while he described this. 'I rather think — '

They waited, curious to see where the vision was taking him.

'Yes,' he decided, 'there were other party-goers in the vicinity who mustn't see her being abducted. Even at night you'd not want to risk carrying off a grown woman over your shoulder or in a sack. It's so much more reasonable to help her out to a car — on her own two feet. We know she's masked, and if she stumbles it's easily accounted for — a little over-indulgence: because even the nicest people can find they've drunk more than is good for them. If anyone saw — and with luck no one would — it would hardly seem significant, especially among sophisticates. They would perhaps smile and look away. No vulgar rubbernecking.'

'How are we with the timing on this?' Mott queried. 'She was found shortly before 11.48 on Friday night, and rigor hadn't begun to set in. We need to find the last person to see her on Friday evening. The previous day Hetty Chadwick would have cleaned at her house. Z, you'd better see her again. Also find out where Leila Knightley went on both days and who saw her.'

Z was turning back pages in her notebook. 'I looked through the fridge and freezer at Knollhurst,' she said. 'There was some salmon in its original dated wrapping. She — or another — went shopping at Tesco on the first. That was Thursday, the day before she was killed. It looked like stocking up for the weekend. Did anyone come across the till receipt? It should have on it the time of day she went through the check-out.'

Mott nodded. 'If not, and she wrote a

cheque or used her Club Card, we can get the information from the store's computers. But try the house first. Her receipt could be in the paper bin for recycling. And Beaumont, I want you to — ' Mott was interrupted by his pager, pulled it from a pocket, read it and grunted. 'The Knightleys' daughter is booked for a flight due in at Gatwick about noon.'

'Right,' Yeadings approved. 'Angus, I'd like you to meet the daughter off her plane yourself and escort her home. With a WPC, of course. And I'll take over at the house. It could be useful if I familiarise myself with the territory. So I'll follow you across there, Z. We can have another look around before the daughter cramps our style.'

He busied himself with a file on his desk, to avoid the DI's pointed stare. 'It's important to get the child's angle on the marriage,' he claimed, 'before she thinks to clam up.'

'Wouldn't Beaumont handle a teenager better?'

'Possibly, though he's not so used to girls. Comfort her. Act the big brother. Besides, you're allocating Beaumont elsewhere. It leaves me idle. When Z has talked to Hetty Chadwick again we'll have another look at the house, then you can take the girl there and settle her in. By that time her great-uncle should have arrived from Scotland.'

'And me, Guv?' Beaumont reminded Mott hopefully.

'Hang in at the Shotters Wood end. They haven't finished their fingertip search, and you'll need to check on what's already turned up. So breathe down Forensics' necks. Also tell them I want every detail they can get out of those fibres. House carpet, car rugs, whatever.'

Yeadings began to clear his desktop. 'I think that's all for the moment. I needn't stress how important the first forty-eight hours are in a murder investigation. This is the point where we mustn't overlook any detail however apparently trivial. So good hunting.'

He turned to Z. 'We'll take separate cars. Lead the way and I'll follow.'

* * *

At the house they found blue-and-white police tape closing off the driveway, with a constable stolidly repelling a handful of local sightseers. A brief mention on television news had left 'the body of a woman' anonymous; but closeness to Mardham, and the obvious scene-of-crime preparations, had sent tongues wildly wagging.

They gained entry from the rear, using a

key for the newly fitted lock. Already, by mid-morning, the house had an over-heated staleness.

'Better get doors and windows open,' Yeadings advised. 'Today's likely to be another scorcher.'

While Z walked down to the little flint and brick cottage to question the cleaner he made a leisurely tour of all the rooms, beginning upstairs, and then installed himself in the study, systematically emptying everything with latex-gloved hands from the old-fashioned roll-top desk. With the cat away this particular mouse had free access. The paperwork included credit card slips, insurance receipts, a batch of old cheque stubs bundled together in an elastic band, bank statements, various receipts from a builder-decorator, several unpaid bills, photocopies of the house deeds and a heap of unsorted correspondence and notices concerning its purchase.

Nothing remarkable there to justify a superintendent taking over a DC's routine duties. Yeadings might have found more excitement in accumulated paperwork on his own desk back at base. Presumably more sophisticated information would be filed in the computer against the adjoining wall. Unfortunately, Yeadings found, access was denied for want of a password.

But weren't all children computer wizards these days? Hopefully Yeadings entered 'CHLOE' but without result. So the girl was restricted to her own machine in her bedroom. How about her stepmother?

Keying in 'LEILA' opened the system. The files on offer were headed ADDRESSES, BIRTHDAYS, DOMESTIC, EXPENSES, FAMILY, INVESTMENT, RECIPES; SHOP. Yeadings sat back and stared. Did this sum up the dead woman's whole life?

So what had he expected? — other files labelled HOPES & FEARS; SECRETS; even LOVERS?

Mott would be putting some lowly nerd onto sifting all this information, but for now he could switch it off and return to what he was more familiar with. He started to replace bundles of paper in the roll-top desk in the order he had found them.

He hadn't seen Z since she took selected items out to her car and locked them in the boot. That was some ten minutes ago. Now he called and she came in from the back garden. 'Well?' he demanded.

'I thought I'd check. Nobody seems to have stuck a fork in the ground since the hot weather started. In fact it's a bit neglected. Certainly nothing's been buried there recently.'

'And the cleaner?'

'She was here all right. Leila let her in at 8.30 on Thursday morning. She'd overslept and was still in her night clothes. She took a bath, dressed and went out about ten, telling Hetty to slam the door on leaving. She hasn't a key of her own yet. Leila hadn't returned when she left at 12.30.'

'And she never saw Mrs Knightley or her car again after that?'

'So she says.'

Yeadings cocked his head. 'Is that a car now?'

Crossing the hall Z saw a taxi draw up beyond the gate. The girl who got out stared up at the constable guarding the open front door, and the vehicles drawn up alongside. The cab driver dropped her cases on the pavement and stared in his turn, barely checking as she handed over the money clutched ready in her hand.

It had to be Chloë. She had travelled alone, having somehow slipped past the escort Mott had laid on for her at Gatwick.

Superintendent Yeadings completed his paper-shuffling and closed Knightley's desk. He listened to the murmur of voices as Z explained that her boss was waiting to meet her.

He went out into the hall and joined them.

'Chloë, come in,' he invited, nodding her into the study. He explained who he was. 'We didn't expect you quite so soon.'

She sat with a tote bag at her feet and a light raincoat over one arm, stiffly as if waiting for a train. Her freckled, heartshaped face was taut, framed by dark red hair that fell straight over her shoulder blades. She wore the teenage uniform of loose T-shirt, blue jeans and white trainers.

'There was a vacant seat on an earlier flight to Heathrow, so I took that,' she explained. She sounded almost aggressive. 'How's Leila?'

Her abruptness didn't surprise either of them. Only twenty minutes after Mott had phoned the news to her grandmother, Chloë had called back asking the DC on duty for confirmation of her stepmother's reported accident. He had given her this without details and she had demanded none.

It was as if she suspected Mott's call was a hoax. Her voice, DC Silver had said, was tensely controlled. She looked the same now to Yeadings. He would have described her as petrified.

He approached her gently, Z seating herself in a corner behind him. 'I'm very sorry indeed about your stepmother. I'm afraid that later I shall have to ask some questions which

156

may sound insensitive, but you could help us in finding out quite what has happened.'

'D'you mean why she ran off, or — '

Yeadings waited. When the girl didn't come out with the alternative he risked being frank. There was a challenge in the way she stared at him, chin held high, that made him sure she detested evasions.

'Or whether she could be a woman we found in Shotters Wood,' he said gently.

Her breath came out in a barely suppressed hiss. 'Why should she be? What would she be doing there? I thought you meant she'd run off and crashed her car. How badly hurt is she?'

'I'm afraid she's more than hurt, Chloë.' The tone of his voice must surely save him from putting the whole truth into words just yet.

'She's dead! You mean she's dead, don't you? No! Leila, dead? She can't be!'

Z went across to the child's chair and reached out her arms but Chloë pushed her off. 'Why does everyone lie to me? They just said that she was in an accident.'

'Your grandmother wasn't well enough to travel with you. We knew you'd be coming alone so we sent someone to meet you. Because you boarded an earlier flight it's been left until now for you to get the full story.'

He went on talking, quietly on a level tone, giving her time to face the unbelievable.

But Chloë was suspicious of him. 'Who else is here? Janey? Uncle Charles?'

'You'll see them soon. They've been touring in Scotland. We hoped they would arrive before you.'

The child closed her eyes and was silent a long moment. Yeadings was appalled by her stiff self-control. When she looked at him again it was with something like loathing in her eyes.

'You — you aren't going to make me see — ? Identify her, I mean.'

'That won't be necessary. Once we trace your father he will be able to do that.'

'You mean you don't know where he is? He'll be in Reading somewhere. Have you tried asking at the University? Someone must know where he's holed up.'

The bitterness in her voice was unexpected. Nor was 'holed up' quite the expression of a respectful daughter. She had a stepmother whom she'd suspected of 'running off'. So where did her loyalties lie? If any.

'We're still making inquiries. Nobody seems to have seen him for a few days. We shall be advertising for him to come forward.'

She closed her eyes again the better to take

this in. 'He's gone missing? But you haven't called me home for that. They simply said Leila had been in an accident. Now you say she's dead. But you don't think he's dead too. Or do you?'

Trying so hard to make sense of it, she stared at him with wide, frightened eyes. 'You really do believe it's Leila you've found. What makes you think that?'

'We're going by photographs in the house here. And we've examined records of dental work she had done in Mardham.'

The girl leaned forward in her chair, hands gripping the seat to either side of her tensed thighs. She looked transfixed.

He gave her a moment to absorb the clinical detail. A grown woman might have burst out with 'Oh, my God!' but not this disciplined child. Perhaps over-disciplined? She was doubting and testing every new fact. Yeadings felt for her; and there remained so much more for her to face.

'But Leila's really fit. There's nothing wrong with her. Granny said — an accident. How could she have an accident in Shotters Wood? There's no road through. People don't even ride horses there. Who was with her?'

'We don't know.' He could answer only the last question. And then there was no avoiding the full brutal truth. 'It wasn't an accident,

Chloë, and she wasn't unwell.'

He watched her work out the truth on the level of logic. An intelligent girl, she arrived there by herself: not a natural death and not an accident, so what else remained?

'Chloë, I have to tell you. It appears that someone attacked her. That is why we're so concerned, and why we need you to help us find out everything we can.'

But still she wouldn't believe. She had gone stubbornly into denial.

'No!' she ground out. 'No, not Leila! Nobody could do that!'

Rosemary Zyczynski moved again towards her but the girl sprang up. 'Don't touch me! Leave me alone.'

Out in the hall there were voices. Z walked past her and went to see who had arrived. It was a sallow-faced young woman from Social Services accompanied by a great bear of a middle-aged man. She introduced him as her senior officer.

'We can probably do with both of you,' Z assured them as he seemed to hang back. 'Chloë is through there with Superintendent Yeadings. She's only just learned it was murder, so you'll find she's in shock. I'll make some tea for us all.'

'You haven't been questioning her?' the woman demanded sharply.

Her companion beat Z to the denial. 'Don't worry. Mike Yeadings knows better than that. We'll give him a couple more minutes with her before we interrupt.'

When Z took in the tray with four cups and a tumbler of lemonade from the fridge she found Chloë sitting straight-backed and pale under her freckles, listening to the Boss. 'Visitors?' he asked, looking round.

Z nodded. 'Social Services.'

'I won't see anybody,' the girl said fiercely.

'We are obliged to have someone here,' Yeadings said calmly, 'to represent your family.'

'I'll wait for Uncle Charles. And Janey. They're written into Leila's will, *in loco parentis* in case anything happened.' The Latin came out in a brittle, adult voice. She was trying so hard to command reality.

'They should be arriving in London at any time now.'

'Maybe they're back. I'll ring them.' She went across to the phone on her father's desk, turned away, took a deep breath, and while she began to dial Z let in the two social workers. They gave their names to Yeadings as Ms Maggie Martyn and George Claydon.

The double brrr of the dialling tone continued, clear to all in the room, until an amplified male voice took over, inviting a message to be left. 'Oh no!' Chloë cried, almost despairing. 'Why is nobody there? Uncle Charles, it's me. I need you. I need you, right now. Please, speak to me!'

Painful to witness as Yeadings found it, he had to leave her a free rein. That way she might feel she had some influence over events. And then, thank God, at last she broke down, standing there abandoned, still fiercely clutching the receiver while dry sobs racked her.

He went across and gently took it from her stiff fingers. 'They'll come. I know they're on their way.'

I hope to God they do, Z told herself. Such wholesale desertion was unbearable.

Chloë refused the drink. 'I'd be sick,' she said shortly, exhausted by sobbing.

'Can you tell us who your doctor is?' Maggie Martyn asked.

'I don't need a doctor. We haven't registered with one yet. We've only been here a few weeks.'

'Is there someone from where you were before?'

'Caversham,' the girl said almost contemptuously. 'And no there isn't. I'll wait till Uncle Charles and Janey come.'

Z looked meaningfully at Yeadings. Chloë needed to rest before they spoke to her further, but she couldn't be left alone. 'How about your nextdoor neighbours?' Z asked, mainly to cover the Boss's voice as he spoke quietly into his mobile phone across the room.

'The Piggotts. I don't know them.' She seemed determined now to insist on isolation. Then impulsively, 'Look, I have to phone Gran. She'll be expecting me to. Only I don't know how to . . . explain.' Her head twisted in horror from side to side.

'Can I help?' Z offered.

'Would you?' It sounded breathless.

'Give me her number and tell me what you want her to know.'

Chloë looked baffled. 'Just that I'm here, I suppose. I've arrived. And thanks for having me.'

Less truculent, Yeadings noticed. This was progress of a kind, habitual good manners surfacing through the nightmare. But shock had prevented her seeing that some explanation was due. Mrs Knightley senior would demand to know what kind of accident Leila had suffered.

'You can leave it with me. I'll explain everything,' Z told the girl. 'What if she insists on coming over?'

'She won't. Gran doesn't go anywhere now, she's so arthritic. Don't tell her — please don't say there's nobody here.' At last there was a faint note of panic in her voice. 'I — I think if you don't mind I'll go and lie down. Is that all right?'

'Of course.' Yeadings looked pointedly at the social workers. 'Rosemary, help Chloë up with her luggage, will you?'

Z followed her. 'Smart room,' she commented as the girl wearily dropped her jeans and kicked her trainers under the bed. She turned back the bedcover and Chloë slid in, turning her back on the world.

'Thanks' hollowly, and still polite, the ingrained civility functioning at surface level whatever churned beneath.

Z drew the curtains to block out the brilliant midsummer light. She left Chloë lying flat and staring frozen-faced at the far wall.

'This is appalling,' the male social worker had burst out as the door shut behind them. 'It's absolutely essential to locate the father at once. She must have personal support.'

Yeadings caught the flicker in the woman's eyes and saw she shared his misgivings. 'We're hopeful he's not involved in the murder,' he said quietly. 'Either as a further victim or the killer. Chloë hasn't asked for him and she assumed at first that her stepmother had 'run off'. We may find the marriage was far from a happy one.'

'That's all she needs at a time like this,'

wheezed George Claydon. 'A dysfunctional family background.'

⋆ ⋆ ⋆

Charles Hadfield made his call to the house on his cellular phone. A background noise of slamming car doors and distant shouting reached Z — the typical scrimmage for taxis at a major railway station. Hadfield gave his estimated time of arrival as 1.20pm.

Z handed the receiver to the Boss who identified himself and added that Chloë had already arrived from France and was resting in her room.

'Superintendent? Good, good.' Yeadings' rank gratified the man, as it should. Maybe he was familiar with police matters and knew that normally a sergeant or DI was the most he'd be meeting initially.

In for a penny, in for a pound, Yeadings told himself, replacing the receiver. Since he'd been more or less caught out abandoning his desk, he'd carry on and meet the main characters. Certainly until Mott managed to get back from Gatwick. Not that there was any hurry to inform him that Chloë had slipped through his net. When Uncle Charles put in an appearance would be soon enough for Z to ring the DI and call him in.

12

The social workers having left, promising to keep in touch, Yeadings and Rosemary Zyczynski were examining the main bedroom when they heard the Hadfield pair arrive. While Z slid shut the doors of Knightley's wardrobe her boss went to the head of the stairs and watched the dead woman's uncle blunder through the open front door and head for the dining-room. There followed a chink of glass on glass and the man's throat clearing.

A smaller, oddly dressed woman followed quietly, sighted Yeadings on the shadowed gallery, stopped short and stood looking up at him. He went down. Despite her cool stare the grey eyes were red-rimmed. She was mourning the dead woman. 'Superintendent Yeadings?'

'Yes. Chloë is resting. She'll be relieved you're here. She needs someone she can trust.'

The corners of the woman's mouth quivered. 'Doesn't she think much of the police then?'

'Not yet.'

She nodded, as if his reply had pleased her. 'So her father's still not available? We decided, if that was so, we'd move in. I had the luggage stacked outside in case you're examining the house.'

'We shall be sealing the main bedroom and study. Beyond that, I think we've seen all we need for the moment. When you feel ready I should like to ask you a few questions about the family.'

He was aware of her looking past him and then Charles Hadfield came up behind, a whisky tumbler in one hand. 'Has Knightley not shown up yet?' he demanded.

Yeadings turned and took him in: tall and heavily built but leaning on a hand-cut blackthorn. He had a large, squarish head with close-cropped white hair, strong features and startlingly blue eyes made more so by contrast with his ruddy cheeks. Pale skin above the eyes showed a red indentation made by a tight hat brim. The cream panama, pushed to the back of his head, made Yeadings think of a cricket umpire.

'We're still looking for the Professor,' he said.

'I see. So how can I help?'

'By suggesting where else we should look. And particularly by telling us anything you know about your niece that could explain what she got herself caught up in.'

'Caught up in,' the man repeated. 'So you don't think this is a random killing? There's method in it?'

Which was precisely what Yeadings did feel in his bones, but he'd no explanation for it as yet. 'We have to cover every possibility, keep an open mind.'

'Yes, yes.' He sounded impatient at the cliché. 'Leila was nobody's fool, Superintendent. Yet I always felt . . . '

'Yes?'

' . . . there was something of the innocent about her. Not that I'm that good a judge of women. Been deceived by them too often. You'd best ask Janey what she was really like. They seemed to have an understanding. If you want me I'll be in the garden.' At which he abruptly raised his hand with the stick to draw the panama back over his eyes, and limped off in the direction of the kitchen.

Their voices had reached Chloë who had been barely asleep. She came out on the landing and gave a sharp cry, 'Janey!' Then she was flying down, barefoot, with a cotton robe still undone, and was hugging the little woman in the long bunchy skirt.

Over the girl's head Yeadings nodded towards the drawing-room. 'I'll give you a while together,' he offered. Janey met his eyes briefly, her face screwed with distress, then the two moved off, their arms round each other.

It was a risk. He knew he could miss something vital passing between them. But this was no time to put on pressure.

He sat down on the third stair, resting elbows on knees, and was conscious of Z upstairs moving from the main bedroom into another. He guessed it was the one that Chloë had just come from. Good move on Z's part. The child might have left something significant open to view. He went outside and ordered the constable on guard to fit a seal to the room Leila had presumably shared with her husband.

In the drawing-room the low voices continued, the words lost to him. Chloë was having the most to say; Janey's voice a mild murmur briefly punctuating the flow. He strained his ears but could get no meaning from it.

Z came downstairs with a man's plastic-wrapped suit over one arm, went out, and he heard her locking it into her car boot. She had just returned as Janey came to the drawing-room door. 'Chloë's ready to see you,' she said, and the two detectives followed her in.

The girl looked defensive. The older

woman's face was unreadable.

Yeadings sat opposite them, addressing Chloë. 'There's a possibility,' he said cautiously, 'that your stepmother was caught up in the unsavoury business of some new acquaintance she didn't know very well.'

It was pure guesswork. All he had to go on was intuition fed by Z's impression that Leila's cleaner scented fresh scandal.

He had caught their attention. They seemed to be waiting for more. Right: he'd wade further in.

'Even something illegal.'

'Leila's not like that,' Chloë protested quickly.

'So what is she like? Tell me. We need to understand. It could lead us to discover who might want to harm her.' He had followed her into the present tense and the girl hadn't noticed.

'Nobody would. She — she's gentle. She doesn't let people rattle her. She puts up with almost anything rather than make a fuss.'

His eyebrows twitched. 'Won't complain? More tolerant than you, perhaps?'

'Too damn true! She lets people — ' Chloë fought to contain herself, fists clenched and tight-lipped.

'Walk over her?'

'Lets people get away with things.' The

words came out reluctantly.

So much anger, he thought; but already she was beginning to retreat, wouldn't give much more away without being shocked into it.

'Yet someone deliberately killed her.'

Chloë stiffened, her eyes shut, and he watched the colour drain from her face. She couldn't speak.

'So these people she never complained about, who are they?'

'Just people.' As she forced out the whispered answer her face burned and she turned away from him.

Answer enough: she meant her father. And perhaps sometimes herself?

'People are so — bloody — awful, if you don't stand up to them.' She spoke with passion.

'They certainly can be. Thank you, Chloë. I'm sorry I had to probe.'

The hands in her lap turned helplessly palms upward. 'It's your job.' She appeared reluctant to allow that much, but relieved that his words sounded final.

'That's all for the present, then. But I may need to bother you again. Later on.'

Chloë nodded, rose and made for the door. There she stood with her back to him and fought against tears, took a deep, sighing breath and ground out, 'She was so nice, a really good person. You have to know that.' And she was gone, not waiting for Janey.

Leila submissive and a peacemaker? That wasn't the impression given by the body found in Shotters Wood. Leila Knightley had fought like a tiger for her life.

Just before Chloë's arrival there'd been a call on his mobile from Forensics. They'd analysed something further: under Leila's fingernails microscopic flecks of black suiting, wool and cashmere mix, luxury quality. And Forsyth, the expert on fabrics, had said they were lucky it hadn't been pure wool super 120-twist, or the fabric's surface wouldn't have scratched off.

Which was why Yeadings had had Z take out Knightley's dinner jacket in its plastic cover, to send on to the lab for comparison.

Janey — he already thought of her as that — stood regarding him, dumpy but strangely impressive. She waited until he acknowledged she was still there.

'So you got what you were after. Leila was the family shock-absorber. All right; the learned Professor is a bully and lives only for himself. But you're wrong if you assume he was the one who killed her. He hasn't the bottle. Aidan is just a womanising wimp.'

She turned away and the scorn had left her voice. 'It's a less civilized world now. There's little kindness left.' She looked suddenly crumpled. Then she left.

Kindness? What had kindness to do with the case? Yeadings asked himself. Yet she was right: we live in an age of anger. With more kindness there'd be less rage. Only where is this kindness suddenly to spring from? There has to be security first. Peace of mind: there wasn't a lot of that about either.

And if Leila Knightley had been kind, what good had it finally done her?

I'm showing my age, Yeadings thought. I should leave the armchair philosophy to others. Our job's keeping the peace. Or at best grabbing wildly as it fast goes down the plug hole.

To the team he often summed up his first impression in a single word. For Janey he chose 'pragmatic'. Now for Leila he had been offered 'kind'. From the brief sight he'd had himself of her alive, she probably had been.

He looked up to see Charles Hadfield standing again in the hall. He hobbled forward, leaning heavily on his stout blackthorn. 'I just can't believe it,' he confessed.

The weathered face, with its fine broken veins over the cheekbones, showed an underlying pallor. Despite the bluff voice, body language said something else. Leila's death had truly shaken him.

'No one who knew my niece could ever want to harm her.'

'So you think it must be a stranger who attacked her?'

'Was she . . . I mean — A man, was it?'

'She wasn't raped. The attack wasn't sexual.'

The policeman's crudeness shocked him, even as he took comfort from the knowledge.

'Sit down, Mr Hadfield,' Yeadings invited.

'I'm not a bloody cripple, Superintendent.' But he took the chair indicated and stretched one leg out painfully. The ankle was heavily bound with crepe bandage. 'Went north for the heather and a good malt whisky. Both conspired to bring me down.'

Yeadings nodded, almost smiling. 'I'm hoping you can help us. We know nothing of the family. Except that Mrs Knightley was your niece.'

'I'm her only blood relative. She was my sister's daughter. Her parents are dead, lost in their yacht off Agadir. She came to me as a little girl. Knightley was a recent widower when they married. That would be nine years back, when Leila had done a year at university. Both children are her husband's. Leila was a wonderful mother to them.'

Good: brusquely informative, he was

co-operating. But then, why shouldn't he? Possibly because by nature he was an awkward cuss; had long chosen that role and revelled in it; lived it as a private joke. Yeadings had met his kind before.

'Tell me what your niece was like.'

Hadfield thought for a moment. 'She was a good girl, dignified, dutiful. Too dutiful. There wasn't much juice in that marriage.'

A curious phrase. It seemed even to faze the man who'd used it.

'I mean — she gave all she had. He was an unmitigated bastard.'

'Was? Do you think he's dead then?'

Hadfield was silent, the blue eyes hooded. He rested his chin on thickened knuckles grasping the blackthorn's carved knob. The stick was planted firmly upright, less as a prop than a device to explode him to his feet. Despite the closed eyes his whole pose was spring-loaded. This was a very angry man.

'You didn't like him,' Yeadings prompted.

Hadfield opened burning eyes. 'I hated his very guts. If he hasn't killed himself already, I'll be first to claim the honour.'

So, speaking apparently without collusion, the family had a single opinion, that Leila was more sinned against than sinning. Yet who ever knew what went on in a marriage beyond the couple themselves? And even they could find it a right old conundrum.

'I was responsible for her upbringing,' Hadfield admitted. 'I was a middle-aged bachelor when she was sent back from Africa, an orphan. Never had any children of my own, that I know of. So I sent her to boarding school and saw her briefly in the holidays. That's if she didn't go off camping or pony trekking, or something of the kind.

'When Janey first moved in with me she gave me no end of a telling-off; said I'd deprived the child of a sense of family. So she took it on herself to act the surrogate mother.

'I think now it may have been too late by then. Why else would Leila have taken on a disagreeable husband with a couple of ready-made children, the first man who ever showed any real interest in her?'

'Perhaps she was in love with him.'

'She thought she was. But once the knot was tied she seemed to — '

Yeadings was good at waiting. He found that the longer the silence drew out, the greater the compulsion for it to be filled. But the man opposite him wasn't holding anything back. He simply found it hard to find the right words.

'It was like one of those dimmer switches. Her light didn't go right out, but she wasn't the same. She would laugh less, and her smile never reached her eyes. She'd been so animated before.

'But she never said she was unhappy. Of course, I'd warned her beforehand not to give up her freedom, her own academic aspirations. You should always be prepared for marriage going sour on you. Not that we knew then of his unsavoury reputation.'

Hadfield beat against the floor with his blackthorn. 'How he is allowed to work among impressionable young people I'll never understand. I suppose it's overlooked because of his exceptional qualifications. Some people only see what they want to see. And he's well thought of in his speciality.'

'Which is what precisely?'

Hadfield waved a hand vaguely. 'Physical Chemistry; Biophysics. These distinctions are all a bit beyond me. That's what he likes, of course: dazzling lesser mortals with his science.'

'You're speaking of him now in the present tense. Does that mean you have changed your mind? He hasn't done away with himself?'

Hadfield nodded slowly. 'I have to admit: suicide isn't his line. He'd never see himself sufficiently in the wrong. And whatever he did know he was guilty of, the arrogant bastard would always expect to ride it out.'

Through the open windows there again came the sound of a car engine followed by men's voices. Z left her post and went through the hall to check on it. Not one but two taxis had drawn up by the kerb and the constable on duty was endeavouring to block a double dose of demands for information.

From the first cab the Piggott family spilled out to stare in amazement at the incident tape and the police presence. Z recalled that they'd left on the previous day in a new-looking white Mercedes; so what had become of that?

The parents seemed aghast, but the prospect of new excitement was bringing the boys out of their subdued state. The zoo visit, like yesterday's trip to Brighton, hadn't proved one of unalloyed pleasure.

Taken up with observing their reactions, Z was slow to remark the smaller man who slid from the second cab and stood staring fiercely at the doorway behind her.

She turned to see that Charles Hadfield had limped out, leaning heavily on his stick. From fifty feet apart the two men confronted each other like stags at rutting.

The defiantly upthrust goatee beard, the gingery hair and pinched features were familiar from a portrait in the study. This newcomer was the missing Professor Knight-ley, alive and clearly in anything but a co-operative mood.

He advanced on the older man, fists clenched. 'What the hell are you doing here?' he demanded.

13

Piggott stared at the two angry men through slitted eyes. His fingers, biting into Madeleine's arm, made her gasp. 'Who's that?' he demanded.

Her head was bent over her purse, locating her house keys. She screwed round to look. 'Which one?'

'The little ginger runt who's just arrived.'

'That's my new neighbour.'

'The professor?' He put into it all the scorn he felt for the over-educated. And something else besides.

'That's right.' Madeleine hooked out the keys and became aware of him paying off the cabbie. That was strange, because he normally turned tail the minute he'd dropped the kids off.

'You're not coming in again.' It was somewhere between a question and a protest.

'We have things to settle.' He scowled at the boys. 'You two clear off down the garden.' He aimed a swipe at Duncan as he passed.

Madeleine looked affronted at the way her husband appeared to be settling back in. He needn't think she was going to offer him coffee. On the other hand her own nerve ends were shrieking for caffeine, and with her hands busily occupied she'd feel less vulnerable.

They went straight through to the kitchen and, relatively secure on her own ground, she opted for frontal attack. 'I'll be needing more money for the school holidays. There'll be outings and fresh clothes for Dunkie even if I pass his old ones on to Patrick. It costs twice as much as in school term.'

His little currant eyes went meaner. 'You'll get same as usual. It's more than ample. And if either boy gets a new outfit it'll not be that dickhead Duncan.'

She knew it was hopeless trying to explain how the younger boy manipulated his brother into the wrong. Jeff would only say you shouldn't let anyone make a fool of you. Yet that's what he was doing. Or else he enjoyed egging Patrick on in his mischief-making. And if she defended Dunkie, Jeff'd start shouting about her turning him into a mummy's boy; why didn't she go ahead and let him do the cooking?

Due to yesterday's lost trainer he'd had a miserable time today breaking in a stiff pair of new shoes. His skin was sensitive and he tended to get blisters. But the trouble had started long before Dunkie acquired his limp. It was when Jeff drew up at Regent's Park with the Merc's wheels half on the pavement.

'I suppose it's all right to leave the car here?' Madeleine had doubted.

'There's nothing to say we shouldn't.' Nevertheless her uncertainty reminded Piggott of the car's value and its recent purchase. It would be a blow if some marauding kids fancied it for joy-riding. A customer last week had had his brand new Porsche wrapped around a lamppost after a police chase.

'I'll just shove it in over there.' Piggott opted for safety by reversing the Mercedes into the forecourt of a sizeable block of flats with the name Flambard Court above the impressive doorway.

The zoo part of the day went fairly smoothly, irritation being mainly avoided by the party splitting into three. Madeleine found a shady spot and some magazines to keep her entertained, while Jeffrey mooched off to appreciate the mandrills' coarser activities. The boys stayed mainly together, Duncan circulating in his normal amiable haze while Patrick, having tired of banging on the bars outside the big cats' enclosure and having been repulsed by a spitting camel, experimented with pieces of discarded sandwich and various animal droppings as ammo in his spud gun. This kept him out of worse mischief until a keeper observed him firing

182

near the penguin pond and he was compelled to beat a hasty retreat.

They reassembled for lunch, which wasn't a bad meal and left them, at least temporarily, glazed and less antagonistic. By 3pm Jeffrey considered his duty done and rounded up the others for the journey home. It was then that he found the Mercedes was no longer parked in the forecourt of Flambard Court.

A tight-lipped approach to the duty porter brought him out to observe the empty parking place. The man allowed the heated flow of complaint to wash over him with the air of one accustomed to being misunderstood, before pointing out the notice warning: vehicles not displaying the Flambard permit were likely to be wheel-clamped and removed.

'But it's Sunday,' Piggott roared.

'Yes,' the man agreed mildly. 'We get a lot of it on Sundays.'

Piggott wasn't going to lose face in front of the others by chasing up where the car had been taken. He had minions for that, and tomorrow was another day.

They straggled along the pavement to a bus stop and waited in surly silence. Decanted twenty minutes later at Baker Street Underground station, Jeffrey felt the last of his patience snap and he hailed a passing taxi.

By the time he had its passenger door open wasn't Madeleine, stupid cow, queuing for train tickets. The boys were even further ahead.

'C'mon, dithers,' Patrick shouted, standing by the down-escalator. Duncan hopped obediently on. He'd been carried five or six stairs down when Patrick's crowing laughter reached him. He spun round and stared up at his exasperated mother, and his redfaced father gesticulating towards something outside.

His heel twisted painfully as he turned. He lost balance, falling against a fat man trying to pass alongside. Both went staggering for a yard or two, grabbing at the moving handrail. At the foot of the stairs the man held him at arm's length, bitingly sarcastic.

Duncan tore himself free and made for the up-escalator. When he arrived at ground level his mother hauled him off like a two-year-old.

In Baker Street the cab driver was fuming and a traffic block building. As Duncan made to get in the cab Jeffrey reached out and struck at him with the back of one hand. Duncan felt the slash of his signet ring and warm blood start running down his cheek.

'Bloody imbecile!' his father roared. 'You've been nothing but a fucking disaster all weekend!'

And a disaster it had been for everyone, Madeleine agreed now as with shaking hands she started filling the kettle. And Jeff hadn't really taken notice of her demand for holiday cash. There was something else eating at him.

'This professor.' You couldn't miss the contemptuous pause before the title. 'What did you say his name was?'

'Knight, I think. No, Knightley. They delivered his post here by accident once, so I saw it. We've never actually met.'

'Knightley.' Nearly another bloody title. You could see the little shit thought he was God's gift to the universe. A small man. They often behaved like that. Pompous little squirt. Well, it wouldn't take much to puncture his balloon. And with the police on his doorstep it could be that trouble was catching up already.

'Why the interest?' Madeleine asked with suspicion. 'What's he to you?'

'Nothing. Less than nothing. Just thought I'd seen him somewhere before.'

'Not in your shop. He'd hardly be the betting sort.'

Piggott gave a throaty chuckle. 'That's what you think, eh? And you're an expert on the punters! He's on the books. Clever he may be, but he can't pick a horse. Too bloody high-and-mighty to come in himself after the first time. Runs a Special Account. Uses the pseudonym Vector, whatever that means.'

He swung himself into a chair at the formica-topped table. 'So what else, family has he?'

'I told you once before but you never listened. They've two kids. The boy's left school and the girl's fifteen or sixteen. You'd best ask Duncan, since it seems he's been in there.'

Piggott spun to his feet, opened the back door and roared for his elder son. Duncan wandered in from the terrace, a split grass stem between his two thumbs. He blew on it to produce an ear-splitting shriek. Jeff cuffed him into the house, closing the door again for privacy. At the garden's far end he'd glimpsed Patrick perched high in the old pear tree, binoculars trained on the garden next door. Well, at least one of the kids was awake.

As he might have guessed, Duncan could tell him nothing. Just that the Knightley's house was 'nice' inside, not modern, and Chloë was 'all right really'. He'd met her mother too. She'd been washing china in the conservatory and had asked him about school.

'The girl goes to a private school. Fancy uniform with a purple blazer,' Madeleine put in, adding some body to the skeletal information. She couldn't think why Jeff was interested at this point. He hadn't been when she told him what a helluva lot the house was sold for. He'd simply said that some people had more money than sense, and that anyway all she knew was the asking price: it could have changed hands for a lot less.

But Sally Ellis who sold it said the new people hadn't quibbled. They'd paid in full, for fear of being gazumped. So then Sally wished they'd slapped another ten thousand on, except that admittedly there were a number of repairs to be done, one or two of them structural.

Patrick slid in from the garden, his face puckish with gossip ready to spill.

'There's been a right barney going on next door,' he said happily. 'But then a big man made them all sit down and I couldn't hear anything. But he was giving them a real pi-jaw.'

'The white-haired one with the stick?' Piggott asked sharply.

'No, another one. I think he was a plain-clothes policeman. He had a woman with him, with a notebook.'

'So it's not just a traffic inquiry. I wondered why that copper was on duty outside. Maybe they've been burgled.' Piggott eyed his son with suspicion. 'You making this up? How could you see all this from the tree?'

'Some I could. But there's a big knot-hole in the fence by their conservatory. You can see right through into their lounge from that.'

'Patrick, it's not nice, spying on people,' Madeleine limply scolded. 'That's how trouble can start between neighbours.'

'Maybe they've started enough for themselves,' said her husband with a smirk. He pulled his mobile phone from a pocket.

Patrick watched enviously as he rang one of his minders to come and pick him up. The man's name was Walter Pimm, a weasely man whose party piece was making his knuckles crack. He shared a flat with a massive bloke called Big Ben. Dad called them his heavies and made it sound like a joke.

Patrick wondered what chance he'd have if he asked for a mobile himself for his next birthday in October.

If Piggott had stayed on ten minutes after Pimm whisked him off he could have watched yet another car pull up at the neighbouring house and a tall, fair-haired man whom he knew as DI Angus Mott arrive to take Professor Knightley away for questioning. It was done without fuss and the three remaining Piggotts were unaware of it, being inelegantly draped around the kitchen, feasting on chilled lemon squash with cheese 'n onion crisps and defrosted doughnuts.

★   ★   ★

Superintendent Yeadings was glad enough to extract himself from the Knightleys' troubles and — even on a Sunday — return to check on a deskload of other serious crimes. He left Z behind to await experts who would take apart the sealed bedroom. It wasn't an obvious scene of crime, but at this juncture you couldn't be certain. Leila had been kept tied up somewhere before her body was dumped in Shotters Wood, and that was only half a mile away. Carpets in all the rooms would also be combed for fibres to match the microscopic threads already at the lab.

He was relieved that Mott had taken over the investigation. It was his call-out anyway, possibly the last case Angus would handle before the threat of tenure caught up with him. Already he'd run over his five-year stint as DI. The coming change would mean welcome promotion for him, but it meant the team's break-up.

Angus was a good detective, with a decent record for putting together a convincing case. He'd chafe at being returned to uniform and removed by rank from the sharp end of investigation. Yeadings couldn't see him taking kindly to admin or hobnobbing with community leaders. Maybe his good looks and law degree would even get him shoved into PR.

But with the Knightley case it was less on account of Angus and more for himself that he was conscious of a strain easing. Because of the victim. It was nothing new to come upon a body of some person he'd known alive, but here there was a difference. This wasn't someone with a criminal record, a hard-nosed loan shark who squeezed his debtors beyond endurance or a sleaze-bag running a string of prostitutes, or even an upmarket lady-of-the-night herself — for all that this victim's get-up had given that first impression.

It seemed now, from the opinion of those who surely must know, that she was an ordinary, well-meaning housewife with family commitments and a respectable part-time job. Which put her in the running to be one of those random victims that stalkers or indiscriminate killers happen upon.

Horror enough. But what made it more poignant to him was how he'd met her in the context of his family life, at a moment when he was feeling bad about letting Sally down. While they conversed he had known she recognised him in his police capacity, and had almost acted upon it.

Preoccupied with his own petty problem, he'd walked away; and so he had this disquieting sense that he should somehow have been able to shield her. Which was totally illogical. Who was he to guarantee invulnerability? Didn't his job sometimes risk the reverse for those near him?

To be truthful, what bugged him was simple frustration. He'd not stayed and listened to her, and so he had no idea of the importance of what she would have said. It might have been no more than a minor query he could have set her mind at rest on. Or — if the killing wasn't random and she was under threat already — it could have proved of use now as vital evidence.

That could implicate someone in her circle; possibly one of those he had already met that day. And since statistically the odds were always on a domestic murder, it seemed inevitable that in Interview Room 1 Professor Aidan Knightley and DI Mott would be getting down to a serious discussion.

He was tired; he had not realised how weary until, after half an hour of paper-shuffling and scribbled memos at the office, he reached home and sprawled at ease in his rattan chair on the patio, a tumbler of Nan's homemade lemonade close at hand. The overgrown ash tree, which he had long intended to cut back, stirred lacy fans overhead, alternately dazzling and dappling his upturned face.

Gently its susurration faded into the sigh and suck of water at a sea's edge. He found himself wandering barefoot along a shoreline. It was the time of evening when only overhead is the sky still blue. Gradually, towards the horizon, it shaded to an indeterminate yellow like the flesh of a pear, and finally flushed to meet the dark sea. Above him craggy cliffs caught the lowering sun, bunched like an enormous arthritic fist.

At the water's edge he was quite alone. Down here the light was already slipping away. Only gentle ripples and the rim of wet sand showed a faint phosphorescence. He moved his weight slowly from foot to foot, watching water press up between his bare toes, then briefly stay pooled in the imprint as he lifted each foot away, until the sand slid back and no trace remained. He knew that behind him nothing marked that he had come this way.

The thought brought a mild kind of grief, but then ahead phantom pressure marks began to appear in the wet sand. Traces left by finer feet than his own, long-toed and delicate. But with no one there to make them.

Then these imprints too began to vanish. He heard himself cry out in an urgent protest.

He fought himself awake and felt Nan's hand on his shoulder to calm him. 'Mike, you were dreaming.'

He couldn't speak, lying limply sweating, anguished. At what? A memory rather than the dream. It was a place he'd once visited as a young sergeant with the Met, taking solitary leave in Cornwall. It had been at a turning point in his life as he worked out whether to stay in the job or try for something with better pay; because he'd fallen in love with Nan and he wanted to offer her so much more.

He remembered plodging his feet there at the edge of the warm sea, with his jeans rolled up to the knee. A mudlark sensation, pleasurable and totally physical for the moment.

That was the point where the dream had started to out-strip reality, because it hadn't mattered then that the footmarks must disappear. It was what happened; something acceptable and accepted. So why the angst of the dream? Some Jungian indication that he feared impermanence? A warning he was getting older, due some day to wear out and himself vanish?

That wasn't what disturbed him. Already the dream's outlines were fading. Losing the action, he was still transfixed by the sense of sadness.

Something about those footmarks. He stared into the dark behind his eyelids, and patterns of feeble light started flickering and taking shape.

Then they came back. Not the phantom imprints, but bare feet he had seen elsewhere; on the peaty floor of Shotters Wood. And on Littlejohn's steel table: fine, arched feet slanting upward and outward in the total relaxation of death. Pathetically toe-tagged.

He stirred in his chair, passed one hand over his dry mouth. Perhaps not so much Jungian as Freudian then? Had Leila Knightley called on his libido from beyond the grave?

Only it wasn't lust he felt; it was more like guilt.

★   ★   ★

While Superintendent Yeadings relaxed at home, Z awaited the scene-of-crime experts. She agreed with her chief that it wasn't an obvious murder scene, but they could not afford to ignore that Leila Knightley had been kept tied up somewhere before her body was dumped in Shotters Wood.

As well as Knightley's dinner jacket she had also removed the computer from the study to pick over its contents at her convenience. Now she had a tussle with her conscience over having commandeered Chloë's stack of disks as well. She decided it was better to be over-cautious, and transferred them all to the car, using a grocery carton she found in the utility room.

With Knightley's departure for questioning, the Hadfields had moved their luggage in, Janey collecting it from beside the front doorstep and transferring it to a twin-bedded guest room at the rear.

'If Aidan comes back and needs somewhere to sleep,' she decreed, 'he can use Eddie's old room or make up a fresh bed for himself. I don't mind cooking but I don't intend waiting on him.' She then took over the kitchen and started preparing an evening meal.

Charles Hadfield had been curiously silent since Yeadings intervened in the flare-up on Knightley's arrival. He had been content to listen and ponder. Now, with Chloë pottering about at the far end of the garden, he voiced his opinion that if the police had any sense at all they needn't expect her father back that night. He appeared to have changed his mind yet again about Knightley's guilt.

'They'll keep him as long as permitted without charging him. Isn't that thirty-six hours? By which time he'll have broken down and admitted the killing. I suppose I should get in touch with his solicitor, if only for Chloë's sake. And we may need someone ourselves to keep those social workers at bay. Not to mention the Press once they're on to this. Can't have them upsetting the poor girl.'

For a long time Chloë had stayed crouched on the edge of her bed with her head in her hands. Elsewhere in the house there were sounds of comings and goings. She thought at one point she heard her father's voice. A little later the front door had closed noisily and a car drove away but she didn't bother to look out.

It didn't matter. Nothing did. It was awful, this swirling void. Whenever she closed her eyes she seemed to be moving in a vortex. Needing air she slipped out into the garden. The ground seemed to be tipping under her. Lying flat she had to dig her fingers into the lawn to keep herself from sliding away.

She pulled herself up on to the stone bench by the garage wall. Now at least she had her feet against the ground but still there was movement, and she knew it was inside her head.

Janey had asked if she would 'like

something'; meaning aspirin, she supposed. She had refused because it was both too little and too much. She had feared being any more confused than she already was. What she needed was to go out like a light.

Back at Granny's she'd believed she was beginning to get herself straightened out, and now total disaster. Leila gone. Leila killed, for God's sake, by some maniac in Shotters Wood.

There was no sense in anything any more. She had almost made up her mind to tell Leila everything once she got home, in maybe two or three weeks' time, but now — She found she was rocking forward and backward over her knees. Like a madman in some gothic film, she thought. She had to force herself to stop and sit stiffly straight with her arms wrapped about her. And still her brain felt to be sloshing to and fro, knocking against the bony inner skull.

Someone came out on to the patio. Janey, calling her name.

'Not now,' she cried desperately. 'Leave me alone!'

But that was the opposite of what she wanted. It scared her being abandoned. She wanted Leila there, close, holding her, talking in that low, level voice that could turn the worst nightmares normal.

Janey wouldn't do. How could she understand, being so old and so odd? Things like this didn't, couldn't, happen to Janey. But Leila — who knew men could be shit and still remained sane — Leila just might have understood.

At first the very idea of admitting what had happened was impossible, a grotesque extension of the original horror. But by getting away she had achieved a sort of perspective, if only a slightly skewed one. She'd had time to draw breath, believe that she'd almost escaped, survived without permanent damage. But still there were decisions to be made. She had to put a finish to it forever or she couldn't live with herself again. And Leila might have helped her there, although it wasn't clear just how. Now she had no one. How could so many hideous things crash down on her at once?

She shook her head wildly, angry at seeing herself at the centre of this new horror. It was Leila it had happened to, Leila abused, done away with. Something that left her outside. It made her hate herself more.

'I want to die,' she growled through stiffly clenched jaws. But she knew she didn't: there was too much anger boiling away under the shame.

She wanted to forget, yes. Only there'd

been so much confused blurring of her mind already, with patches of time gone missing, that she'd thought she was going insane.

No; what she fervently wanted was for none of it ever to have happened: to go back to that afternoon of the French orals. It had been a Friday, so afterwards she'd walked to the Uni's Faculty of Science to beg a lift home with her father. Leila had gone north for the weekend, to the annual trade fair, so there was no one at home, and Chloë hadn't yet been given a doorkey for the new house.

That had been the beginning. That was the last moment life had been normal, without unnerving distortions. The afternoon that she'd got involved with Beryl Ryder.

Chloë

14

I had admired Beryl Ryder from afar. She was one of those willowy, superior blondes worshipped by some of the juniors at my girls' day-school. My own respect wasn't so sloppy, but I would have given a lot to be like her. What I most envied, beyond her tall beauty, was her obvious lack of concern for any of the people or things which cramped my own horizons.

She had no idea who I was. Her gaze was far above the level of someone with the main subjects of GCSE still to master. She had already survived those exams to reach the Sixth Form. Although automatically a prefect through seniority, she had somehow steered clear of other student chores — School Captain, Head of House or Games Captain. If the positions had been elective and not from the Head's choice she would probably have filled them all, but I could never see such a brazenly free spirit organizing school charities or team lists.

When she swanned into my father's room that afternoon I assumed she'd become one of his students, and I realized then that I hadn't seen her about the school corridors for some months.

She stood draped in the doorway, one hip exaggeratedly jutting, fabulously slim — almost anorexic — and sneered at me. 'For godsake,' she challenged, 'lectures ended at four. What the hell are you doing still here?'

She sounded so officious that I bobbed up from my chair and explained I was waiting for my father.

She took one look at my uniform and placed me as a student applicant due to be picked up after an interview. I didn't trouble to put her right because her lofty attitude was beginning to make me bristle.

She brushed past me with assumed authority, seated herself at Miss Morris's empty desk and began opening drawers and riffling through them. On Fridays my father's secretary left soon after lunch, and I wondered if Beryl was appointed to replace her part-time.

After a minute or two of silence she picked up the internal phone. 'Joanne,' she complained, 'have you any idea where Aidan's got to? There's a schoolgirl here who's expecting to be picked up by her family. D'you know anything about it? Well, can you . . . ?'

And it was then that he walked in. My father. Clearly her lover. Their eyes locked with such indecent familiarity.

If he felt wrongfooted at sight of me he covered it well. With practice, I suppose. He instantly picked up on the cross-purposes we'd been at and sorted us out with casual introductions. 'My daughter Chloë,' he explained me away. But 'A student here who's helping me with the paperwork,' he offered for Beryl.

'She was at my school,' I told him.

'Oh.' He looked at her, then back at me. 'So you know each other, good.' He went through to his inner room and I expected him back with his briefcase, but after a few scrabbling sounds in there he called, 'Beryl, I can't seem to find my — '

She swayed in with her long-legged stride and closed the door behind her. I heard their voices, mainly his, but couldn't — didn't want to — make out any words.

They came out together and faced me. 'Look,' my father said, 'I've got stuff here to clear up, so I could be another half hour. Why don't you both trot off and have tea somewhere in town? Then later Beryl can give me a buzz, so I know where to pick you up.' He had obviously forgotten he was to drive me home, and there was no enquiry about how the French oral had gone.

The last thing I wanted was Beryl Ryder's

company, although at that point I chose to see her as someone who'd been through the examination mill ahead of me and might offer some lowdown on tackling the next stage. As for Beryl, she seemed almost amused, certainly recovered from the distaste she'd shown on finding me in Father's outer office.

She had a little car, a blue Fiat, and drove leaning back as if it were a sun lounger, both hands at the top of the wheel. I couldn't miss the weird variety of rings she wore. She wouldn't have been allowed them at school; and certainly not the pearl-mounted one piercing her left eyebrow. Her style in clothes had changed too, ultra-mod, just short of punk. I thought her make-up was too harsh for a blonde, but it certainly made you see her.

She drove out of town and pulled up in the yard of a country pub. 'Right,' she said, sounding no end chuffed, 'let's get to know each other. You can leave your school blazer in the car. And you'll find it cooler if you pull your shirt out.'

I don't like anyone bossing me over my appearance, but I thought twice about arguing with an erstwhile goddess, however much she seemed to have changed. So I did as she suggested and did feel cooler.

The pub had a little garden round at the

back with a scrappy lawn and a couple of overgrown rose arches. We settled at a rough, creosoted bench which had a matching one facing us with a wooden table between. The whole set looked crude, like furniture in an illustration from Goldilocks: surfaces suited to wild bears immune to splinters.

Beryl brought us out long glasses of something chilled with a ball of golden sorbet floating at the top. I asked what flavour it was and she said passion fruit, then laughed. To make conversation I said I'd sat the French oral that afternoon, and she stared as if I came from an alien planet.

'Didn't you?' I asked.

'Suppose I did,' she granted. 'A long time back. Seems so, anyway.' Then she switched on some appearance of interest. 'How did it go?'

'All right, I think. Except when we got on to politics.'

'I thought that was banned: politics, sex and religion. Dangerous stuff for the innocent young mind.' She was mocking me.

'It was about the European Union. I said I hadn't much interest in the idea of a superstate and was happier with literature. So then we got on to something I knew a bit about.'

'Good move; manipulate the bastards.

Anyway, why work at French? I suppose you'll turn into a scientist like your father.'

'No, I shan't.'

She gave a scoffing laugh. 'You can't help it. It's in the genes. Like your red hair.'

'Actually I'm more like my mother.'

She looked hard at me, one eyebrow stagily raised. 'But she's only a stepmother, isn't she?'

Beryl started lighting a cigarette from the butt of her previous one and didn't catch me staring back. I couldn't believe she'd be so undiplomatic, but that wasn't what jarred me. Although back at the Uni she'd had no idea who I was, yet she knew about my actual relationship with Leila. How could she, unless from my father having discussed it with her?

How much intimate family information had been passed on as gossip? Would she even know how I'd persuaded Leila to henna her hair, so we'd look like real mother and daughter? I'd meant my father to know that, to hurt him, but I hadn't thought he'd noticed.

There followed a silence which had to be filled. 'Have you met my brother?' I asked.

She was sucking in smoke, her eyes lazily half-closed. 'No idea. What's he called?'

'Edward.'

'I know three Edwards. The name's common enough. How did he get into the conversation?'

I wasn't quite sure myself. The lowering sun shone full in my eyes and seemed to leave swirling disks in the dark when I closed them. 'He's going to be a scientist,' I said. 'How frantically exciting.' Her drawling tone said the opposite.

I considered. She was right: as conversation it was pretty limp. But then so would be any topic I had to offer. She'd apparently forgotten her suggestion that we get to know each other.

We had sat there quite a lot longer than the half hour my father had mentioned. Beryl had twice renewed our drinks. A number of cars had driven into the inn's yard, and the saloon bar behind us was noisily beginning to fill up for the evening. Others came outside with their drinks and I hoped no one would think to question my age. Beryl had been wise to make me leave my blazer in the car. There was nothing specifically schoolish about my plain white shirt and grey skirt.

I must have been dozing when her mobile phone started warbling. She pulled it out of her shoulder-bag and murmured into it, 'About time too.' And then, 'Oh no! Shit! I'm not sure I can.' Her voice had turned sulky.

'Well, all right then, but it's a bloody bore all the same. You'd better make it worth my while.'

She snapped the phone off and stuffed it back in her bag. 'He wants me to see you home.'

I supposed she meant my father, but it made no difference one way or the other. I was already past caring who said what, where I went, what I did. It would be good, I thought, to find somewhere soft to lie down and sleep.

I vaguely remember getting to the car, being helped in and its stored heat hitting me. For security she had left all its windows tightly closed and it was facing into the sun. My head lolled forward on the fascia which bobbled disagreeably as she started the car and we lurched out on to the road. At some more distant moment she was shaking me, demanding something, then shouting again into her phone.

The last I was conscious of was her exasperated swearing. 'Now he's shut the fucking thing off! How can I get the little cow home if I don't know where she lives?'

At some time after that the nightmare must have begun to build, but I had no recollection of it when I awoke at last in my own bed. Early light was beginning to show at the edges of the curtains.

I knew I'd been in the pub garden and that I'd unknowingly drunk something strongly alcoholic. In the past I'd had wine in small quantities at home with special meals, and it had never affected me. This was different. I hoped I hadn't been sick or objectionable to anyone.

I remembered Eddie coming home drunk once, back at Caversham. Father had been away, and Leila helped the cabbie get Eddie indoors and upstairs to his room. Disturbed by the shouted abuse and horrible retchings I had lain sweating in my bed, until a flaming dawn was breaking over the Chilterns, and I was convinced that something horrendous had changed our lives forever.

But Eddie had recovered; Leila had put me right. 'We all make mistakes,' she said. 'It's best not to dwell on them. I'm sure Eddie will have a word with you about it.'

And he had. He apologized. 'I'm sorry if I frightened you,' he said. 'I never knew the state I was in.'

I'd told him it was just the noise that woke me: a bit of banging and crashing on the stairs.

He made a lemon-sucking face. 'Well, there's one thing I do know now,' he said. 'Drink's something I can't take. Perhaps it's just as well.'

What he'd said then, about not being able

to take it, stayed in my mind. So I guess I'm the same with alcohol and it's a family thing.

I slept in late that Saturday after my meeting with Beryl Ryder, only waking properly in mid-afternoon feeling headachy, sick and confused. Over the next couple of days tender red patches on my flesh gradually went purple and later greenish yellow. They felt like bruises. On my upper arms dark fingermarks showed, so I guessed I'd been unsteady on my feet and needed firm holding; but the patches of bruising on my inner thighs were bigger and quite painful. They frightened me, because I couldn't account for them. When Leila came home and suggested we went swimming I had to cry off. I didn't dare let her see, for fear of what they might signify. I don't think Father had mentioned the episode to her, and I was too ashamed to.

The effects weren't only physical. My mind was affected. I guess it was like one of those ancient cinema films Granny called 'the flicks'. From almost total darkness a shutter kept opening on slits of light and fragments of images. These terrible flashes came when I least expected and were gone before I could account for them. And there were alarming sensations following certain movements. I felt vertigo as I tried to rise from a chair or walk across a stretch of floor.

Often after sleep I've been conscious of having dreamed but can't remember specifically what happened, yet the certainty is there because the dream's atmosphere hangs on. I know I've been to a frightening place, or been worried, or experiencing delight or been warmly comforted: the glow or the unease remains as I come awake. And sometimes I know exactly who I've been with, yet have no idea of any incident we were involved in. It was the same now: the sensation that came back in waves was one of absolute terror.

Now I tried to explain away these flashes of confused dream as a chemical effect, the action of alcohol on my hormones. I'm adolescent, so surely my body chemistry is still dodgy. But that doesn't excuse, doesn't account for, everything that disturbed me. As well as the physical evidence of bruising, there were strangers' faces, or part-faces, that flashed up without warning.

The most terrible and recurrent was of eyes pressing so close over me that they had merged into a single black beetle-shape. And then they would reappear less close, separate, with pinpoint dark irises set in a strangely mottled pale blue, which made me think of tie-dye jeans with the colour washed out.

Off and on came a partial face which was

familiar. My father's, livid with fury, hanging over me, mouthing, but his words never reached me. I supposed he must have fetched me home and been disgusted at the state I was in. But home from where, I had no idea.

By the time I felt well enough to show my face that Saturday evening my father had left the house, so there was to be no explanation required from either of us. Before Leila went north she had left a number of pre-cooked dishes in the freezer to be heated up, and Mrs Chadwick was coming in over the weekend to look after us. Not that I felt much like eating.

Since Father was out there was little for her to do. I told her I would clear away and load the dishwasher, to prevent her staying to see me empty my plate into the trash bin.

From then until Leila got back from Yorkshire on Sunday evening I spent much of the time on the garden swing or face down in the overlong grass making a pretence of reading. I slept a little, but that was no more restful than my wakeful unease. It seemed more and more likely that there was something wrong with me, in my brain.

Unexpectedly my father returned that Sunday about a quarter to eight. For some reason I had thought he wouldn't be back. I suppose it was because of seeing him with Beryl. Although they'd both tried to give the impression she worked at the Uni, I wasn't fooled. Quite when I'd first known about his 'little friends' I'm not certain, but I knew there was always someone there in the background, important to him but outside the family. A mistress, but only of sorts, because he'd always have to be the master. She would be something less.

How Leila felt about this was unclear. I suppose she accepted it, expecting nothing better from him. I couldn't be like that, not with anyone I'd ever loved. She was always so calm. She should have shouted at him or thrown things, like deceived wives in television plays. It would do him good to feel afraid of someone.

He arrived as I was helping unload goods from the boot of Leila's car: boxes of fancy stationery, novelties and heavy albums containing samples of new greetings cards. She was tired from long hours of driving and he made the most of grumbling that she took on so much. Not that he was concerned for her, just for himself, because he had always to be in control.

That's how it would have been on Friday night too. He was furious with me for stepping out of line, but he wouldn't care at all how I was feeling now. As they went indoors he was still quibbling over some detail of the route she'd taken.

Leila had passed me her key-ring. Since we'd come to this house she'd been letting me put her car away in the garage. It would be eighteen months before I could apply for a licence, but I took every chance I could get of practice off public roads. I was specially proud of my skill in reversing, to park exactly level with the BMW and dead centre in the allotted space.

Tonight, however, the BMW wasn't there. Either my father had taken a cab home or someone had dropped him off. With my head bent over the Volvo's boot I hadn't noticed his arrival. Perhaps it had been in Beryl's little Fiat. So had Leila picked up on it? It all seemed tedious and unnecessary. I would leave them to the routine exchanges, he bickering, she silently shock-absorbing.

My old Raleigh bicycle was leaning against the garage's inner wall where I'd left it after the nextdoor boy fixed the chain for me. I wheeled it out and stood astride it facing the roadway. The lamp was a bit dodgy but it came on after I hit it once or twice. Perhaps by now indoors they'd reached the subject of my misdemeanours and Leila was getting the flak off it. Better I shouldn't be there. They might even think I'd slunk off to bed. It seemed a good time not to be around.

15

All day the oppressive heat had been building. Evening brought no relief. Dark bands of cloud were closing over the yellowed skyline and the sultry air was disturbed by quirky little gusts of wind. One moment all was totally still, and then dust eddies were swirling across the surface of the road. I stood on my pedals and looking up saw the early stars blacking out in twos and threes overhead around a half-moon in tatters of smoky cloud.

Our house stands high on a thickly wooded ridge that falls steeply towards open farmland. At the drive's end I turned left to freewheel downhill towards where the Chess snakes out to the Thames. There was no sound but the soft whirring of the bike's spokes and once the faint two-note hoot of a distant turbo train with its tantalizing hint of travel. I would have given anything then to get right away.

Halfway through the tunnel of arched beeches my head-lamp flickered three times and went out. Now the darkness was total until, between sparser trees, lit windows became visible pricked out like stars. Then to either side were sloping fields that gleamed dully under fleeting moonlight, with hedgerows black and flat as stage scenery.

Between me and Mardham Village in the hollow straggled a few small cottages showing yellow, uncurtained windows. Then came the halogen glare of a farm's floodlit stockyard. A diffused orange glow over the distant town was reflected on the underside of felty overcast clouds, and strung out towards the horizon a receding double strand of sodium lights marked out the curving motorway, diminishing with distance like an exercise in perspective.

Ahead, occasional white scuts of rabbits flickered as they caught the whirr of my bike, and instantly, like juggled balls, they were bouncing away, behind invisible bodies. The road began to flatten. I braked towards level ground and then, before the river's hump-backed bridge, the first fat raindrops spattered my bare arms. Lightning instantly lit the sky from behind. There were a hundred new scents released by the rain.

The storm came on fast with a sheeting downpour and heavy thunder. There was no shelter but the occasional tree and I'd sense enough not to go for that. If I returned by the route I'd come the steep gradient would force me to dismount and push uphill for most of the way. The alternative was to pedal fast through Mardham and take the more gently rising loop back to the far end of our road. A further half-mile, but in the long run it must be quicker.

Already my cotton shirt clung like a second skin to my back. Water was trickling down my forehead. I'd been a fool not to take account of the weather; but at least this was a normal kind of disaster, one I'd be capable of handling. No challenge to my sanity.

There was no let-up. If anything the deluge increased. Thunder doesn't worry me, but the vivid flashes set my heart racing. Fork lightning flashed against the blackness like gigantic incandescent roots, violet-white. One strike was close, exploding with a violent hissing, and the air was filled with an acrid tang like cordite after a gun's been fired. Somewhere not far off a tree flared like a beacon.

With my head down, I pedalled on through a cowed village where all windows were close-curtained and the street lamps' pale globes had little effect.

Beyond it, for even the gentler climb, I should have dismounted because the lane fast became a gulley with storm-water gushing down between raised banks. My front wheel went suddenly from under me and I was pitched into the flow, an elbow grazing on invisible flints.

I sat up in the lane which had turned into a stream and I shouted with anger.

One moment I was alone and then next there was this man looming over me, motionless. He looked immense, tall and sinister in a black mackintosh that reached down over his rubber boots. On his head a wide-brimmed rain-hat kept his face obscured.

'Should I help you?' he asked doubtfully.

'What do you think?' I spat back. 'I'm not sitting here for pleasure.'

He disentangled the bike from my legs and hauled me up. 'One can't tell,' he said mildly, 'quite how independent ladies require to be these days.'

It sounded too bland and I suspected irony. His grip on my arms in lifting me had been vice-like. I didn't dare let him see how scared of him I was.

'I suggest,' he said, 'we give up on the lane and take to the higher fields.'

Anything would be better than the ankle-deep torrent we were standing in, but I remembered the stranger I'd always been warned against as a child. Although I'd mocked the idea then, it didn't seem so melodramatic now.

But it was sordid inner cities where thugs and perverts existed, not the rolling Chiltern countryside. Here they were as improbable as vampires. And outrages happened with a different sort of people, not the kind we lived among.

That's what I'd believed until . . . Until what?

Despite the hot anger of a moment before, there came a flash of terror. It was illogical, but for a bare instant my mind lurched with a sort of half-memory. Something terrifying from the past, although I didn't know what. But I could no longer believe I was invulnerable.

No one knew where I was. If anything happened I was on my own. If I disappeared who would think to go looking for me, supposedly safe in my own room at home? Not my father. He hadn't brought his car back today and he detested any kind of rain. Not that it would cross his mind to check on me unless he needed something. Now that Leila was back that was less likely.

What was the matter with me that I should get this fit of nerves?

I tried to shake off the fear but a disturbing resonance hung on: danger. I could become a victim.

The man stood waiting sideways on to the steep bank, one leg braced ready to climb. His heroic stance made me think of a highwayman. The wind flicked open the ends of his long coat. I could see now that, like the hat, it was of black leather, the sort I connected with old war films and the Gestapo. He held my bicycle almost effortlessly under one arm. The front wheel looked mangled. Perhaps he was burdened enough to be incapable of violence. Unless he hurled the bike at me.

I had to do something; used the edges of my trainers like skis to dig into the soggy grass, and staggered, sideways-on and slithering, to the top. And there I turned to run — straight into barbed wire. Some bastard farmer had thought fit to break the country code here.

The man reached out to where my shirt and jeans were caught fast. The more I pulled away the more I tore them and slashed my arms. I could feel warm blood running down one to the wrist.

Then I heard the bike dropped.

'Stand utterly still,' he ordered. 'Each barb has to be unhooked separately.'

A brilliant flash of lightning lit the figure bent over me with his fingers in my clothes. I saw a lean, curved profile like Mr Punch,

222

brows knitted in concentration, a prominent nose with deep lines etched from bridge to chin.

'You're in a real pickle.' His fingers stilled as he considered his own words. 'That's a curious expression, when you come to think. Soused in vinegar and onions: you're hardly that.'

He was unbelievable. I started laughing, uncontrollably.

'Steady,' he warned. Did he know I was almost screaming inside? He gripped my upper arms tightly a moment, hurting the bruises already there. I hiccuped into silence. Then he began again plucking the torn cloth off the wires. 'You must shout if I hurt you,' he said. 'I can't properly see what we've got here.'

Then a humorous snort. 'If it's any consolation, you weren't the first to be hooked.' And he handed me an oily wad of sheep's wool he'd untangled with my shirt.

'You chose a fine night for a cycle ride,' he commented drolly.

I didn't explain that I'd simply had to get away from the house, so turned it on him. 'What were you doing out here anyway?'

'Needing fresh air. It's been a helluva day.'

'Doing what? I mean, what are you?'

There was a pause while he decided how

truthful to be. 'I'm — a company director. It was my bad share day.'

So he chose to joke, but it was evasive. Any fool knew the stock exchange wasn't open on a Sunday. Besides he didn't look the part: more stagey, like an actor in a thriller film. I asked no more questions and volunteered nothing about myself.

We located a gate in the barbed wire fence and squelched through wet meadow-grass that whipped my bare ankles, then circled a field of ripening maize. By now the thunder sounded more distant and the rain had lessened, but the damage was already done.

Finally we reached the top, gaining level ground through a spinney where a beaten path led off to the road, my road. When I recognized where we'd come out I managed an ungracious, 'I'll be all right now,' as a brush-off. 'Thanks for helping.'

'You can't go home like that,' he said. 'You'll scare your folks to death. My sister can put something on your scratches and lend something to cover you up.'

'I don't need — '

But we had arrived right opposite his cottage and a woman was silhouetted in the brightly lit doorway. 'Is that you at last?' she called. 'What on earth are you doing with that old bike?'

She sounded so normal that I shrugged off any remains of fear. Just a little resentment hung on, at having publicly made such a fool of myself. And I didn't want my father to catch me looking like this. Especially after Friday's mess-up.

Inside, the cottage was tiny and bright with unframed colour sketches taped to the whitewashed walls. There were bean bags to sit on, or disappear in, and — funnily — they didn't look out of place against the antique furniture.

The sister, whose name was Morgan, conjured up a fluffy bath towel and almost pushed me through to the shower room. 'A period piece,' she excused it. 'You pull a chain here to get the water. But it's hot and there's plenty. I'll just go and rustle up some dry clothes for you.'

I stood a long while under the deluge until the gravel rash and the rips on my arm were cleared of blood and mud. The skin smarted afresh and I noticed that the bruises which came up yesterday had darkened to a rich plum colour. I was wrapped in the warm towel when Morgan passed me the clothes round the screen: a red silk blouse and snugly fitting jeans which for me just needed the ends turned up. I emerged feeling more human.

The blouse was sleeveless and I couldn't miss her glancing at my bruised arms and then meeting her brother's eyes with something like a nod of affirmation. It made me wonder what each had been saying about me while the shower had drowned out all sound of voices from the adjoining room. She insisted on smoothing antiseptic cream on the new cuts, her pretty face puckered with mild concern.

Her brother — I still didn't know his name and felt embarrassed about asking — was making coffee in the minute kitchen. I'd meant to leave at once but the coffee smelled so good I was won over, so we all ended in the bean bags, Morgan neatly, and her brother's long body making an angular zigzag, his splayed knees above the level of his head.

Now I could observe him more closely. It was a long, humorous face with a baroque mouth, but, even without that Gestapo leather coat, I still found him formidable. I had let him get away with a lie over his profession, but I felt I'd best not stray far from the truth in anything I told him.

It was tempting to stay on. The old cottage was snug and comforting. I didn't look forward to the chill newness of Knollhurst and possible further encounters with my

226

father. Without saying as much, I found I was explaining myself a little. They asked the usual questions about school, then about the move here from Caversham; which in turn brought up my father's transfer to the University of London.

'Our father was a professor too,' Morgan said. 'An archaeologist, so even in the holidays we didn't see a lot of him. He was always away on digs. I'm afraid we both found that sort of thing rather slow and preferred travelling to more racy places with Mother. She's a doctor of sorts.'

So then I told them about Leila, how really cool she was, although strictly only a step-mum. I didn't remember my biological mother except as an invalid in a nursing-home.

'Are you an only?' Morgan asked sympathetically.

Being proud of Eddie and his brilliant A-levels, I told her about his year off before Cambridge, how he'd been sponsored to sit in on American space research, observing biomechanics and robotics.

'M'm, impressive,' she said. 'So do you take after your father too?'

'No.'

Even to myself it sounded abrupt. I rushed in to cover up. 'Eddie doesn't either, not as a person. Just in the brains department. I'm not so bright. If I go to college it will be on the Arts side. My best subjects are Languages and History. I'm taking French and Italian GCSEs this year in advance. As soon as those exams are over I'll be free of school until September. Two years of sixth form after that.'

'Then what?' Morgan's brother asked from the depths of his bean bag.

'I don't know. I'd like to go abroad. Granny Knightley lives in Provence. Leila might work it for me to go out there.'

'Good practice for your French. Will your father agree to it?'

'He doesn't think Granny would be much . . . I mean, they aren't all that close. Anyway it's not a good time to ask him at the moment.' I was embarrassed at having to explain that much, so said no more. The very thought of approaching him when I was in disgrace brought back the confusion of Friday.

It wasn't really fair to blame me for getting drunk. I hadn't known the stuff was so strong, though I should have guessed Beryl Ryder was out to make mischief. The moment she had clapped eyes on me there had been a sort of spark between us. Of malice, I was sure now.

Morgan had set up a low Moorish table

between us with a beaten brass top and a matching tray with coffee and biscuits. 'It's decaff,' she said, 'in case you're afraid it might stop you sleeping tonight.'

'I don't think anything would do that.' In fact my eyelids were already heavy. I seemed to have done little else but sleep since Friday, when whatever had happened happened.

I was taking a bourbon biscuit from the plate offered me when I caught the intense look in her eyes and I knew, just knew, I had seen her before, recently; seen that same piercing expression on her face. Only she had looked different then in some way. 'Have we met before?' I blurted out.

She hesitated, as her brother had done when I asked him what he was. 'That's not likely is it? You've only just moved here from Caversham, you said.'

It wasn't a direct lie like his, but she was turning my question off. I wondered what they had to hide, and I was quite certain now that I had met her before, even been involved with her in some way. There was this stupid business of forgetting and only half-remembering what had happened lately.

They took it all right when I abruptly said I had to go. Morgan insisted I borrow a plastic mackintosh although it seemed to have stopped raining.

'Your bike,' her brother reminded me. 'I'll let you have it back when it's fixed.'

'Please don't bother. I mean, I'll get it seen to.'

'My pleasure.'

I was sure it wouldn't be. He didn't look the sort to be any good with fiddly jobs. His fingers were long and slender, for all that, like his face, they were suntanned to a rich mahogany.

He had risen. 'I'll see you to your door.'

'No thanks.' It was one occasion when he'd have to accept female emancipation. He picked that up at once. 'Well, see you around,' he compromised. Morgan handed me my own wet things in a plastic carrier.

The air outside was fresher now, the moon only momentarily obscured by moving cloud. The front of our house was in darkness except for the porch lantern which burned all night. I still had Leila's key-ring so I slipped noiselessly in, listened to locate where the others were and decided that, at eleven-fifteen, they'd retired early.

Leila would have assumed that I'd discreetly withdrawn from any threatening row with my father. I wondered what account of my drunkenness he'd given her. Or if he'd even bothered.

16

She bent close over me and I screamed, lashing out with my fists. But it was Leila. I didn't see how it could be. Leila wouldn't hurt me.

'Chloë, it's all right. You were having a nightmare.'

From the next room she must have heard me call out. Because I was threatened. With a tumbler of something salty being poured down my throat. And the face! — not hers but Morgan's, yet looking different, with the fair curls scraped tightly back into a bun under a starched white cap.

'What was the dream about?'

'I was — in a sort of hospital, I think. Oh, it was all confused.'

'But you aren't. You're at home. There's nothing wrong with you, is there?'

'No. I — I'm fine.'

'So go to sleep again. You've another four hours. Tomorrow we'll go swimming. How's that?'

'Lovely.'

Leila knew, because I'd once told her, how sometimes in good dreams I'm blissfully cutting through turquoise water, butterfly stroke, with the sun glistening on my wet arms. She thought I had only to close my eyes, think of that, and then any dream would be a happy one. Perhaps she'd forgotten that tomorrow I'd be sitting my last two exam papers.

She squeezed my shoulder and went quietly away. I was afraid to relax because asleep something bad lurked just out of sight to get at me. It was like moving in the dark through an unfamiliar room, knowing someone stood behind a curtain there waiting to leap out.

It was not just Morgan. Another face, a man's, seemed to come and go, emerging and fading in a fog. Someone younger, pale, gaunt-eyed, suddenly there in a subliminal flash, the features frozen expressionless, his very blankness horrific. An unknown. He hadn't any place in my life, yet he had me deadly afraid. I was far outside the safe world Leila wanted to wrap me in.

Had I actually agreed to her suggestion? Stupid, stupid! I couldn't let her see me in a swimsuit because of the bruises. Tomorrow, after school, I'd have to make excuses, and hope she didn't guess I'd something to hide.

I switched on the table lamp by my bed and reached for a book. From the page where

I'd left the marker I read empty words, sentences, mechanically turned pages, but it all passed my eyes without reaching my mind. Again I was seeing flashes that I couldn't account for, incidents from some violent film I don't ever remember watching.

Eventually I must have fallen asleep. I awoke to hear the house stirring to life, and my bedside lamp was still on. I felt heavy and sluggish, in no way prepared to face my Italian Composition paper. Leila insisted on my eating a breakfast of grapefruit and marmalade toast. Then she dropped me at my bus stop on her way to the shop. 'Don't worry about the exam. You'll be fine. We'll swim this evening,' she promised. So in the night it hadn't been said just to calm me.

Being with the other girls, letting their chatter wash over me, helped; but still it was an effort to pull my mind together. It was only half an hour into the first paper that I began to tackle it as if it was real. I forced myself to eat some lunch: shepherd's pie with green beans, and much too heavy for another steamy day. Last night's storm had done little to break the heatwave.

The afternoon paper was Comprehension, which I found easier to get into. Afterwards I joined in the others' moans and groans as expected, although I knew I'd made quite a good job of it. And then there yawned a great void ahead: the extended summer holiday, because public-exam candidates were allowed to skip the rest of term, and my few papers had been early ones. I decided to drop into the town library and pick up something to focus my mind on.

We were a group of five as far as the council offices and after that I continued alone. Crossing by the fish market I had the silly idea that someone was following me. It was so strong that I stepped inside among all the smells of dead flesh and disinfectant, the rattling of buckets and robust slapping of scaly bodies on wet chopping blocks.

I pretended to be examining the bright pink steaks of salmon, then turned quickly and looked all around behind. Monday's not a busy day for selling fish, and most people shop there in the morning anyway. Among the small number there I should have been able to pick out anyone I knew.

No one appeared out of place or interested in me.

'Yes, miss. What'll it be then?' demanded the man in a striped apron and straw hat. I mumbled that I was only looking, and moved off. I glanced back once as I left, and it seemed that a shadowy figure slipped away behind one of the hall's iron pillars.

Not a real sighting. Just another of those flashes that kept bothering me; either half-memories or overexcited fancy. When I reached the library I would look up epilepsy in a medical dictionary. There was something called petit mal but I didn't know exactly what it was, or how it started. I wondered if that was what my mother had suffered from. Nobody had ever explained to me why she'd been an invalid or how it had started. It could be one of those genetic things.

In the library Philip, the dishy young assistant, wasn't on duty at the desk. Instead, when I'd chosen three books at random from the fiction section I took them with my card to Miss Humphreys. She was a massive-fronted dragon whom I usually managed to avoid. She barely looked at me until she was taking my card from the key slot. Then she fixed me with her severe wire-framed gaze and said, 'I think we have some property of yours, Miss Knightley.'

She reached for a package farther along the counter and handed it to me, a quite fat A4 envelope. Before I could deny it was mine she launched her reprimand: I should really take better care of my belongings. The library staff had more than enough to do without scurrying round tidying up after the public. I was lucky it hadn't been locked away in Lost

Property, since it hadn't my address on it.

She was right; it hadn't. But my name was there, typewritten with a new-looking black ribbon: Chloë Knightley. She tucked it firmly between two of my books, looked past me and said, 'Next, please,' as friendly as a flatiron.

There seemed to be quite a lot inside the envelope. I knew I had never seen it before, so someone had left it, intending it to be handed to me next time I came in. And since it hadn't yet reached the Lost Property cupboard, that person must have left it a matter of minutes before.

Out in the torrid street I hugged my books to me and squatted on the low wall by the bus stop, with the park railings hard against my back. One bus must just have gone because there was no queue waiting. So with twelve minutes or so to spare I laid the books down and eased the envelope open with a fingernail while the traffic droned past, building towards rush hour.

Inside were six glossy black and white photographs and no note to cover them.

I had never seen porn before, but that's what these must be. No way could you call it Art.

The shots were of a woman's naked body squirming in obscene positions, brightly front-lit. Two of them showed the photographer's squat, cruciform shadow projected across her white flesh. Long hair, tangled and rat-tailed, barely allowed a glimpse of her eyes closed in mock ecstasy. The rest of her face was in deep shadow. The last shot was every bit as obscene, although she wore a filmy, translucent dress. It was long and seemed to have a snaky pattern. In only this picture was the face revealed.

With horror I found I was staring at my own. I appeared to be asleep.

*   *   *

Automatically I boarded the bus, showed my pass, found a seat. I felt nothing, except some difficulty in breathing.

Time must have passed as I sat there unbelieving. And yet it made sense now. It accounted for so much: the confusion, the film-clip flashes of memory, the bruising.

I didn't think any more that I'd been drunk. This was due to more than alcohol. I'd read sometime in a newspaper about what they called the date-rape drug. I could even remember its commercial name: Rohypnol. Dentists sometimes used it, and there was a similar veterinary product which sometimes got loose on the market.

There had been women who innocently accepted drinks from a stranger. Perhaps as much as a day later they'd woken to the sort of state I'd been in, with whole passages of time missing from their lives. They'd suffered the same symptoms. The friendly stranger — as they'd thought — had drugged and abducted them, then raped them while they were helpless. To anyone watching as they left the bar, the women had seemed a little drunk, not unwilling to be led away. Even co-operative.

Now it had happened to me. I'd been given something like that, when I'd been with Beryl Ryder. How could she let it happen? And why would she?

But she hadn't been alone. I recalled the shadowy sightings — a man, a decadent with pale eyes like washed-out blue denim, the pupils pinpoints. And Morgan, dressed to look like a nurse.

How much of that was nightmare fantasy, and how much real? And I'd thought I'd seen my father looking furious. Perhaps that was a memory escaped from some earlier time I'd offended him. How would I ever know?

But then I didn't want ever to know.

I found the bus had gone past my stop and I rushed to get off, clutching my library books and the package with the revolting photographs. Now I'd nearly a mile to walk back.

I'd need all of that to get a grip on myself before facing Leila. She hadn't offered to pick me up today, expecting us to hang about after the last exam or go off to discuss it over milkshakes. That was one thing to be glad of.

I started to walk, and to try sorting things in my mind. My mind which I'd thought I'd been going out of. Now I knew I wasn't sick in quite that way.

But there were other horrors every bit as bad: what had actually happened. I could have been made pregnant.

Bile came up in my mouth. Whatever had happened was too far back now for any precautions to work. I knew there was a 'morning-after' pill but it was too late even for that. And what about AIDS? HIV? I should really see a doctor, but I didn't dare. I would just have to wait and see what happened. How could I, though, with so much hanging over me?

I had to find Beryl Ryder. She had a lot to answer for. She had certainly laced my drink at that pub. Where had she dropped me off afterwards? Maybe she'd taken the photographs too. The idea shamed me. I wasn't sure I could trust myself to get in touch.

Was I imagining the way she'd looked at

me once she knew who I was? With silent amusement. Could she be so coldly malicious, the sixth-former I'd admired because she was beautiful and, as I thought, sophisticated?

I still wasn't ready to face Leila by the time I reached home. I couldn't believe I ever would be. She was in the front garden planning where she'd plant a Viburnum hedge. She saluted me jauntily with a soily trowel but I went right past.

'I'm going for a shower and then early bed,' I said shortly. 'I couldn't face going out tonight.'

'Whatever you like,' she offered. I'd worried her, but she doesn't fuss.

I'd reached the foot of the stairs when I thought of something and went back to her. 'Do you think I could borrow your mobile? I've a couple of calls to make. I promise I won't run you up an immense bill.'

'Of course. The phone's in my shoulder bag in the kitchen.'

I helped myself to it and to the current area phone directory from the study. Then, as I'd said I'd do, I showered; but no amount of standing under the water and soaping myself off would ever get rid of what had happened to me.

In bed I looked up the Ryder number.

There were only two entries for that name and one was for Truck Rental, so I chose the other. It still took me a long time to get round to ringing it.

It must have been her mother who answered; a languid, rather artificial voice. 'Beryl's not here,' she told me. 'Who shall I tell her called?'

When I gave my name and was halfway through my number she snapped back, 'She has it, as you must know. I'm quite sure she won't want to trouble you by ringing back, Mrs Knightley.' Then the line went dead and the dialling tone returned.

It rather stunned me, but her mistake was understandable. So Beryl's mother knew about her affair with my father and had probably heard her ringing him at this number. She'd taken me for Leila, not knowing her first name. Now she might not pass on to Beryl that I'd rung. Perhaps that was a good thing.

But it seems that she did.

I was lying sleepless at a quarter to eight when the downstairs phone rang and Leila called up that it was for me. 'Beryl someone,' she said as she passed the handset across.

The voice on the other end sounded a little breathless, and something more, perhaps uneasy.

I made certain the kitchen door was fast closed on Leila before speaking. 'I want to know,' I said as firmly as I could, 'exactly what you were up to on Friday. And as for the photographs, you've no hope of blackmailing me. I've no money of my own. You must realise that.'

There was a silence. I tried to picture her face and couldn't. Then, 'What photographs?'

It sounded like genuine incredulity. But with someone like Beryl how could I tell?

'Listen,' she said threateningly. 'It's not my fault you got sloshed. You ought to be thanking me for what I did for you.'

It was unbelievable. 'Did what for me?'

'Got your dad to come out and pick you up. I even undressed you and put you to bed at home. I'm not surprised you don't remember. You were out cold at that point. He was disgusted. Lucky it was your mum's weekend away.

'And don't forget I want the dress back. It cost somebody a helluva lot of money. Make sure it's dry-cleaned, in case you puked all down it.'

I didn't know what she was talking about, any more than she'd appeared to know about the photographs. I put the receiver down and went, sickly, back to bed.

The thought of Beryl here in my room,

touching my things, undressing me, filled me with added disgust. And then, remembering how uneasy she'd sounded at first, I knew why: because of the little sachet of white powder I'd found in my bedding. It could have been in her pocket and dropped out when she manhandled me. Maybe some of my bruises had happened then. But she wasn't sure she'd lost it here. As far as she knew it could be anywhere.

Next morning I knew I had to get away. I would tell Leila I'd arranged with Granny to stay with her for a week or two. I might even do that, but only after I'd been for a medical check-up.

I couldn't trust any local doctor not to gas to Leila or my father, so it would have to be in London or even further away. I'd have to go private and use an assumed name. And the fee must come out of my holiday money.

Meanwhile I saw no point in pushing Beryl any further, but there was someone else who might be more forthcoming. I wasn't fooled anymore by her apparent niceness when she'd offered me coffee and dry clothes after my drenching. She'd been anything but a friend to me the first time I saw her, forcing that salty drink on me. The image had hardened in my memory and I knew for sure now that it was Morgan. Morgan who might, or might not, be a nurse. And nurses had access to all kinds of drugs.

So that was why I dressed and went out, saying I needed fresh air. Which was how I came to get really involved with the Gregorys, all three of them, just trying to get myself sorted out.

Investigation

17

Sunday 4 July

Chloë wandered out into the darkening garden and sat on the broken stone seat they'd retrieved from a tangle of brambles. Through the big windows she could see Janey moving about the kitchen illuminated like a stage set by the harsh strip lighting.

Leila had intended changing it, rejigging completely with new cooker, fittings, the lot. Now it would never happen. Everything had been struck dead. A part of her, Chloë knew, had gone the same way.

At Granny's she'd been getting over the shame and the shock of what had happened in her own life, sorting herself out and facing up. Then this unbelievable horror of Leila's killing. Today was the worst ever, so immeasurably long, starting in Nice and then ending in nightmare.

She tried not to see the physical murder in her mind, but that was impossible. It had happened in only one actual way, but a hundred dreadful images of it overwhelmed her. To break free of them she needed to know exactly who, and how, and the full agony of the reality. But she didn't yet dare face up to it. Oh God, not yet.

The sight of Janey getting on with life was offensive. Yet she was showing guts. No one could deny Janey had loved Leila. As I did, Chloë admitted. It was terrible to think *did*, not does. Because the love was still there, in the great gap that had appeared.

Janey seemed to be hunting for something, pulling out a kitchen chair and climbing up to peer in the top cupboards. Chloë brushed grit off the seat of her jeans and went in to help.

'Ah,' Janey said. 'That big brown pottery thing she does the casseroles in; have you any idea where it's been put? I thought I'd start tomorrow's steak off tonight; let it cook slowly for an hour or two.'

'*Does* the casseroles in . . . ' She was having the same trouble with tenses.

Chloë went through to the conservatory and retrieved the pot from where the cleaned china had been stacked. Under the trestle table Leila's yellow rubber gloves hung over the edge of a bucket, plumped out as if her hands were still curled in them, but weirdly collapsed.

She hugged the pot to her, its bright highlights on the heavy brown glaze comfortingly familiar. Continuity: that was something.

'Anything you'd like me to do?' she asked Janey, back in the kitchen.

'Could you trot down to Hetty Chadwick's and say I'd like a word with her when it's convenient. I could phone but it's better face to face since we barely know each other.'

'Right.'

Passing the first of the old cottages she noticed the absence of lights. No sign of Morgan or her brother. Next-door the chenille curtains had been closed but sounds of the television escaped from an open casement. She recognised the opening music of the Sunday evening serial. Mrs Chadwick wouldn't care to have her regular viewing interrupted.

Chloë hadn't accounted for the woman's priority of the real world over the screen one. Or perhaps it was just unhealthy curiosity. 'I'll come right away,' she offered. 'Just a sec while I put me shoes on.'

She riffled through a bulging handbag for her key-ring which she dropped in her skirt pocket. 'Time was,' she said, 'when you never needed lock your doors. That's long gone. So how're you all bearing up, dearie? What a terrible thing to happen. I couldn't believe me ears when they told me.'

She slammed the door and they turned into the lane. Chloë was glad she wasn't expected to interrupt Mrs Chadwick's flow. The sky was growing overcast, like a lid pressing down the day's stale heat. Because the unmade edges of the road were tussocky and shadowed, they walked together in the middle.

'Gotta nasty bunion on me left foot,' the woman confided, to account for her hobbling.

'I hope it doesn't stop you . . . '

Chloë broke off, dazzled by headlights instantly switched on by a car racing towards them.

As she left she'd been vaguely conscious of a vehicle parked beyond Knollhurst with its engine idling. The speed at which it was roaring at them now was terrifying. She grabbed Mrs Chadwick by one arm and dragged her towards the verge, almost made it, but the woman tottered and was on the point of falling as the car struck, tearing her from Chloë's grasp. Falling, the girl saw in slow motion the big pale figure strike the bonnet and seem to leap off into the night as the car screamed past, its red rear lights swallowed up in the dark.

In the awful silence after it she gazed around. Grit in her eyes made them stream and she couldn't see. Hetty Chadwick had disappeared.

Then she made out a dim shape heaped

against the far verge. There was no movement, no sound.

Chloë crawled across on hands and knees. She took the heavy, ungainly body in her arms, rocking over it, lifted her head and howled like a dog.

★　★　★

Over breakfast on Monday Superintendent Yeadings paused after the first bite into his marmalade toast and wondered aloud where the proverbial prejudice against stepmothers had sprung from.

'Fairy tales,' Nan supplied. 'Snow White and the Wicked Queen, that sort of thing. Or maybe it goes further back, to the Ancient Greeks. They were pretty smart about funky families.'

She reached out to retrieve young Luke's yoghurt spoon which had unaccountably come sailing across the table in a wide parabola. 'I hope you aren't considering a replacement for my useless self.'

'That'd be the day,' her husband said, grinning fiercely. 'I just hoped you could shed some light on the stepchild's point of view.'

Nan planted her elbows on the table, earning a squeak of priggish protest from their daughter. 'Well, at best a new mum means comfort and support for a lonely little person who's rather adrift. For an older child who's into independence it can seem an invasion, a rupture of a standing relationship with the father, as well as an insult to the memory of the real mother. That leaves a sizeable area in-between.

'Does this sudden interest stem from the two boys who killed themselves in the stolen car?' She meant the case which had made front-page news in last week's local paper.

'No. Both had a full complement of biological parents, however inadequate they may have been. You recall the incident in Shotters Wood that we came across on Friday night? Nine years back the dead woman had married a widowed professor with two young children. The son's abroad at present, but I've met the daughter and she gives every sign of being devoted to her late stepmother. In fact she's devastated by her death.'

'How old?'

'An intelligent fifteen.'

'It's not simply shock at the idea of murder?'

'I'm sure it's much more.'

'In that case the new mother could have replaced her own early on when she needed basic nurturing. Or else the girl's at odds with her father and welcomed the new mother as an ally.'

'Or both,' said Yeadings. 'Thanks, Nan. That backs up the impression I get from the whole set-up.'

Nan made a grimace of distaste. 'Will the murder turn out to be a domestic?'

'Could be. It depends what Angus has made of the husband overnight,' Yeadings allowed, rising from the table. 'Then again it could be a lot more complicated than that. There are some definite undercurrents that make me wonder.'

'Are the Press on to it yet?'

'They will be shortly. The PR office is putting out a brief statement today after I've checked it. So the *Evening Standard* will give it a para or two tonight, the morning dailies tomorrow.'

So she could read about it there, and that would be her lot. She could see Mike wasn't going to loose-mouth on this one. Not at this juncture anyway.

He brushed off his toast crumbs, solemnly kissed his way round the table, wiped the resultant stickiness off his mouth and went with Nan to the door. 'What's for tonight?'

'I'd better make it lamb, slow roast. Safest when I can't be sure how late you'll be.'

'Right. New case: lots'a spadework.'

She watched him drive out on to the road and reflected that any digging was rightly the team's. But Mike was no slouch when it came to active policing. No way was his desk the full-time obsession the top brass had meant it to be.

★　★　★

Mott was in early and Yeadings stopped off at the CID office. 'Anything promising with Knightley, Angus?'

'Nothing worth charging him with. I took it gently, but I'll be pulling him in again today. Why is it that clever people are often so stupid? He doesn't seem to realise how serious this is. He's scared for himself, but he doesn't really believe he could be in the shit. He refuses to give an account of where he's been for the past four days. If ever anyone was qualified for a doctorate in arrogance . . . '

'So you sent him home?'

'Yup. Silver dropped him off at his gate. Not exactly welcomed by the Hadfields, it seems. The cat among the pigeons, hopefully. Something useful might come out of that.'

'A womanising wimp, according to Janey. That's a line we'll need to follow up. It seems to have been generally accepted, but by now the family may have decided to close ranks and cover up his philandering. Anyway, however much the others may slate him on that count it's too late to help the dead woman.'

'We've no reason to think she was any better than her husband. Z picked up a hint from the cleaner . . . '

'Not in so many words. Body language and then a suddenly buttoned-up mouth.' Yeadings realised he was defending Leila's reputation and pulled up short of taking sides.

'Staying stumm out of loyalty to her employer? That's an old-fashioned principle. Is it possible the woman expects to use her knowledge elsewhere?' Mott offered.

'Small-town blackmail?'

'Probably not. But if there's any truth behind the hint . . . '

'*Cherchez l'homme?*' Yeadings' black eyebrows shot up to his hairline.

'That's something I'll check on anyway. If Z doesn't get any further with Mrs Chadwick she can try having a word with Leila's neighbours.'

Yeadings grunted agreement. 'The Piggots. I spotted one of the lads yesterday up in a tree, with field-glasses trained on the house.'

Mott hummed. 'Right; I'll send her round after school hours. You'll find a tape of my interview with Knightley on your desk, sir.'

'Thanks.' Yeadings knew that when Mott called him 'sir' it was as good as a dismissal. He grinned wryly. 'Bring the others along when they get in and you can rough out your general briefing.'

In his own office Yeadings skimmed through the newspaper résumés and cuttings which the PR office had extracted from the morning papers. There was a leader on the handling of juvenile crime from the local *Clarion*, but the two teenage joyriders' bloody end merited only a couple of paragraphs in most London sheets.

Max Harris, Z's columnist friend, had an article headed Where's the Joy in Joyriding? in which he considered the j194 police chase as a reaction. At least he saw two sides to the problem and dwelt on the courts' inability to deal with eleven-year-old habitual offenders. It was a problem to hand back to Parliament. The legislators, he insisted, had failed to respond to current needs.

From that consideration Yeadings progressed to the coffeemaker, spooned liberal quantities of ground Mocha mix into a filter paper, topped up with Highland bottled water and switched on. The machine's gentle burbling accompanied his running of Mott's taped interview with the widower Knightley.

The man managed to sound at the same time pompous and offended. He had refused the offer of a duty solicitor to represent him and clammed up when the questioning became personal, even when warned that present silence might be prejudicial. One thing he had denied outright was having accompanied his wife to any private or hotel party during his four-day absence.

As he eventually realised that he could be setting himself up as prime suspect to murder, he had querulously pleaded shock, grief and loss of sleep. At that point Mott had let him go. Timed at 20.47.

Not at all bad, Yeadings thought. The man had been given plenty to ponder. The release was a bit of a bungee jump: he'd be coming back time and again, on each occasion with a little less bounce. The resultant tension could ensure a more co-operative mood in future.

At a knock on his door Yeadings shouted, 'Ready.' At present it amused him to use the same cry that young Luke gave when welcoming either parent to a successful potty session.

Mott ushered in the two sergeants, and Beaumont produced three mugs while the others found seats.

'Well,' Yeadings invited, 'what's today's menu?'

Beaumont reeled off a list of hotels and country clubs which he had contacted regarding a masked entertainment on Friday night. 'Negative throughout,' he confessed, 'so I checked what stage or cabaret shows had been put on, in case Leila K was an exotic dancer or suchlike. So far no joy, but there are three clubs I haven't got to yet. Not to mention the unlimited London list.'

'Did the dead woman have any history of involvement in show business?' Mott demanded. 'I doubt it. And we still have to look into private parties. I've got Davidson's Traffic Department checking for unusually heavy street parking over that period, and patrol officers are collating the same. Also at the general briefing we may collect stray observations from off-duty officers circulating in the area.

'Uniform branch are continuing a search for the cut-off hair, with no success as yet. SOCO did the same in rubbish containers at the Knightley house. We need to extend it to outdoor containers at other houses in Acrefield Way where access would have been easy from the road. And one street away there's a builder's skip opposite some minor demolition work. That has been sealed for examination and will be gone through today.'

'Knightley's car?' Beaumont enquired of the DI.

'Has proved elusive. He claims it had a recurring electrical defect. For a scientist he was surprisingly unspecific. Nor does he know which garage it's been sent to. He left it at a friend's house to be picked up and will inform us when he knows the firm's name. I expect him to ring me this morning.'

'By which time he will have removed all traces of anything naughty it carried,' Beaumont said bitterly.

'Only he doesn't know our boffins, does he?'

'However much or little they may find,' Yeadings reminded them, 'we could have difficulty proving who was responsible for its presence in the car — or who drove it Friday night — after so much shifting it around.'

'Which is nothing to the shiftiness of the professor,' Z suggested.

Beaumont gave his puppet grin. 'Just like Cluedo: Professor Plum, in the car, with a ligature.'

'So prove it,' said Yeadings shortly. 'Who is working through the Knightley address book?'

'DC Silver,' Mott claimed, 'together with all references taken from the computer. Doubtless there'll be an almighty complaint from Knightley when he discovers we've helped ourselves to it.'

'Then he'd better have it back,' said Yeadings mildly. 'We don't want him unnecessarily upset. I might trot along there with it while you're giving the briefing, Angus; see how nervy its absence has made him. I assume everything in it has been downloaded by now?'

'Everything,' Mott admitted. 'Silver has turned into Superhacker. It was worth losing him to that computer course. He eats, breathes, dreams nothing else these days.'

Better he than I, Yeadings thought. Young Silver was clearly a man of the future. From such might Chief Constables one day be chosen. He regarded his select team. Beaumont could get back to chasing up the party/cabaret origins. Z was itching to check on Leila's love life, if any. For himself he'd like a private word with Mott before he went off to brief the extended murder team.

'Right. On your respective ways then, except Angus perhaps.'

'Boss?' the DI said, when the other two had departed. 'I'm due downstairs in ten minutes.'

'This should take only five. Have you done any thinking about your own situation, Angus?'

'The future, you mean?' At Yeadings' nod he pulled a sour face. 'The original plan's in abeyance, if not permanently junked. As you know, Paula's boss has put off his intended early retirement and she's staying on as his junior, building quite a reputation at the Bailey when he gives her the chance. Even at her present level there's a lot more money in defence than prosecution. And with promotion, I still doubt if I could make up the difference. So it seems the wedding is on hold.'

'I was thinking more about your career options. I get a whiff of something in the wind.'

Mott hunched, silent with bowed head. Then he stirred and sat straight. 'There are three options, as I see it. One, as Paula suggests, I quit here, transfer to the Met and we marry, take a flat in London. Two, I stay put with Thames Valley, take promotion and am put back into uniform. She stays on in London.' He stopped at that point.

'And three?'

'There's this need for an expanded international contingent to help train the new mixed-race Bosnian police force. A friend out there says the Brit group badly needs strengthening at the top, if only to counter more brutal versions of the job being introduced from Eastern Europe and beyond. I thought I might have a bash at that.'

'That would certainly be to the Bosnians' advantage. What about your own?'

Mott stood up, tight-lipped. 'It's option three I'm favouring, Boss. It'll broaden my experience and it won't be forever. Paula's coming over this evening and I shall explain to her then. I meant to tell you tomorrow.'

Yeadings' spirits sank. Angus deserved more than to end as a sniper's target or from stepping on a leftover landmine. He managed a shrug. 'I'd — the team would lose you in any of those options. Can't you wait to see whether the tenure ruling gets changed? There's considerable pressure for CID service to be extended from five years to eight.'

'I have to make a decision now. I've faffed about long enough, Boss.'

'I see. It's your choice, Angus. Thanks for letting me know.' He watched the tall DI pick up his papers and go off stern-faced.

Yeadings knew it wasn't just a boyish yen to be a hero; an updated version of flouncing off to join the Foreign Legion. It owed more to a horror of becoming Paula's poodle.

Separation and their opposing career needs had meant that the relationship had been dragged out like a string of dough, so far that it was thinning to break-point. Despite their promising start Angus and Paula seemed fated to go the way of so many police partnerships.

There but for the grace of God . . . thought Yeadings. He made a mental note to buy flowers on his way home that evening.

There was a knock on his door and a constable looked in with a note from Traffic: 'Isn't this one of yours, sir?'

Apparently the joyriders' deaths hadn't put other thrill-seekers off. Yeadings glanced through the copy of a Traffic report: a further incident last night. Two women mown down in a hit-and-run in Acrefield Way.

Coincidence? When you had something specific on your mind, you started seeing it pop up all over the place. One woman's condition critical, now in the ITU at Wycombe: named as Hetty Chadwick.

He whistled between his teeth. This was the cleaner for Knightleys. The other joyrider's victim, a teenager — Chloë Knightley — had sustained only minor injuries.

Yeadings roared down the corridor for a constable and had the Professor's computer loaded into the Rover's boot. He revised his original plan. He didn't see Acrefield Way as a dedicated joyrider's racetrack and skidpan. It was too rural and twisting to offer high speeds, and disappointingly short of the needed hyped-up crowd of spectators.

So this could be a different breed of driver, one burning rubber while escaping from some crime. Or — more germane to present interests — an attempt to eliminate a witness with information on the Knightley murder? An attempt which could yet prove successful.

He knew well the statistics Traffic quoted for pedestrian casualties: at 30mph nearly 50% were killed; at 40mph nearly all were fatalities.

It might not be possible to get anything yet, if ever, from the critically injured woman, but Chloë was another matter. A bright youngster, she could have spotted the driver; was probably well clued-up on cars. So to Wycombe Hospital first. Her father and the computer could wait.

18

At the hospital Yeadings met with stalemate. Hetty Chadwick lay in a heavy coma in a shuttered area of the ITU. Chloë, kept in overnight, had received orthopædic manipulation and was already on her way home, still under light sedation but insisting on being discharged. The ward Sister said she had rung an aunt to come in and collect her.

A uniformed constable seated outside the ITU had been provided with a generous provision of magazines. 'You can bin those,' Yeadings told him. 'Stay alert. I want everyone who goes in or out of that room checked against their ID photos: doctors, nurses, porters, the lot. There could still be an attempt on her life. Get yourself a leak now, while I'm here. Then hang on till your relief turns up. I'm having surveillance doubled.'

He put the order through by mobile, then slid the car into gear and set off to the Knightley home.

Driving along Acrefield Way, Yeadings observed Z's blue Ford Escort parked opposite one of the ancient brick and flint cottages. At the adjoining one the nose of a green open-top Alfa Romeo was emerging from the side drive.

A pony and trap might have been more fitting, he thought; but it wasn't unknown for modern opulence to be enjoyed alongside the romantically historical, especially if finances restricted choice. For himself, he would rather go for comfort at home. A car, after all, was a mere means of transport. He took in the floppy-haired, old-young face behind the steering wheel and wrote the man off as a fancy-free bachelor visiting an elderly relative.

He drew in to the kerb, braked and stared back at the Chadwick cottage, curious to know why Z was calling there when the occupier was away.

Just then the front door opened and the woman DS appeared carrying a travel bag. Double-locking the door, she had her back to Yeadings. When she came down the path she saw him and pulled a gruesome face. 'I had permission, sir.'

'From whom, since the owner's unconscious?'

'When I couldn't get an answer here, her neighbour came out and explained she was in Wycombe General. So I went there, got turned away but offered, as a friend, to bring her some things in from home. It seems she could eventually come round. Her housekeys had been in her skirt pocket, so they let me have them.'

Yeadings sucked in his cheeks. 'Better you, perhaps, than whoever ran her down. So what did you find?'

Z's eyes went round with innocence. 'Her clothes, sir. Nighties, tissues, washpack, fluffy slippers, handbag and small change.' Then she grinned. 'Nothing of special note, sir.'

He gave her a thin smile. Z wouldn't have missed out on the chance to give the cottage a good turnover. 'We appear to have lost a source of information for the moment, but there are still the Knightleys' nextdoor neighbours.'

'I'll be calling there as soon as school's out, sir.'

'Good.' He drove off, readjusting his mind to face a grieving household — if not the unsavoury background to a domestic murder — turned in at the gates to Knollhurst and pulled up before the open front door.

Before he could knock or ring, the inner glass door burst open and Knightley stood there, unshaven, flushed of face, his hands balled into fists. 'Can't you leave us alone?' he ground out. 'Isn't it enough that I should be questioned at a police station, but you must chase me out to my own home? And my phone never stops ringing now you've dragged the Press into it.'

'I thought,' Yeadings put in mildly as the other man drew breath, 'that you might care to have your computer back.'

'My God, did you even help yourselves to that?' So he hadn't been up long enough to check on his study.

'My team had a warrant to search the empty house,' the superintendent said calmly. 'Which includes all contents. Under those terms a computer ranks as an electronic filing cabinet.'

'That is an unpardonable invasion of my privacy! And I have no intention whatever of saying anything beyond the statement I have already made to your Inspector.'

'If you have somewhere clear to put it I will bring it in.' Yeadings ignored the outburst and went back to the rear of his car. When he returned with the heavy computer Knightley tried to snatch it from him, but too late discovered it wasn't so easy.

'In the study,' he snarled. 'First door on the left.'

'Perhaps you will check that you've received it in good running order, Mr Knightley.'

The man was torn between defiance and protection for his property. Truculently he thrust plug in socket and switched on. The screen lit. 'It will take longer than this to see whether any data's been irrevocably lost.'

'You have my guarantee that nothing has been obliterated.' The urbane tone was enough to goad Knightley further. Obliterating, Yeadings reflected happily, was not quite the same as downloading.

'It's actually your daughter I'd like to have a word with at the moment,' he told the professor.

Knightley looked stricken. Not perhaps entirely on behalf of the girl's feelings. 'There is no call for that. You should know by now that Chloë was abroad until you — you assumed the authority to have her recalled. There is no way she can provide any information germane to your inquiry. In any case she's not available at present. She was involved in a serious road accident last night and is in need of rest.'

'She has my sympathy,' Yeadings assured him, 'but I must remind you that we are investigating a violent death, Mr Knightley. Who is to say at this point what may prove to be germane?'

Knightley turned on his heel and, left to wait, Yeadings reflected that even a violent death can be less a momentary act than a process. Once born we are all on a journey towards one end. Our nearest and should-be dearest have the ability to accelerate or delay that process. In several claustrophobic families he'd dealt with in homicide, the victim had been slowly murdered over years before the final vicious act. And often cumulative torture, mental or physical, had driven the killer himself to that point.

When Chloë came Janey was with her. 'I'd like my friend to stay,' the girl said and nodded when asked if she felt up to seeing him.

They took chairs on the far side of the room. Yeadings looked at the girl's father. 'Mr Knightley?' He indicated the door. Knightley stood his ground, affronted.

'Chloë has chosen a responsible adult to be present, as required.' Yeadings nodded again towards the door, saw an unwilling Knightley through and closed it firmly after him.

'What did you want to ask me?' Chloë challenged. Whatever sedative they'd given her, she was fighting it off.

Yeadings wandered back and stood leaning with both hands on a chairback. 'I'm not altogether sure. I just have the feeling you can help me if you will. It's a question of observation really.'

'You know about last night's accident?' Janey demanded. 'It's disgraceful what these young hooligans get up to. Can't you police do more to stop it?'

Yeadings treated the question as rhetorical and expressed his sympathy. 'Chloë, I'm afraid we need to trouble you for an account of what happened.'

She sat straight-backed and spoke in a cold, controlled voice. 'I told the policeman at the hospital. We were run down by a car. It turned its headlights up and came straight for us. I guess Hetty was dazzled. I know I was. She'd got a bad foot and stumbled. I tried to pull her to the side but she fell and that made me let go. I'm so sorry.'

She shook her head, took a deep breath and went on. 'It was only a glancing blow on me but she — she hit the bonnet and then sort of bounced off and disappeared. When I got up I couldn't find her. She must have been on the opposite side, but I don't remember getting to her. A neighbour — a man I hadn't seen before — came rushing out of his house and then there was quite a crowd. I must have blacked out then and came to for a while in the ambulance. It's no good asking if I saw the driver. It all happened too fast, and I was blinded by the headlights.'

'You had no impression of the driver's age or sex?'

'None at all.'

'And the make of car?'

'I've thought about that. It was big. Powerful. I got the impression it was pale: maybe white. Not a Volvo anyway.'

Yeadings stiffened. 'How can you be sure of that?'

'Because a Volvos' lights come on with the ignition. And I remembered afterwards I'd had this impression of an engine idling when I came out of the house to go to Hetty's cottage. There was a car parked at the far end of Piggotts' front, near where the wood begins. I suppose it didn't mean anything to me then because couples sometimes park there with the lights off, but usually later at night.'

'Thank you, Chloë. There's nothing else you remember? A familiar engine sound?'

'Nothing. It revved up like a racing car. I've never heard an engine roar so, except on TV.'

'I see. Well, if you think of any other detail later, please ring me or Inspector Mott.' Trust the formality of the words to reduce the tension, he thought. From Chloë's description it would seem the hit-and-run had been no accident, but he was unwilling then to suggest to the women why the older victim might have been targeted.

As if she read his mind, 'It was deliberate,'

the girl said shakily. 'He meant to kill us. One of us, anyway.'

'How is Mrs Chadwick?' Janey asked quickly.

'Her condition's unchanged. Still critical, but there is hope.'

'I feel responsible. If I hadn't sent Chloë with a message to her none of this would have happened.'

'You asked for her to come to Knollhurst?'

'Yes, but at her convenience. We need more help in the house. I thought we should discuss it.'

'It was Hetty's idea to come right away,' Chloë said. 'So nothing was planned. Whoever ran at us wouldn't have been expecting to see her. He was just waiting about on the off-chance.'

She stared at Yeadings with fear in her eyes. 'Right by our house. That's why I think it was me he went for. To kill me.'

It might appear so to her, and there was logic in her reasoning, but he couldn't accept that. She'd been away at the time of her stepmother's death. It was the cleaner who had been on the spot as observer. This was an attempt to silence a witness.

'I don't think so,' he countered. 'As you say, the driver wouldn't have expected you. You've heard about the joyriders, I'm sure. I think we may find it was someone like that. But there's another way you can help me if you will. Again it's a question of observation, and you're good at that. Sometimes adults don't realize just how much the younger family members are picking up from their actions.'

'Regarding what exactly?' She didn't quite trust his change of subject.

'How happy they are, or worried, or lonely.'

Chloë looked down at the twisted hands in her lap, suddenly darted a glance at Janey and said, 'You mean Leila. I don't see how she can have been particularly happy. None of us made enough of her. I guess she felt really lonely inside.'

'I know too that I let her down,' Janey confessed in a rush.

Yeadings looked out of the window, his back to them. 'As we all feel when anyone dies: because it's too late. Guilt over not having done enough: kinder things we might have said or done; begrudging, when we might have smiled and offered help. I've had all that, when my own father died.'

'But Leila didn't just die!'

He turned back at the protest in the girl's voice. 'You're right. However unbelievable, someone wanted to take her life. How can that be?'

'Some madman.'

He watched her with pity, unhappy that he must push her further. 'You said your stepmother might have felt lonely. Is it possible she found someone to fill that gap in her emotional life?'

'You mean a man, a lover. No; she wasn't like that.' Chloë was scornful.

Janey sighed and shook her head. 'Leila didn't set great store by men. The only two she came close to condemned her to triviality, Aidan regarding her as an airhead, Charles by setting her up in the shop. She was worth more than that. There was nothing trivial about her mothering of the children.'

'No despairing lover, then? So we're left with Chloë's 'madman'. Or could she have been seen as a threat to someone, because of what she'd seen or knew?' he suggested. 'You see why it's essential for me to understand how she seemed in those last few days; where she went; who she spent time with.'

Chloë was looking puzzled.

'Can you suggest any circumstances in which she might have seemed a threat to another person?' Yeadings probed. 'No? A barrier, then, preventing some course of action?'

All the blood drained from the girl's face and she started to tremble. Janey put out a hand to her. 'They're going to find out, Chloë. Maybe know already.'

'Janey, I can't . . . '

'You don't have to.' The older woman turned to Yeadings. 'Leila's husband — I've told you already — there was always some girl. It seemed he couldn't keep his hands to himself that way. Leila knew. We all knew, and did nothing to help. Charles would have taken it up with him but I begged him not to. She would have hated it. I think she forbade him to say anything. It was a sort of family truce. We all pretended to be blind. For the sake of peace and quiet.'

'But he wouldn't have hurt Leila. Not physically,' Chloë begged.

'Not unless he was driven into a corner,' Janey admitted. 'I'd thought at first he wouldn't, because I didn't believe his feelings could be that deep, not for any young girl. I think he's one of those men who need women and rather hate them for it. But then, if he was desperate to have someone and she was holding out — for marriage, say, and Leila could block a divorce — who knows how crazy it might have driven him? He can get very angry. The male menopause they call it, don't they? He could have been out of his mind.'

'But she wasn't holding out,' Chloë

276

shouted, then clapped her hands to her mouth.

Yeadings hid his excitement. The girl was appalled at what she'd given away. It was clear she knew the identity of her father's present lover. Maybe he should leave it for now and hope to extract the name less painfully through Janey later.

But it seemed not. 'Who then?' the older woman insisted. 'Do you mean you know who he was — was — '

'Was shagging,' Chloë said in cold fury. 'I do, and I'm not telling anyone.' She stopped abruptly and her face hardened. 'But if she had anything to do with what happened to Leila, I hope you do catch her. Whoever did it, I just wish they'd bring hanging back!'

Such passion, Yeadings thought. The child — she wasn't much more — burst into a storm of crying. No tears, but a terrible dry, racking sound that he'd only heard before at grave-sides. He had to leave her to Janey and just go.

In the hall he ran into Charles Hadfield at a total loss what to do. 'If you've threatened her . . . ' he began.

'Dear God, that's the last thing . . . ' Yeadings lifted his hands in exasperation.

'It's catching up with her,' the man said wretchedly. 'She's been too controlled up to now. Holds it all in. Can't do her any good. D'you know what she said last night? 'I'm on my own now. I'm in the front line.' And now this other shock, the accident . . . '

'She'll be all right. Your wife's with her.'

'My — ? Oh yes. Quite. Very decent woman, Janey. Practical, you know.'

Yeadings offered his hand and the older man grasped it. 'Anything at all I can do?'

'Back-up. Just be there for them both.' Lord, Lord, Yeadings muttered silently as he got into his car: why hadn't he left this to Mott, to Z, even to Beaumont. He was a paper-shuffler himself and should stick to the Olympian desk he'd been promoted to.

Clumsily he'd brushed against the rearview mirror on getting in. Now as he straightened it he saw Knightley approaching from the drive. He wound down his window expecting abuse.

But the professor had recovered his dignity. He had also used the intervening time to shave himself. 'If you are returning to — er, to base, perhaps . . . '

'You're still without transport, Mr Knightley?'

'Quite so.' He was covering embarrassment with a sort of pompous bonhomie, a poor parody of Charles Hadfield. 'Struck me I

278

should have another word with your Inspector Mott. Save him a further journey out here.'

For a brief moment when Yeadings waved towards the nearer rear door he stood undecided. Perhaps the memory of travelling so with Mott brought back the sense of being in police hands. He gave a little barking laugh, walked round the car and climbed in beside Yeadings.

All buddy-like, the Superintendent thought; on equal terms, in case anyone was watching.

19

Yeadings left Professor Knightley to cool his heels — or work up a hot flush — on a bench overlooked by the duty sergeant, while he wandered off to find Mott. He found him in the CID office reading printouts from the Incident Room's computers.

'Coffee?' the Boss enquired. 'You can bring those along with you.' They settled into his office where Yeadings removed his tie, eased his collar, refilled the percolator and invited Mott to bring him up to date.

'These are all negative,' Angus said in disgust. 'Interviews with the assistants from the PARTY FUN shop, the Mardham newsagent, her previous neighbours back at Caversham. It seems Leila Knightley kept her nose clean and wasn't the confiding sort.

'Her staff said she was a decent boss, fair to them about swapping duties, but she kept her distance and was strict about politeness to customers: no personal chat while any were in the shop.'

'Discipline,' Yeadings approved. He remembered her warning glances at the blonde assistant who was nattering on about her boyfriend.

'The only mentions of any private life came from Leila's hairdresser, who must practise the same technique my barber tries on. But those referred to purely family occasions.'

'Which were?'

'In her last three weeks she'd had a hairdo for a Saturday outing with her husband: Trooping the Colour, viewed from Carlton House Terrace. They went as guests of the Royal Society. Then a repeat shampoo and blow-dry a few days later for Ascot. Her uncle had bought a share in a racehorse.'

'Quite a social round. This makes her sound rather more than the down-trodden housewife.'

'Vicky — that's the hairdresser — thought Leila regarded the Royal Society lunch as a duty. But she'd been excited about the races. Her uncle took her once to a steeplechase at Auteuil when she was a teenager, but this time it had the extra cachet of the Royal Enclosure.

'That's all I've got. We really need some gossip from that cleaner, who's still *non compos*.'

'Well, let's hope Z gets lucky with the boy snooper nextdoor. By the by, I've left Professor Knightley out front for you. I went to see young Chloë and he was acting surplus to requirements. He wants a word with you, but don't feel obliged to rush at him. It seems he still hasn't his own wheels. Did you get anything on his car?'

'That's probably what he wants to talk about. Odd, this scarcity of cars in that neighbourhood. On Sunday evening Piggott was without his too.'

'And then suddenly there's one nobody needs — running down Hetty Chadwick; though young Chloë claims the driver was out to get her.'

'Why's that?'

Yeadings explained about the idling engine she recalled just beyond her gateway. 'But I think she's wrong. The driver made no move while she was walking down to the cottage; then revved up as both women were coming back. Of course, it might have been that he didn't see her clearly until she was facing that way.'

'M'm.' Mott tapped his pen on the printouts in his hand, reached for his coffee and drained it. There was no doubt in his mind that the driver had been a tearaway in a stolen car. 'I doubt it had anything to do with the murder. Let's leave it for the present. Guess I must let Knightley have his say now.'

He rose, stretched stiffly and reached the

door before turning back. 'There's one thing, Boss. I hadn't realized Charles Hadfield had only just gone to Scotland. He must have been around here recently because he took Leila to Ascot. We could have overlooked his importance. I'll see to it.'

★ ★ ★

'Is that necessary?' Knightley said testily as Mott's DC slid a tape into the recorder.

'This isn't an interrogation,' Mott told him blandly, 'but we need to be sure that any item of information you offer isn't overlooked. You might, unknowingly, mention something that could give us a lead. So we date and collate everything.

'We've only just heard, for instance, that your wife accompanied you to a Royal Society lunch recently.'

'I was invited for the Trooping ceremony. Didn't see much of it myself. Too busy consulting with colleagues.'

'And your wife?'

'She — ' He waved a hand airily. ' — circulated. Socialized.'

'With whom?'

'I have no idea, but it can have no connection with a random attack on her nearly two weeks later. You'd do better to

283

check on local thugs and vagrants.'

'Believe me, sir, we are doing so. But your wife's interests interest us. Did you accompany her later to Ascot?'

'Yes, but that was Charles's outing. Horses don't really appeal to me. I'm not a compulsive gambler.' He smirked and something made Mott wonder if this was true. 'I deal in facts, Inspector; practicalities.'

'A scientist, yes.' Mott observed Knightley's smug acknowledgement. 'Perhaps,' he said, 'you could fill us in a little more about your wife. The sort of person she was. We're short of a detailed description.'

Knightley, seeming more exasperated than grieving each time her name was mentioned, took off his spectacles, held them up to the light and started to polish them rapidly on a square of chamois he took from his breast pocket. It gave him time for a shift of perspective. His reply, when he'd prepared it, was waspish.

'The reason you haven't a good description is that she didn't leave much impression. She was quiet; never took much of an initiative.'

'Reclusive, then?'

Knightley bridled. 'I wouldn't say that. As I explained, she could do the social thing, talk to people, so long as it all stayed at a mundane level. Just as well she did really, since I never could suffer fools gladly. Leila did. She even seemed to like them, no matter how boring.'

'Not being an academic like you.'

'Quite. More of a homely little woman.'

'Not in the American sense, surely. She appeared quite exotic on the night she was found.'

That startled him. 'Leila? Exotic? But I — I saw her, in the mortuary.'

He meant naked except for a body sheet. Mott decided on shock tactics. 'You were never shown the scene-of-crime photographs? I'm going to fetch you one now.' He rose, nodded to the DC and left the room.

'I came in simply to explain about the car,' Knightley complained irritably to the young detective, who said nothing beyond a murmur into the tape before switching off. He watched coldly as the man patted a folded handkerchief across his sweating upper lip.

Mott came back with a large manila envelope from which he slid a number of glossy 8 by 10s. He made a card-player's fan of them.

'This one, I think.' He lifted it out and pushed it across the table to Knightley, who stared in disbelief.

'You see?'

'That's — my wife? Macabre! What's that

bird thing on her face?'

'A carnival mask. Didn't she ever show it to you? How about the dress?'

The colour drained from Knightley's face. He looked transfixed. 'But that's not . . .'

'Not her style?'

'Certainly not. It's — vampish.'

'We think she was bound for a party. Or possibly had been to one earlier.'

'This is the first I've heard of it. You might have . . .'

'At the time you weren't available for us to inform, Mr Knightley. And since then you have never asked for details. Which strikes me as curious — your being incurious.'

Knightley looked dazed, as if the full truth of the killing had just come home to him. 'I saw a paragraph in the *Times*. It simply said the body of a woman had been found in woodland near my new house. There was nothing to make me think then that it might be — anyone I knew. It was Charles Hadfield who broke it to me when I got home.'

'Back from where, Mr Knightley? Don't you think it's time you came clean about that?'

Knightley's back straightened. 'Clean? I resent your implications, Inspector. When I spoke to you earlier, I was distraught — at news of my wife's death. I hardly knew where

I was. Otherwise I would have explained fully. I have no taste for obfuscation.'

Mott waited.

'This is a delicate matter. The fact is that I have been extremely busy at the university, terminating my connections, both professional and personal. That is to say, with my colleagues. In addition I have been at some pains to deal with a rather embarrassing situation which arose from a stupid misunderstanding.'

'This involves a woman?'

There was a brief silence. Then, 'In a way. Yes.' An icebox voice.

Mott listened sceptically while the man ploughed through the sort of excuses that he'd heard used so often. There was one minor variation — it was a misunderstanding by the mother of a young student in whom he'd taken a purely academic interest. Then the need to placate a Fury, which necessitated staying on until the matter was satisfactorily cleared up. And he was adamant now that naming the family would be an unpardonable breach of their right to privacy.

The DI was unimpressed. Such discretion sounded foreign to Knightley's social code. 'When we do identify the young woman, as we certainly shall, you may regret not having been totally open. Now, about your missing car, sir.'

'Yes, yes. That's what I came to tell you. It was sent by a colleague to McIlroy's garage on South Road, Reading, where he has a discount account and suggested I make use of it. I shall be picking it up today. If that is all, Inspector, I really must be on my way.'

Mott left him with the DC, ostensibly to await an official stamp before initialling the tape-recording — a fictional requirement, but Knightley wasn't familiar with police procedure.

It did, however, allow Mott time to phone and prevent the car's release from McIlroy's until SOCO could inspect it. He needed a specimen of its carpet fibre. Not that that would fix the killing on Knightley. A third party could have driven it to the wood to dump Leila's body, with or without his knowledge.

Knightley's shock at sight of his wife's party get-up had been convincing enough. He was actually more shaken than Mott had expected. Which made him a poor prime suspect. His bumbling attempt to gloss over the sexual 'misunderstanding' showed he'd never win a Best Actor Oscar.

Mott returned to the interview room

convinced that at their next meeting Knightley would be rescinding much of the garbage of the present statement. All these petty evasions just made the job harder, piling on the need to chase up false trails.

When they began to put pressure on, Knightley would need to produce a genuine alibi, if he possessed one, because no way had he spent time at the university sorting his 'misunderstanding'. Not short of starring as the Invisible Man.

With the professor sent on his way, albeit carless, Mott returned to his office to find a note on his desk from the lab. A second, more detailed examination of blood spots taken from the mask had produced evidence of a second type differing from the dead woman's. Although in the same AB general group this was rhesus negative while Leila Knightley's had been rhesus plus.

★ ★ ★

When Rosemary Zyczyinski looked in again at Wycombe Hospital to drop off Hetty Chadwick's things she found that although the patient was still unconscious her prognosis was more favourable. The absurdly boyish houseman hoped that she would be coming round within a matter of hours. She was, he said, an exceptionally tough old bird.

From there Z drove out to Acrefield Way and parked at the foot of Piggott's drive. After some twenty minutes the two boys appeared on foot, Duncan bowed under a bulging backpack; Patrick, less laden, kicking a crumpled lager can along the gutter. She waited while the older boy produced a latchkey on a cord from round his neck and opened up the house. It seemed that Mrs Piggott was not at home.

Patrick streaked indoors but Duncan stood in the doorway as Z approached. 'Detective-Sergeant Zyczynski,' she announced.

'Yes. I remember you. Ma's out, though.'

'I'll wait then. Will she be long?'

He thought not. They went through the house, leaving all doors open, circulating the stale air, and arrived in the back garden. Patrick was already swinging crazily in a rubber tyre suspended from an ash tree.

'Fruit juice?' Duncan offered. He brought out a tray with a full jug bobbing with ice cubes, and three plastic tumblers. Patrick flung himself ostentatiously on to the grass, performed a parachutist's roll and joined them on the terrace.

'Nice garden,' Z commented.

A horticultural gem it wasn't, being totally child-centred and harbouring several heaps of what an adult might write off as scrap. Sheets of corrugated iron formed a stockade in one hollow, its walls bristling with aggressively outward-pointing lengths of lead piping to represent machine guns.

'Have you got a tree-house?' Z asked and was taken by the younger boy on a voyage of discovery.

'Ackcherly,' he confided in a patronising tone, 'it fell to bits, but I'm going to make a new one. Twice as high.' He shinned up an overgrown pear tree and posed like a pirate in the rigging.

'Can you see far?' Z asked and climbed up to join him.

To one side, across the wattle fencing, was dense woodland. On the other lay the Knightleys' garden partly hidden by the roof of their double garage, but with the terrace, lawn and conservatory in full view.

'They're out.' Patrick was disappointed. 'The woman before them used to sunbathe topless. And they gave parties with coloured lights in the trees.' He looked at her out of the corner of his eyes. 'Brilliant nosh. I used to nip over the top of the garage and sneak some back.'

Z smiled. 'Don't this new lot entertain?'

'Nuh. Not yet. Except her fancy man.'

The expression was unchildlike, quaintly

gossipy. Picked up, she wondered, from his mother or the cleaner? 'Who's that, then?' She made her voice sound casual.

Patrick spoke over a pear twig gripped between his teeth. The words came out scornfully with a spray of spit. 'The Frenchy from down the road.'

'I don't think I've met him.' Still a throwaway line.

'Pascal. He's got a smashing car. One day I'm going to have one like that, only red. Green's for wallies.'

'Right.' Z let herself down to the rough grass and brushed off her slacks. She wasn't happy about leading him on. Kids had to be questioned with an approved adult present. But where did idle chatter stop and questioning begin? She hoped Mott wouldn't split hairs over it.

Still Mrs Piggot hadn't returned, so Z thanked the boys for looking after her and escaped to her car. As she went to unlock it the Hadfield Peugeot drew up with Janey at the wheel.

Z followed it up the drive on foot. She noticed Chloë look back towards her with a frown before slipping from the car and disappearing quickly into the house.

'Sergeant, is there anything fresh? How's Mrs Chadwick?' Janey demanded.

Z explained there was hope of her recovering soon. Standing at the open front door, she heard the girl's furious cry from upstairs, then Chloë came rushing down. 'We've been burgled!'

Janey stared around in amazement. Nothing seemed disturbed. 'Where?' she said.

'My room's trashed.'

'Shall we?' Janey invited Z grimly. They found the wardrobe doors open, clothes dragged across the floor, drawers pulled out and their contents piled untidily on the bed.

'What on earth did he think he was doing?' shouted Janey. 'Where is the bloody man?'

'Who?' shrieked Chloë. 'You don't mean Father?'

'Who else? There was never any break-in.' She was getting herself under control.

'In my room? How dare he? How dare he? He's gone mad, Janey. Oh, Janey!'

'Chloë, calm down. I'll help you put everything straight, but just now we'd better find out where he is and demand an explanation.'

There was no mystery as to his whereabouts. He came in shouting from the back garden. It was clear he'd been drinking. 'Where's the bloody Volvo?' he roared. 'I went to get it and it's not there! Goddammit, don't say those bloody police have taken that one as well.'

'The Volvo is Leila's,' Charles Hadfield declared sternly, appearing from the drawing-room.

Knightley blundered past them and started upstairs.

'My room!' Chloë wailed.

'He wouldn't be fit to drive, anyway,' Hadfield offered irrelevantly, bemused by the hubbub.

Z put a hand on the girl's arm. 'Chloë, was there anything in your room he might have been looking for? Will you check if anything's gone missing there?'

On the gallery Knightley turned and beat on the banister rail with both fists. 'That damn dress. That's what's gone missing. I should have burnt it! What in the name of God did Leila mean by wearing it?'

'The dress?' Chloë faltered. She took a step towards the staircase. 'Oh my God!' and she crumpled on the hall tiles.

20

Z helped Janey carry the girl to a sofa in the drawing-room, Hadfield trailing anxiously behind. Even Knightley seemed sufficiently appalled to come back downstairs and hang over Chloë's limp body. 'What's the matter with the girl?' he demanded. 'I never meant to . . . ' Z resisted an urge to flatten him.

'I think it's better if you disappear,' Hadfield decided, as near as dammit dismissing the man from his own house.

'I'm all right,' Chloë managed to get out. The faint had only been brief and she was trying to sit up. 'I need to go and . . . '

Janey stifled her protests. 'You're staying right here while I get you a hot cup of sweet tea. You need sugar.' She nodded at Z to stay on. 'Come along, Charles.'

Given a free rein to talk with the girl, Z was loth to upset her further. 'I'm afraid your father's under a lot of stress at present.'

Chloë didn't pick up on it.

'So he was looking for something in your room?'

'The dress. You heard what he said. But it's not mine.' She clasped her head. 'And what did he mean about Leila? She never takes things from my room.' The girl closed her eyes. 'Never took.'

'Perhaps he's not making good sense at the moment.'

'He's been drinking.' Chloë herself seemed confused.

'That may account for it.' Only it didn't. Knightley had been fully focused on what he was raising the roof about: some dress of Chloë's that Leila had worn? Or vice versa?

'What dress was it he meant?' Z pursued. 'I don't know.'

And that, Z saw, was a flat lie. Chloë had already said it wasn't hers. A specific dress that belonged to someone else, then. It all seemed so trivial to be causing a family crisis.

'Here,' Janey said, arriving to deposit a filled mug alongside the sofa. 'Drink up and we're going to leave you in peace and quiet. Give a shout if there's anything you need.' She ushered Z out of the room.

'Well, did she explain what that was about?'

'No, I think she's more likely to confide in you. I'd better make myself scarce.'

They walked towards the open front door and then Z remembered what Patrick Piggott had told her. 'Have you met any of the neighbours, apart from nextdoor?'

'Not formally, though a number introduced

themselves at the cricket match.'

'When was this?'

Janey explained about the two sides of the road and the twice-yearly contest. 'We met several people there. They seemed very friendly. There was a plump girl called Holly who kept the scoreboard and an eccentric Frenchman. I can't remember his name. And Charles was quite taken with a couple of old codgers sporting school ties to keep up their flannels. The Piggotts weren't there. Maybe they're not into cricket.'

'A Frenchman lives in Acrefield Way?'

'Apparently. In one of those old flint and brick cottages, next to poor Hetty Chadwick. What's so special about him?'

Z shrugged. 'Seemed funny, that's all — a Frenchman at a cricket match. I wonder what he made of it.'

She left Janey staring after her and probably marvelling at her butterfly-brained curiosity. But that would be only one of the kinky things the afternoon had turned up.

Z drove off in the direction of town and slowed to observe the cottage Janey had spoken of. On an impulse she got out, went up the path and knocked. There was no answer, so she walked round the side, peering in the diminutive windows at white, rough-cast walls lit in places to warm ochre by the late afternoon sun. They appeared to have coloured sketches attached haphazardly. Three beanbag seats were lined up opposite as if for an absent audience. At the back door her toe clinked against glass on a flagstone half-hidden under a lavender bush. A note folded in the neck of a milk bottle read, 'None until Friday, thanks.'

There was also a small triangle of white paper showing under the door's edge. The milk deliveryman's bill? Or some advertising bumf? But it was worth checking. Z risked an index fingernail, scratching to retrieve it. The folded paper was lined and had been torn from an exercise book. On it was written, *I must see you. Please ring me. It's urgent. Chloë.* She slid the note back where she'd found it.

*   *   *

Back at base Z found Beaumont in the canteen and learned that the Boss had been called out to Kidlington. For some flak from the ACC Crime, Beaumont supposed. It was easy for these off-stage characters to demand the impossible of troops in the firing line. With a domestic murder Statistics expected a clear-up rate of forty-eight hours. In this case at this rate they'd be lucky to make it in as many days.

Angus Mott was in his office when his two sergeants looked in. He waved them to seats. 'What's new?'

Beaumont reported on the missing cars. 'Knightley's was where he said. SOCO were plastic-wrapping it ready to take away when the professor turned up. He went ballistic.'

'The outcome of which I witnessed at his home,' Z put in. 'Doubly ballistic when he discovered his wife's car was missing too. He assumed we'd taken it.'

Beaumont beamed. 'I checked on Piggott's Merc for good measure. It was parked round the back of his betting shop. I put a modest fiver on the 3.30, gave a wink and watched it go into a private pocket. He's a sly dog, that Walter Pimm. Piggott's put him in as manager. I'd rather have his other heavy, Big Ben Carter any day. For the price, Walter didn't give much away. He'd had to pick the car up Monday after it was clamped and removed from a hotel's forecourt in Regent's Park on Sunday. It seems Piggott had parked it there for safety while he took his family to the Zoo.

'Next, I pushed the lab for anything on the fibres. They'll be examining a sample of the carpet in Knightley's car to compare with what Littlejohn found between her toes. And

Knightley's dinner jacket wasn't responsible for the fluff under Leila's nails. No cashmere in it.'

'No progress, then.' Mott sounded gloomy.

'Depends what you're after,' Beaumont comforted him, leering somewhat. 'I checked on who'd brought the Knightley car in to McIlroy's. It was a woman, name of Ryder, forties to fifty, a bit of a dog. She ordered an engine-oil change and said it would be picked up by the owner.'

'Where does that get us?'

'Knightley said he had trouble with the electrics. Maybe we've 'trouvéd la femme'. We know he's a womaniser, but he told you a colleague dumped the car off to get a discounted bill. The garage has no such arrangement with the woman, but an apprentice knew where she worked. So I went along to her travel agency and picked up some holiday brochures. Her desk-keys were lying beside her handbag and the silly woman had attached a tag with her address on. It's a semi out on the Sulham road. So I tootled out there for a looksee and had a word with the old biddy next door.'

'And?' Mott pursued.

'I said my friend had left his BMW there earlier to be picked up. So I got chapter and verse from her. It seems he's done it before at weekends. This time there'd been a terrible row there Friday night when madam came home and found her daughter entertaining a man upstairs. Eventually the man drove his car off with the daughter in as passenger. She took an overnight bag with her.

'This worthy Mrs Crane said the couple came back the following evening. The mother let them in and that's when she first saw the man properly. Her description sounded exactly like the prof, and he was carrying an enormous bouquet of cut flowers. The car stayed there overnight. Next morning — we're into Sunday now — the man and young Beryl — definitely not Mrs Ryder — went off in her Fiat, while she was out in the garden hanging up some washing. That on the sabbath, to Mrs C's horror.

'Knightley's BMW was left in the drive. Mrs Ryder drove it out after lunch that day, coming back after dark. Then she left in it on Monday morning half an hour earlier than she usually went to work.

'This confirms what McIlroy's mechanic said about the car being dropped off there at 8.30am.'

'Useful neighbour, this Mrs Crane. Is she reliable?'

'Without doubt. A widow, living alone: I'd say she gets her kicks from peeping through net curtains. Probably makes diary entries on her neighbours' doings. It helps that she disapproves of the Ryders who 'let down the neighbourhood'.

'Sorry, Guv; but it seems that Knightley had more on his mind this weekend than murdering his missus. Or, if he did, he took the Ryder girl along with him to share the entertainment. We can at least fill her in as his present love interest.'

Mott grunted. His DS's account seemed to square with the professor's quoted 'misunderstanding'. If the mother had caught him out in a spot of nooky with the daughter that could have sparked the 'terrible row' the neighbour overheard. But by the following night all had apparently been smoothed over and Knightley stayed on. The car-swapping on Sunday sounded complicated but there was probably a reason for it. Perhaps Mrs Ryder had wanted to impress a third party with the BMW. So had Knightley actually talked her round and bought her compliance by lending it to her?

'Does this totally eliminate Knightley from the murder?' Z asked.

'Possibly,' Mott said heavily. 'We'll have to check times and places for the whole alibi. I already had my doubts. His reaction to the crime-shot in Shotters Wood was genuine shock. He'd not seen her geared up like that before. He was knocked back, doubted who was under the mask. It's all on the interview tape.'

'Geared up?'

'In that dress. He called it 'vampy'.'

'Dress,' Z echoed. 'I have some follow-up on that.' She told them of the scene after Knightley searched Chloë's room, and the girl passing out at mention of what he was after.

'Write it all out,' Mott ordered. 'I want it verbatim. We could have something here.'

He sent Z off while he and Beaumont re-ran the taped interview with Knightley.

'Stop it there,' Beaumont suddenly hissed. 'Knightley was starting to say something and you cut him off.'

Mott wound back and replayed the words; his own voice prompting — 'How about her dress?' Then Knightley: 'That's not . . .'

'You see?' Beaumont insisted. 'That's when you suggested, 'Not her style?' and Knightley lapped it up. But suppose he'd been going to say, 'It's not her dress,' meaning he thought it was Chloë's. He had seen it before and remembered, because it was quite unsuitable for a kid. Like he said, it's vampish.'

Mott thumped the desk. 'Then from seeing

the murder-scene photo and finding we'd taken his car, he went straight back home and trashed the girl's room — looking for the dress he'd seen earlier on Chloë. He couldn't find it and now he thinks his wife had taken the dress from the girl's wardrobe'.

'I want the Boss to hear all this,' Mott decided. 'I'll ring Kidlington and have him drop by before he goes home.'

'Is it all that important?' Beaumont doubted. 'Don't mothers and daughters swap clothes all the time?'

'Not the way Z tells it. Let's wait for her write-up, but I thought she said that Chloë denied it was hers.'

'Right, so it was really the mother's, but she'd hidden it from her husband. It was sexy and pricey, after all. Something to fascinate the lover with.'

'There's something I don't get. When had Knightley seen it before? And why did he still expect to find it in his daughter's wardrobe when he'd just learnt that Leila was killed wearing it?'

Mott looked up as Z came in with a printed sheet in her hand.

'I know,' she admitted. 'It's a labyrinth. While you're reading this through I'm going for three doughnuts. As Janey would say, we all badly need sugar.'

Superintendent Yeadings took longer to get in touch because the message he received from Headquarters switchboard was ambiguous: 'DI Mott would like you to drop in on your way home, sir.'

Since the DI's flat lay on his route and the uncurtained windows showed lights, he pulled into the space before Mott's garage. When he rang at the door it was opened by Paula, looking gorgeous.

He remembered then that tonight was scheduled for an emotional workout and he could find himself stepping in as unintentional referee. It was even more embarrassing since she appeared appalled to see him. 'Mr Yeadings! Is something wrong?'

She'd mistaken him for the bearer of bad news! 'No, no. Angus is fine. He's not here then?' Obviously not: he was making a thorough sow's ear out of this.

'I'm sorry, Paula. Our paths seem to have crossed, mine and his I mean.'

She looked relieved. 'Well, come in anyway. I've just put some supper out.'

'I'm not staying, thanks. Angus must have got hung up at the nick. I'll send him along right away. Good to see you, Paula. You're looking great.'

'You too.' She seemed amused at his confusion as he backed out.

Her car hadn't been out front, so she'd have come by train. Did it mean she was staying over, or on a day-return ticket?

No concern of mine, he warned himself, driving off. But Mott's future did concern him. Thames Valley could lose a good officer as the outcome of a barney tonight. And he'd lose a colleague he valued as a friend.

He walked into Mott's office to meet the conundrum of the dress. He heard it through; then, 'Leave it to Z,' he told the DI shortly and explained he'd mistaken the message to drop by. 'Paula's waiting at the flat for you,' he warned. 'So knock off now.'

Mott muttered something as he started to clear his desk-top. Yeadings thought it sounded like 'Oh shit!' but he hoped not.

*　*　*

At Knollhurst Janey had set the table for a late dinner, laying only two places. 'You men,' she told Charles Hadfield, 'can have a formal meal, so try to behave civilly to each other. Chloë and I will snatch something in the kitchen. We can't expect her to face her father yet across the table.'

'Good, good. I shall be formality itself. I

306

will even make stilted conversation if you require it. Whether Knightley is capable of appreciating it — or your excellent cooking — is another matter.'

He hrrrmped and fixed her with the gaze of a chided but hopeful spaniel. 'Tell her we — er, all love her a lot, you know.'

Janey squeezed his hand and went to call the professor. He came in stiff-faced, glanced at the table settings, hesitated and then seated himself facing Hadfield.

Having already served the hors d'oeuvre, Janey went to call Chloë. 'The men are at table,' she said. 'We'll be eating in the kitchen.'

'I don't want anything.'

'Well, keep me company then.'

As the girl stood and stretched, the phone rang. Janey took it in the hall. 'It's for you,' she said as Chloë passed.

Chloë took the receiver, shook her head and tried to pass it back, but Janey had gone. She drew in breath.

'Hello.'

There was a small shuffle of movement at the far end of the line. Then a wispy laugh. 'Chloë?' — whispered.

A pause. 'You don't remember, do you?' It was barely voiced. She couldn't tell if it was male or female. Would Beryl sound like this if she kept her chin tucked under? It was mocking enough to be her.

'Who is this?'

'No; you don't remember. He said you wouldn't.'

And then she knew. The voice went with a face seen in a nightmare: slack-mouthed; sharp cheekbones slanting over blue-grey hollows; centre-parted hair falling lankly over dead eyes, the pupils pinpoint. Male? Indefinitely, but she thought so. Scary.

And he had a name. She'd heard Beryl use it. 'Neil,' she said tremulously, but already the phone was purring. He'd hung up. Leaving her shuddering. Angry and afraid.

21

He let the phone drop to dangle on its cord, swinging against his knee as he crouched at the foot of the stairs. He felt better to have heard her. Warmer, excited. He'd waited until the stuff started to kick in before he dared to ring.

But it was all right. She didn't remember anything bad. Her stuff had worked like the weasel promised. It should do at that price. She had been his doll, and would be again.

At the memory a delicious shiver passed down his spine. Such exquisite risk. Her fine, soft flesh, faintly scented, salty on his tongue. He could taste it still.

It wasn't enough just the once. There had to be more. He'd waited, and the waiting made it more vital. More wonderfully dangerous than ever, now that the drongos had messed up with that other woman.

He wasn't sure what happened that time. Afterwards they'd caught him in the garden and hustled him off without explaining.

They'd said they'd see her home, pay her off. He'd made a bad trip that night and she'd confused him, made it too hard for him.

The first time was different, perfect. He remembered it, all the thrill through; the girl yielding, like a velvet doll under his fingers. Only he hadn't come. He didn't any more. But there were the photos. He got there looking at them.

He'd sent her some prints and she'd come back for more. That's what she said: she'd buy the negatives. She couldn't think he'd be such a fool as to give them up.

Only, that time it didn't seem the same girl. She'd tried to trick him. So he'd had to get rough. He'd tied her up to keep her quiet, and cut off her hair as punishment. Stupid bitch gatecrashing the downstairs party, done up like his real doll, but with that weird mask so she looked like some cruel bird. She should never have tried to frighten him. She was supposed to give in like the time before.

But it was the right one he'd talked with just now: his Chloë. She'd answered to her name, and after her voice he'd put a finger on the button and cut her off, like the other one's hair. He had shut her up there inside the phone, ready for another time.

He heard his own name called. His hand jumped, knocking the cord and cracking the receiver against the newel post. He sat curled up and silent, but someone was coming down for him.

'Neil, can you come now? Your mother's ready for bed. She wants to say goodnight.'

Ready for bed? She lived in the bloody thing, was dying in it. And anyway she couldn't say goodnight: would just slaver and make those farmyard gruntings, clawing at him with her one good hand. And he'd have to bend over and kiss her.

If she had any humanity left she would know it was too much for him.

Not that it was she who demanded it. For that he must thank his father, because he believed her poor brothy brain still grasped that he was her golden boy, her darling son, petted and possessed into becoming a life-serving prisoner.

Which he was. There was no way out since he'd given up at college, and he needed the man's money to pay for his habit.

The real, white habit; not that pathetic substitute they doled out like it was platinum dust, too little, too seldom. It was lucky he had other resources. And that was ironic, supplied right under the old bugger's nose, using the man he employed to bring his silly games.

This evening it was the dark-haired nurse on duty, but she was as cautious as the other one. She treated him as if he might leap out on her and have his wicked way. She didn't know he wasn't that kind of wicked. He'd never raped, not even the sickly rabbit that had been his first patient. Or the collie bitch drowned in the lake.

No, the nurses were safe enough. Different if either had been a redhead. Then they could have played together, like with Chloë. But he didn't do rape. It would have shocked Mother to death.

The stuff was kicking in at last. It seemed to take longer each time; or was that imagination? Imagined, like the way he was gradually growing taller, stronger, more beautiful.

He stood up and dropped the receiver back on the phone. Its buzzing had become annoyingly louder. Nothing must upset him now, spoiling his good time.

'Coming,' he shouted up. He didn't attend because they required it. He would choose to put in an appearance, go through the disgusting actions, perhaps tonight even lay his head beside hers on the pillow, stroke the hair of the imposter who'd replaced the pretty woman of his childhood. God, what a bitchy world it was.

★ ★ ★

'Look, Janey,' Knightley said as she cleared the table, 'this is all so petty. Just a dress, for God's sake. You'd better explain to Chloë. It would come better from you.'

'Explain exactly what?' Her face was as frozen as her voice.

'That Leila was wearing it. When she was killed. Didn't you know that? I didn't myself until the police showed me the photograph.'

'What has that to do with Chloë? Am I being stupid or something?'

'It was Chloë's dress, though I don't know where it came from. You'd better ask her. I only saw it the once, the night she came home drunk.'

Janey put the dessert dishes down and reached for a chair-back. 'Chloë drunk? When was this? What has been going on here? I think it's you that has to do some explaining.'

'It was about three weeks ago, on a Friday. After school she went off with a friend who had a car. I was hung up at the university or I would have brought her home. They rang me to say where they were . . . '

'Where were they?'

He bit at his lip. 'At some other friend's house. They seemed to be having a party. I was to come and pick her up there.'

'Did you know these two friends? Were they girls from school?'

'The first one was. I hadn't met the other.' He seemed to be picking his way with some care.

'They brought her to the front door, and she was in a terrible state, could hardly stand up. I thought — I was afraid . . .'

'She'd taken drugs?'

'They swore she hadn't. Just gone at the drink too hard. She said as much herself next day. She had a frightful hangover.'

'You took her home? Not to hospital?'

'It wasn't necessary. There was a nurse there. She'd given her something to make her sick. Anyway this isn't about her getting drunk; it's about the dress. She was wearing the one Leila was found dead in a few days ago. Leila must have taken it from Chloë's room while she was abroad at her Granny's. I suppose my mentioning the dress reminded Chloë how she'd misbehaved. That accounts for the fuss and fainting fit. Guilt, you see.'

Janey let him run on, thankful that Charles had left the dining-room and hadn't to hear all this. She couldn't quite grasp it. There were so many details missing. 'Where was Leila while all this was happening to Chloë?'

'She'd gone up north for the shop. To the annual trade fair. They always put next Christmas's stuff on show in June, to get advance orders. She must have told you about it. She drove up to Harrogate Friday morning and brought some samples back Sunday.'

'What did she do when you told her about Chloë?'

'I didn't.'

'But for God's sake why not?'

'To save any fuss,' he snapped.

'I don't understand you. The child must have been in an awful state. What did you do for her?'

'I think that's my business, Janey. She is my daughter, and I did know the girl she was with. When they went off together I had no idea of the state she'd get into.'

'Some fine friend! I hope Chloë's had the good sense to drop her.'

'Never mind that. What I want you to do is explain to the girl why I was checking whether hers was the same dress as in the police photograph.'

'I? Explain why you were trashing her bedroom? I suggest you do so yourself. I think you've been treating her appallingly, Aidan. It's time you tried straightening things out.' She picked up the dishes in hands trembling with anger and retreated to the kitchen.

Chloë was out on the terrace whittling savagely with a kitchen knife at a soft piece of wood. Aidan made no attempt to find her. When Janey opened the kitchen door to the hall she heard him phoning for a taxi. Running away again when things got too hot for him.

Chloë abandoned the carving, dropped the knife in the dishwasher as she passed and announced she was going for a walk. From the drawing-room window Janey watched her turn right and disappear in the town's direction. Then she retrieved the card with Miss Zyczynski's phone number and decided that she at least deserved some explanation of the madhouse goings-on.

★　★　★

Z was away from her desk. The constable guarding Hetty Chadwick at the hospital had rung in to report that she was off the ventilator and there was a chance she might come round. In Mott's absence the Boss decided Z should try to have a word with her. So, although he was overdue at home himself, he stayed on and was the one Janey's call was put through to.

She kept it brief. 'It's possible that Leila was wearing a dress of Chloë's when she was killed. You were asking about it earlier.'

'That's right, because it's quite eye-catching. I understand too that there was an upset at the house this evening, concerning the dress. I have DS Zyczynski's report here. She seemed uncertain who had borrowed it from whom. Chloë denied it was hers.'

'Her father says it was. I couldn't sort that out without asking Chloë again.'

'And she is the only one now who would know.'

'I got a long rigmarole from her father about seeing Chloë wearing it once.'

Janey took a deep breath and explained what Aidan had said about Chloë's condition when he picked her up to bring her home. She sighed. 'It must have shocked him when he was shown the police photo of Leila. Not, I suppose, that it matters whose the dress really was. I just wanted to put it right with Miss Zyczynski, since she witnessed the embarrassing scene here.'

Yeadings thanked her and she rang off. The dress could be irrelevant, but it gave him an excuse to ring Z on her mobile for further news. Then he recalled the ban on cellular phones near hospital equipment and decided on a detour there on his way home.

Z was leaving the hospital car park as he drew in. She had been allowed two minutes with Hetty who was awake but had no memory of the hit-and-run. She did, however, know 'the Frenchy' young Patrick had mentioned. He was her nextdoor neighbour, actually half-Swiss. He lived alone and yes, he'd struck up a friendship with Mrs Knightley. She'd invited him to the house one Thursday, which was Hetty's cleaning day, and had been out a few times with him in his car. She couldn't say where he'd be if he wasn't at the cottage, but they could try the studio.

Was he an artist? Z had asked.

'No. He owns a firm that makes television films. They've just finished one that's going to make them a fortune.'

'One hopes,' Yeadings commented.

'There's something else,' Z remembered. 'When I checked the outside of his cottage I found a note from Chloë Knightley tucked under the back door. She wanted to see him urgently about something.'

'Then we'd best find him fast. I have news on her for your ears too, but we can't stand out here talking. Are you free to follow me back? I'm sure Nan would be happy to fix us some supper.'

★ ★ ★

The smoked salmon salad Paula Musto had set out at Mott's flat was to be wasted.

He knew if he didn't speak out at once he wouldn't get through what had to be said. Sitting opposite her, making conversation, wasn't on; so he'd broached it abruptly without finesse, trying to ignore the overnight bag she'd dropped by the bedroom door. And Paula had listened silently, arms folded, farther distanced from him at every moment.

'You must have expected it,' he said at the end.

'Not a bald ultimatum.'

'It isn't that. We've three options. One: I stay on with Thames Valley, you join Crown Prosecution here and we get married. Two: I give up here, transfer to the Met and we marry. Or three: I join the international policing team in Bosnia and you carry on as you are.'

'No. We don't have those three options. You have. In your mind you've already decided. Where does my choice come in?'

'To be my wife; or not.'

'You see? An ultimatum.'

'One of us has to make a career change or we continue exactly as we are — which is going nowhere. I'm trying to be reasonable, Paula. A relationship has to grow or it's dead.'

'And ours is stagnating? Thank you. I thought I meant more to you than that.'

'You know you mean almost everything to me.'

'Almost.' Her voice was a whiplash.

'Can you say more than that?'

She stalked about the room, flushed and tight-lipped. 'Why now? Can't you wait a while? Why rush me? As for throwing yourself at the Bosnia thing, that's petty. Like threatening you'll walk under a bus if you don't have your own way. Petty and vicious.'

'Paula, don't push me too far. Can't you see how difficult it would be for me in London, painstakingly building a criminal case, then watching you work to demolish it? It might not happen that way, but it could. That's why the Met's impossible for me. You've admitted it bugs you to win a case when you know the defendant's guilty as hell. So give up. Darling, come here and use your skills on the other side.'

'The police side. You're wonderful, d'you know? — playing hard cop and soft cop with me, both at once.'

His reason ran out. He was breathing hard, towering over her. 'A cop is what I am. It's the only thing I know how to be. And I'm bloody good at it. If you can't take it, you know what to do.'

She stared back as if he had hit her. Seconds ticked by, then she struggled to pull the ring off her finger. It landed on the supper table, rolled and fell to the floor. Without another word she turned, swept up her bag and left. Mott stood staring at the blank panels of the door.

★　★　★

In the CID office Beaumont was the only one remaining. Not dissatisfied with his own efforts over building up Knightley's amorous background, he was still weighing the possible outcome from Forensics on the cars.

When the call came the voice he heard was one he didn't know. Young and uncertain at first, then displeased that Z wasn't to hand.

'I'm afraid she's gone home. My name's Beaumont. I work alongside Zyczynski,' he told her. 'We're partners.'

'Well, would you tell her Chloë rang? Chloë Knightley. I've remembered something about the car that ran us down.'

'That's great, Chloë. Can you tell me?'

'Well, it was the front grill, the radiator. When I close my eyes I keep getting flashes of Hetty's body hitting the bonnet. And I see the grill's squarish chrome with that circle on top and a sort of three-pronged cross in it. It was a Mercedes. I'm sure of that now.'

He thanked her. She sounded relieved to

have made the call. A Mercedes. Now where had he come across one just recently? He returned to the printouts and the word jumped out at him. From his own notes. He'd seen the car himself, parked round the back of Piggott's betting shop. And it was white. It had been facing the wall, so he hadn't observed the state of its front.

Piggott, of course, lived right next to the Knightleys. It wouldn't have been strange at all if he'd been sitting there Sunday night with the engine idling after Walter had returned it from being carted off and wheel-clamped.

But Pimm claimed he retrieved it on Monday. Which he might well have said if his boss had paid him to lie.

22

Sir Arthur Waites left the car by the colonnaded entrance, collected briefcase and *Evening Standard* from the passenger seat, and went into the silent house. A dim light reached the hall from a passage leading to the domestic quarters. He followed it and found the kitchen neon-lit with the dark-haired nurse seated at the large scrubbed table with her supper on a tray.

She looked up from an open book and smiled coolly.

'Evening, Nurse,' he said and, as ever, 'How's your patient?'

'Just the same, sir. She's settled down for the night.'

He nodded at the expected answer and went across to inspect the fridge's contents. It seemed well supplied. He supposed Piggott's heavies had stocked up. Which meant they would be staying over to set up the tables. He felt curiously flat about the prospect of tomorrow's gambling. Perhaps if he cared about money it would be different, but it was the way the numbers behaved that mattered to him. And at present so much gloom overshadowed a purely intellectual pleasure.

'My son about?' he asked.

'In his room, sir, watching the telly.'

'Right.' Feeling dismissed, he left her to her supper and reading, returned to the hall, dumped briefcase and car keys, then mounted the stairs to check on Neil.

He found the boy half-dressed, sprawled in an easy chair facing the TV. Whether he'd been preparing for bed and given up, or had only just struggled into his underclothes and then lost energy for more, wasn't obvious. He was nocturnal much of the time now.

Cool air stirred the gauzy curtains at the open sash window. Beyond the dark cumulus of the garden's trees the undulating Chilterns swelled to a clouded sky underlit in the distance with diffused orange from the motorway's sodium lamps.

After London's incessant rumble and hum the country always struck Waites at first as still. But not silent. There were minute rustlings and sighings, evidence of hidden night creatures and the slower pulse of rooted things growing. Only this house was paralysed, hopeless.

The screen that held Neil transfixed was dimly blue-lit, showing narrow inner-city alleys and dark warehouses with the glint of greasy water between. Feet were pounding on cobbles: flight and pursuit; hot breath panting.

Too much excitement for the young man. Waites reached for the remote control and selected another channel. Neil never stirred as the screen lit brilliantly for the end of *Crimewatch*. Nick Ross was gently recounting the details of an armed robbery some two months back in which a security guard had been clubbed to death.

'And more recently,' he said, 'Thames Valley Police want to know if anyone recognizes this dress. It's very unusual, made of fine silk chiffon and was worn by the murder victim found last Friday night in Shotters Wood, South Buckinghamshire. It has an Italian label, but the firm no longer exists. If anyone has seen such a dress, or if you saw the victim on the afternoon or evening of the same day, Friday July 2nd, please get in touch with our team here or ring 01865 846000 for Thames Valley Police. This was a particularly callous killing and the police are anxious to find the person responsible before he can repeat the crime. Finally, in West Yorkshire . . . '

Waites snapped off the remote control and the screen went blank. There was a little gasp of protest from Neil but his father took no notice, shocked to the core at the face he had seen flashed up: Leila, Knightley's wife, whom he'd chatted with not three weeks back at Carlton House Terrace.

Leila, dead? Murdered in a wood? Good God, how could that be? She was so ordinary, so nice. Who in his right mind would want to harm such a woman?

'Chloë,' Neil muttered.

'What?'

But the young man shook his head, bemused. His father looked at him. It had taken little more than a year on drugs to make a zombie of him, ruining a promising career. Depriving him, Arthur, of the only member of his family left fully alive. Before Alice's accident he'd been dabbling in hash, as most kids did nowadays. But since then, away at college, he'd gone the whole hog, irretrievably damaging a fine brain. Yet another foul-up from that car crash which had left Alice shattered and his own life in ruins.

He was as much to blame himself because, cut off in private grieving, he'd given little thought to how his son was coping with the shock. Alice and their only child had been unusually close, although she had originally longed for a daughter to share her love for music and pretty things. She was so feminine herself that he'd once feared she'd make a milksop of the boy, petting him and encouraging him to play with her collection of dolls. Once even he'd come home and found the toddler Neil rigged out in a frilly pink frock and white socks.

He sighed. Even that, to grow into a cross-dresser, would have been better than this present wreck of a young man.

He looked down at the over-elegant, now emaciated, body sprawled in string vest and boxer shorts. The boy was running his fingers over his eyes in the habit he had when distressed. Waites put a hand on his shoulder in comfort but Neil shrugged it off.

'I'm going for a shower,' Waites said. 'When I've changed I'll see about something to eat. How's that, eh?' There was no answer, and he left Neil facing the darkened screen.

His own room was at the house's rear, so he knew nothing until Nurse Howe came running up and rapped on his dressing-room door. 'Sir Arthur, can you come, please? It's an emergency.'

In his bathrobe he opened up. 'Alice? My wife?' he demanded sharply.

'It's your son. He must have taken your car keys. There's been a slight smash. He's all right, I think, but I can't get him out on my own.'

He reached the front drive to find that

Piggott's men were there before him and had the boy stretched out on the gravel. There was blood on his forehead and his eyes were closed. The car's bonnet was crushed against the brickwork of the archway to the gardens.

Nurse Howe had already collected the First-Aid box. Now she brought out a kitchen chair. Seated on that Neil opened his eyes, whimpering as she applied disinfectant swabs and taped the cuts. 'It's not serious,' she said. 'He can hardly have got the car moving when it hit the wall.'

'Should we get him to X-ray?'

'I shouldn't think we need to. But Dr Parrish, perhaps?'

'Yes, of course. I'll ring her.' He turned to Ben and Walter. 'Could you get him upstairs to his bed?'

The men exchanged glances. Walter hung back while Ben bent his huge frame and lifted Neil like a baby in his arms.

★   ★   ★

Dr Parrish was playing Bridge at Bix and unregretfully passed over her disappointing hand. She'd drawn an ineffectual but garrulous partner and was finding no pleasure in the rare evening out. It took only fifteen minutes to charge in her Mini through

328

the empty country lanes to oblige Sir Arthur. When they went upstairs together they found Neil out of bed again and on his feet.

'Say goodnight,' he insisted, and turned towards his mother's room. Dr Parrish regarded him keenly, then shrugged. They followed the young man and were joined by Nurse Howe at the top of the stairs.

Neil went ahead into Lady Waites' bedroom, bent over the still form and laid his face against the cool cheek. She was quiet now. No more of those earlier snorts and throaty gurglings. He had done well to let her rest. Only the slightest pressure on her nostrils, and the heel of his hand over the closed mouth. She had barely noticed. More peaceful now, quite pretty again.

Dr Parrish walked to the other side of the bed, bent over and felt the woman's neck. 'She's slipped away,' she said quietly. 'Not entirely unexpected. I'm sorry, Arthur. It's fortunate you called me out for Neil. I'll drop by with the certificate tomorrow.'

She wouldn't stay for a drink and, having checked on Neil and declared him only in need of rest, she passed the open door of the drawing-room on her way out, noticing the tables set up for roulette and cards. One of the helpers — the burly one — saw her glance in and tried to cover the gap with his substantial body.

Interesting, she thought: so that's how the great mathematical brain relaxes. Rather more of a busman's holiday, to her mind.

She wondered who came here to play, and how much money passed through the house on these occasions. Arthur would do better to find less hazardous pastimes. Now that he was widowed like herself she might persuade him to take the Hellenic cruise she'd been considering off and on. There were a couple of suitable places where Neil could be well looked after temporarily, and an eye kept on what substances he was indulging in beyond the prescribed methadone.

Anything to get them both out of this dreary old house with its depressing background of tragedies. It was time it was pulled down and the land put to good use.

At the front door Waites stood tongue-tied for an instant. 'There will be things to arrange,' she reminded him gently.

'Yes, I suppose.' He frowned. 'Doctor, you must have heard about Mrs Knightley. The murder, I mean.'

'The woman over at Mardham, yes. It was in yesterday's papers. Did you know her?'

'Slightly, through her husband. A thoroughly nice woman. I only heard tonight.'

'I'm sorry, Arthur. So much happening to

upset you all at once. They say bad things often come in threes.'

'Threes?'

'Yes. Hearing of the murder; your son's accident; now Alice. At least Neil's not badly hurt.'

'I see. Yes. Threes.' He watched her get into her little car, reverse and drive off with a wave. Another nice woman, and she appeared to have some feelings towards numbers.

It was true what she said: the happenings seemed to make a set, even a sequence. But there was something that troubled him. He'd been hardly aware of it at the time but it came back now with startling clarity. The dress they'd shown on *Crimewatch* before flashing up Leila's photograph: the dress she'd been found dead in.

He knew it, had bought one like it some twenty-five years ago in Venice. On their honeymoon he'd had it made up for Alice from an Italian fabric she'd fallen in love with. And for sentimental reasons, he supposed, she'd never got rid of it; wore it on special anniversaries which they'd shared alone.

It was impossible, because Alice had chosen the style, so there should only have been the one. And yet he knew he wasn't mistaken. Hers must be here still, in one of her wardrobes.

He went back upstairs, passing Neil's room, the door of which stood wide open. This was unusual. He always shut himself in, hermetically. The boy waved a languid hand now from his chair as his father looked through. Sir Arthur nodded back and went on.

He spent a long time searching wardrobes in the room next to the one where Alice lay. There was such a crush of dresses, but not the one he was looking for. Some had dropped off their hangers and lay on the floor of the cupboard, swirled into a sort of nest as though a large creature had crept in there for asylum. He knew who that must be.

The connections sprang into his mind. Alice's dress; Leila Knightley who, however unlikely, had acquired it; then — through Neil? But how would he ever have met her? He had a few young friends who still visited here, but surely no one of Leila's generation.

His mind swung back to Dr Parrish; her mentioning a threesome of bad news: what had happened to Alice, Neil, Leila. The same three, but in a separate connection.

He went into the next room and asked Nurse Howe to leave for a few minutes. Then he bent over the bed and searched the insides of his dead wife's arms for any sign of a puncture.

Nothing. It was all right. He'd imagined a horror that didn't exist. It had been an illogical leap of the mind. Alice had, as Dr Parrish — Nancy — said, just slipped away after prolonged, exhausting suffering. He felt ashamed of his suspicion, and immeasurably relieved.

★   ★   ★

Walter Pimm reversed the silver Mercedes from the crushed masonry and went round to survey the damage, brushing brickdust and cement rubble off the dented bonnet. Not too bad. Broken left headlamp, twisted grill, a few scratches. A couple of thousand to repair and repaint. Waites could afford that, and anyway they could try the insurance. No one need mention that the driver was debarred.

It could be fortunate in a way. He decided to make Waites an offer. He wouldn't after all want to swan around in the car the way it was. So, get it repaired for him and arrange a temporary substitute.

Simple enough. No pong of suspicion coming off it. Lucky they'd come out to set up the tables tonight for tomorrow's flutter. It gave him something to use to his advantage. And Piggott's. He'd have to call on Ben to help, but then Ben already owed him one. By the time it was all worked out the boss would be in his debt forever.

Ben Carter sat in the shadowed angle below the staircase, worrying about Neil. For some reason he had always felt for him, perhaps because like himself the boy seemed so alone and everyone had given up on him.

At the same time he was angry at Walter, so greedy making money from his sideline that he didn't care what damage the stuff could do.

He watched him come back from outside, then heard him in the kitchen, raking around in the fridge which they'd restocked today. It was only for the household's use: tomorrow caterers would bring the party stuff in a refrigerated van — unless the affair was cancelled now. With a death in the house you often got police nosing round. Whatever Mr Piggott decided, Walter wouldn't want anything putting a brake on his private dealing.

The fridge door slammed. Walter came hurrying through with something in his hands. Ben caught the glint of a plastic bag with redness inside and lumbered to his feet to follow.

In the driveway he saw the Mercedes had been reversed and stood again opposite the entrance. Walter was bending over a smashed headlight and appeared to be wiping something into the rims and through the twisted grill.

Walter always claimed he was the brains of the partnership, which consisted, to Ben's slower mind, of thinking up twisty ways of doing things the big man had been taught as a child were wrong. But it made Walter feel superior, even though physically he was the runt of an unhealthy litter.

The first time he'd shouted, 'Come on, Carter, get carting!' it had struck Ben as clever, but by now he was tired of it, hearing the contempt behind what wasn't a real joke.

He watched Walter straighten, looking pleased with himself. When he half-turned and saw Ben there he attempted to cover up what he was holding. Obligingly Ben looked away. 'You want me to get it repaired?'

'You're not to touch it. I'll take it in myself.'

Ben nodded slowly, wondering why there was a cloth over the steering wheel. Walter was careful sometimes about wiping his fingerprints off things he'd touched. But now he seemed to have forgotten to remove the duster.

Walter followed the direction of his gaze, flicked the cloth off, slammed the driving door, locked it and pocketed Sir Arthur's keys. 'Tomorrow,' he said, 'is another day.'

Back at Knollhurst the phone rang. Charles Hadfield lowered his newspaper and stared at Janey over it. 'Hadn't you better answer the thing?'

It continued to ring. 'Aidan went off in a taxi, and Chloë's gone walking.'

'I'd better then. But it's probably from some newspaper.'

The caller was a man apologizing for ringing after hours. His, Janey supposed; because she functioned for twenty-four.

'I'm calling from Pettifer and Jolly, Mrs Knightley. Well, actually from home, but on the firm's business.'

He gave a little high-pitched bark of laughter. Janey started to explain that she wasn't who he supposed her to be, but he was off again at full steam.

'Now it's short notice I know, but I have a very promising offer here and I'd like to bring the client round to view tomorrow at eleven if that suits you. Otherwise he could make it at 2.30pm.'

'To view?' Janey echoed faintly.

'Yes. Knollhurst. I assured your husband it would meet with a lot of interest at the new price, and I was right. Now, is 11am suitable, Mrs Knightley?'

'Well, I suppose so.'

She stood there gripping the handset after the man rang off. 'Charles,' she said faintly, 'that dreadful man has put this house on the market. The children's home. And Leila not buried yet. That was an agent wanting an appointment to view.'

Hadfield roared and hobbled across. 'Ring him back,' he ordered. Janey obtained the number from 1471 and pressed 3. She handed the phone across but Hadfield shook his head. 'Tell him he can't come. And ask the fellow the price.'

She spoke, listened and made a face at him. 'That's thirty thousand less than he paid.'

'And the date it went on the market?'

'Thank you,' Janey said to the man on the end of the line. She was pale when she faced Charles again. 'Last Friday, the second.'

'That's the day Leila was killed.'

'Yes.'

★   ★   ★

Aidan Knightley returned home to meet judgmental stares. The three of them faced him out about his intention to sell, although Chloë alone was silent, hunched in her chair as though she had stomach cramps.

He was taken aback that they knew, but specious as ever. He claimed he was under no necessity to answer to them for his actions, but must take stock and look to new requirements under changed circumstances.

'What circumstances?' Charles thundered.

'In view of being widowed,' he pointed out stiffly.

The date of his decision hung unspoken in the air between them. 'You said,' Janey whispered, 'that you didn't know Leila was dead until you arrived back here on Sunday.'

He saw at once the mistake he'd made and began to bluster. 'It was a decision I'd already come to. Neither of us found the place came up to standard.'

They had no sympathy for him. Had he expected any? Janey demanded. What sensitivity were they to expect of him when he acted so precipitately, without consulting wife or children? Where were they to set up home again, and who was to look after Eddie and Chloë?

'I have had unexpected expenses,' Knightley ploughed on. 'It is a question of husbanding my resources to do the best for us all. For them in particular. One must be forward-looking.'

'Resources,' Hadfield barked at him. 'Husbanding resources! When did you ever properly husband Leila? Or is that too far past? Who do you intend to husband in future?'

'Nobody if I can help it!' The words came out of themselves in a vicious burst of frustration. He flushed with anger. 'I am not answerable to you. It is for me to decide what I do, where my children shall live.'

'Don't, don't!' pleaded Chloë. 'Please stop. All of you.'

Janey put her arms round the girl. 'At least give yourself breathing space,' she said over her shoulder. 'This is not the right time to make fresh decisions. Let a little time go by, for things to settle.'

Settle, he thought bitterly. That's something I'll not be able to do, unless I release the house value to get Piggott off my back. Those bloody horses. They're as perverse as women.

23

Yeadings took one look at his DI when they assembled next morning and knew that Mott's engagement to Paula was off. Intensive work being the best remedy he knew for anguish, he threw all decisions for that day on to the younger man's shoulders, opting out of active policing himself to catch up with paperwork. It irked him to need to, because he felt in his bones that they were nearing a solution, or at least some recognition of the tangled web of deception that had been set up.

Mott waded in hard-mouthed, assigning duties, setting priorities: Z to accompany him on the immediate pursuit of the dead woman's presumed lover, one Pascal Gregory, British citizen with a Swiss mother, and owner of a green Alfa Romeo tourer, present year's registration.

Beaumont was smarting at being sidelined into chasing up the car that had run down Hetty Chadwick. He felt it the more keenly because there'd been a rumour flashing round the canteen over breakfast that Mott was considering an offer to go as an instructor on this international police-training malarky in Bosnia. That would leave a gap at DI level, with himself and Z as candidates in line for promotion.

A few years back there'd have been nothing in it. He had seniority by length of service. But Z was a woman and PC — political-bloody-correctness as well as Police Constabulary — had ordained that sexual equality should be interpreted with a hefty advantage granted to the weaker sex. Which, to add to the overloading of top ranks with academics, social scientists and blacks, already resulted in poorer performance in thief-taking and proactive policing. He was certain that if Z got the leg-up, instead of the leg-over she needed, he wouldn't be staying on in Yeadings' team.

Sourly then he delegated to DC Silver the task of checking through owners of all light-coloured Mercedes in Berks, Bucks and Oxon, while the other two departed on what looked like a promising trail. Leaving Silver to liaise with Traffic on the computer check he set off at once to take a look at Piggott's car. He found it parked much where he had seen it before, this time backing on to the rear wall of the betting shop, its front resplendent in gleaming, pristine glory. Which seemed, on the face of it, to eliminate the car from suspicion.

But there had been time since Sunday for a well-rewarded mechanic to make any necessary repairs to the bodywork. Although there was no visible evidence of it he was considering having it hauled in for forensic examination (thereby incurring the wrath of the almighty budget-keepers if the result was negative) when Walter Pimm appeared at the shop's back door, a wet cigarette stub attached to his bottom lip.

'Admiring the boss's motor?' he asked matily.

'It's not yours then?'

'I should be so lucky! Get to drive it though. Old Piggott likes to lord it on the back seat.'

'Is he a decent boss? Plenty of perks?'

'He sees I'm all right. Like he should, seeing we was at school together.' Walter was bragging. 'Stinker, we used to call him. His dad owned the fish and chip shop, and they lived over the top. There wasn't no way you could sit next him for the stench of rancid fat.'

'He's come up in the world since then. Nice line in pearl grey mohair suiting,' Beaumont tempted.

'Yeah. Flashy, for all that his flat's like a pigsty. One thing he could do was Maths.

Him and me, we was always top of the class for figuring. Real quick he was. His dad was a mug, went bust over the gee-gees. Didn't take young Jeffrey any time to see where the real money was. With the touts, not the punters. So he got hisself apprenticed to a bookie down Epsom way. When he'd made some dibs he set up here and of course he remembered me.'

'So now you're his manager here, and well on the way up yourself?'

Pimm closed his eyes, looked sneaky. 'I'll do bloody better than him before I'm through.'

'Actually,' Beaumont confessed, deciding to risk all on reading the man's features, 'I'm checking on Mercs at the moment. For crash damage.'

He'd have sworn there was no flicker of reaction, and yet the man's mean little features looked suddenly sleeker, as though his ears had lain back like a nag's when nervous.

'Check here all you want. This old girl's fine. Not a dent, not a smear. In tip-top condition.'

Now who said anything about smears? Beaumont asked himself. Maybe Walter had over-played himself there. 'You polish her?'

'Nuh. We have muscle for that. Have to

find something to justify Ben Carter's wages.'

'Ah. The big guy.'

'A bit simple but he's handy. Thinks he's Jeffrey's bodyguard. Especially — ' Walter's voice took on a spiteful edge. ' — since your lot run the boss in for carrying a knife. Shoulda turned a blind eye. Get a lot of nasty threats from the lowlife when you set up as a turf accountant.'

'Guess so. Where is Ben, by the way?'

Maybe he'd sounded too innocent. Walter's ratty eyes narrowed. 'Sent off on a job somewhere. Carter by name, eh?' He ended on a leer.

Not a great partner to work alongside, Beaumont decided. He wandered off, took a tour to satisfy himself that Ben wasn't in the vicinity and settled in his car to consult by phone with Silver.

He learned there were no less than seven Mercedes in the near neighbourhood, three of them white.

★ ★ ★

While Z drove his Saab, Mott called the number for Pascal Gregory's cottage. On the third ring a man's voice answered. 'Gregory.'

It couldn't have been simpler. He agreed to stay at home and put himself at their disposal. He sounded more curious than alarmed. When he opened the door to them, however, he seemed at least cautious.

'We're making inquiries,' Mott said after they'd shown their IDs, 'into the new people who've moved into Knollhurst, along the road from you. No doubt you've heard that the lady of the house was found murdered about half a mile away.'

'I read it in the papers, yes. And there was a mention on *Crimewatch* last night. It's terrible.'

'Had you met the family?'

'A number of them, yes. Briefly.'

'One of them less briefly?'

'Leila.' His breath came out unevenly. He left his seat and went to stand by the window, looking out. 'It was totally unexpected. I meant only to get to know her because of Chloë. I thought she might be what one hears of stepmothers, neglectful, perhaps worse, although Chloë implied she was fond of her.'

'But — ?' Mott insisted.

'She was delightful. Natural, warm, sympathetic. I — found her very attractive.'

Mott scowled at him. From the man's manner he could only suppose that they'd begun an affair. 'Were you lovers?'

Pascal turned back to face him. 'Yes. It seemed inevitable. She was not a happy woman, Inspector. I wanted to give her everything. I'm not inexperienced, but no one had made me feel like that before.'

Mott's mouth twisted. Z, watching him, thought he looked bitter. 'Did you kill her, Mr Gregory?'

The man was appalled, shattered by the brutality of it. Z was dismissed to the kitchen to make hot drinks while the other two spoke together. She could barely hear the low voices, one hesitant, the other pressing him further. She wanted to believe that the one questioned was being open and genuinely as broken as he seemed.

When she carried the tray through they seemed to have reached some kind of trucc. Mott had removed his tie and loosened his shirt. She wondered for the second time that morning whether he was sickening for something.

'You said at first,' Mott reminded the other, 'that you were curious to meet her because of Chloë, her stepdaughter. How did you come to meet her?'

'In a rainstorm. You remember the deluge that night some weeks ago? A cloudburst, and she was out in it with her bike. We were both caught and she was in a bad way. My sister Morgan was staying over that night, a nurse, and she insisted Chloë should shower and borrow some dry clothes. Then we started to talk.'

'Wasn't that intervention unnecessary, since she lived only a few doors away?'

'Chloë was in a strange mood, reluctant — almost afraid — to go home. It made us curious, especially as — '

He stopped and they waited for him to continue. He picked up his cup and drank before going on. Choosing what not to say, Z thought.

It was an incredible story, or would have been if they hadn't so much experience of similar incidents. The reason Pascal knew so much of it was because his sister, Morgan, had been on hand at the time, although Chloë hadn't recognized her out of uniform.

A few days earlier, the girl Beryl Ryder, whom they took to be Knightley's girlfriend, had taken Chloe out drinking. Unused to alcohol she was deceived by the innocent flavour of the passion fruit concoction. But at the house they'd stopped off at later, something else had happened of which Chloë had only partial and fleeting recall. Morgan believed that some other substance had been used on the girl; something like Midazolam or Rohypnol the 'date-rape' drug. But being unsure and not knowing who was responsible, Morgan had simply given her an emetic

347

to reduce the effect.

The Ryder girl had phoned Chloë's home and by then the father had returned. He left at once to collect her, promising she should be taken straight to A&E at High Wycombe hospital. Which, it seemed, she wasn't.

'Your sister will need to confirm all this. It's useless as hearsay.'

'Useless in court maybe, but it should put you on the right path. Morgan hoped it could all be settled at family level, without scandal to innocent parties.'

'It doesn't sound,' Mott said witheringly, 'as if there are any innocent parties. Your sister, for instance; how did she become involved? I'll need the address of this house and to know who — '

He was interrupted by the house phone ringing. Gregory stared at him and raised his shoulders expressively. 'Answer if you wish. It may be for you. No one would expect me to be here after 10am.'

Mott strode across and lifted the receiver. Without waiting for acceptance a woman's voice rushed at him. 'Pascal, thank God you're there. I've tried everywhere else. Listen, we'll have to talk to the police. There was a *Crimewatch* programme last night . . . '

Mott crashed through. 'Am I speaking to

348

Miss Morgan Gregory? This is Detective-Inspector Angus Mott, Thames Valley Police. Can you come to your brother's cottage at once? We have a lot to straighten out between you both.'

She couldn't, being on duty and involved in arrangements for an unexpected funeral. She sounded almost distraught.

Mott's reaction was electric. 'Then we will come to you. Will you give me the address? Yes. Havelock House, Stonor, near Henley-on-Thames. Has your local police station been advised of the sudden death? Right. Please ask the coroner's officer to wait there for us.'

'Who's died? Do you want me to come?' Gregory asked when Mott had hung up.

As Mott hesitated he said, 'I want to. Morgan may need my support.'

'In that case my sergeant will accompany you in your car.'

★   ★   ★

Beaumont had run Ben Carter to earth at last. The big man was in the cellar at the Three Tuns organising a spirits, wine and beer order. It was impressive the effortless way he lifted full barrels around. Bill Preston, licensee, stood at the top of the stairs to

349

ensure the detective took no liberties with his stock once he'd let him go down.

'I just want a word,' Beaumont began, squatting on a metal barrel and finding it struck a chill through his terylene pants. Ben Carter wiped his hands on his trousers. 'What about, Mr Beaumont?'

'Jeffrey Piggott's car. You keep it all smart and shiny, don't you?'

'He's got two.'

'It's the Merc I'm interested in. You clean it, yes?'

'Most times. He likes it kept nice.'

'It looked great when I saw it this morning. When did you last do it over?'

'Friday. He wanted it next day to take the two kids to Brighton.'

'Oh yes, I remember now. That's a long time for it to stay so spotless. Today's Wednesday. You must use something special on it.'

Ben looked puzzled. 'No, it must be real mucky. Always gets spotty at the seaside. It's the salt, see? Then it got left in London, wheel-clamped, on Sunday and I haven't seen it since.'

'So who tarted it up?'

'I dunno. It wasn't about yesterday. I asked the boss and he said Walter'd borrowed it. Mr Piggott was running the Citroën.'

'Mr Piggott had the Citroën and Walter

Pimm had the Merc. That right?'

'Like I said.'

'So Walter would have cleaned it.'

'That'd be the day! You wouldn't get him driving through a car wash. Anyways the boss makes sure it's hand-polished. We don't trust them gritty cloths at garages.'

'Thanks, Ben. You're right to take care of a beautiful car like that.'

The licensee had been called away to duties at ground floor level. Beaumont readjusted his cooled buttocks and grinned at the big man. 'Looks like a real party you're setting up, with all that booze.'

Ben arf-arfed like a cartoon dog. 'One of Mr Piggott's specials over at Henley. We go over and help, me and Walter. Real toff clothes with black bows.'

'Dinner jackets and black ties? I bet you look good.'

'Mine had to be made special because I'm big, but Walter's got Mr Piggott's old one cut down.'

Parties and quality dinner jackets, Beaumont registered. Weren't they just the things he'd spent hours fruitlessly trying to hunt up over the Leila Knightley murder? He took a deep breath.

'And the guests all dress up, wear masks? Things like that?'

Ben was nodding, his heavy face transformed with a vast smile. 'Lovely, the ladies are. Some play the tables and some dance.'

'So who gives these parties, Ben?'

'A gentleman Mr Piggott's partners in it with. Sir Arthur something.'

'Oh, I see. Posh people.'

'I'll say.'

Sir Arthur, near Henley: that ought to be enough for the local nick to come up with an address. Beaumont slid off his barrel, satisfied. He reached the stairs to go up when Ben said reminiscently. 'He's got a nice one too. Sir Arthur.'

Beaumont turned back. 'A nice what?'

'Merc. Only his is silver. And it's usually got mud splashes.'

He disapproved. But Beaumont was in seventh heaven.

24

Beaumont received an odd look from the desk constable at Henley when he made his request. The name of Havelock House and its owner was ready to hand. 'Lotta activity out there today. What's up?'

'You tell me.'

'Second request for info from your lot today. You're on Mr Yeadings' team, aren't you?'

Beaumont treated him to his wooden puppet stare. He didn't intend trading questions all day. He simply needed directions. The constable got the message and produced a local map.

'Take no notice of these lanes,' he advised, running a pencil point through them. 'Go straight out towards Wycombe to this cross, then take a left turn and left again. It's longer but it's quicker, and less chance you'll get lost.'

For starters that wasn't entirely encouraging, and when he did turn in at the open gates of Sir Arthur Waites' home his spirits sank at sight of the cars drawn up before the doors. Central to the group was Angus Mott's Saab.

'Pipped at the bloody post,' Beaumont told himself in disgust.

A fifty-ish woman in a willow green trouser-suit came out of the house and went to delve inside a battered Mini. She emerged with what looked like a doctor's bag. Beaumont accosted her with his ID open.

'Ah,' she said, 'another. I do hope you'll take a discreet line. Everyone is naturally upset.' Behind her two almost identical men in black started bringing out a coffin.

Beaumont felt his hunter's blood stir in his veins. 'Before you start sedating anyone,' he said sternly to cover his bluff, 'we need to know exactly what happened here.'

She wasn't impressed. 'That is presently the concern of your Inspector Mott. Excuse me. I have a patient to attend to.'

He followed her in. On her way upstairs she passed Rosemary Zyczynski coming down. 'Hi,' Z greeted him, surprised. 'What brings you here?' She came out to the door.

'Waites' Mercedes.'

'But it's out of action.'

He looked at her sadly. It wasn't his day for getting things straight the first time. He explained why the car was his subject of interest. 'Are you telling me it isn't here?'

Z gazed around. 'Behind the undertaker's van.' She waved towards where the coffin was being slid into a windowless vehicle with a high top. 'But it's had quite a dent.'

'Splendid. So who's the stiff?'

'Lady Waites,' she said, glaring. Then to cut off whatever gaffe his delighted expression threatened, 'Natural death after a long illness.'

'So where's His Nibs?'

'Which one? Angus is with Sir Arthur. So Sir Arthur's with Angus. Look, if you want the car, shouldn't you take a look while it's still here? It's due to be sent for repair.'

Beaumont hesitated. He had a fancy to sneak in on whatever Mott was about. The DI certainly wasn't following up a death from natural causes. But the sooner the Merc's damage was checked the sooner he could get it plastic-wrapped for forensic examination. At any moment now some oaf might try to get in and drive it away.

He wove his way between the parked vehicles and went round to the front. It looked promising: damage at the right level for the accident as Chloe had described it. What he wasn't keen on was the faint powdering of brickdust in places. Which might be a cunning attempt to explain away the broken headlamp and twisted grill: cover an accident with an accident.

The condition of the nearby archway

suggested it had featured in some cosmetic rearrangement. But if any trace of blood lay underneath, the lab experts would find it.

He used his mobile to call up Traffic support and reconciled himself to indefinitely standing guard.

Z collected her tape recorder from Mott's car, relocked it and returned indoors. She found the atmosphere in the upstairs sitting-room tense. Sir Arthur, seated by the window, looked ashen; Dr Parrish, hovering protectively over him, forbidding.

'I can only say,' the man admitted in a stricken voice, 'that it's not impossible. But I know nothing about it myself.'

Mott placed the recorder on the table beside him. 'Tell us again about the dress. When do you last recall seeing it?'

Dr Parrish tried to intervene, but Sir Arthur was quite willing to produce what facts were available. At the end he raised his hands, palm upwards. 'You've already spoken to Nurse Gregory. She must be able to explain better than I could. I didn't know until now that this girl had been here.'

'The nurse has confirmed that you weren't present on the evening of Friday, June twelve. Which is why we wish to speak to everyone who was. I understand that late that night Professor Knightley called here to pick up his daughter who was in a semi-comatose state. Was he familiar with the house? It wouldn't have been easy to find for the first time in the dark.'

'I had entertained him here twice before.'

'With his wife, perhaps?'

'No. He came in a group of academics interested in mathematical equations.'

Euphemism for Piggott's gambling set-up, Mott assumed. 'He was unaccompanied, then?'

'The second time there was a young woman with him.'

'Do you know her name?'

'He referred to her as Beryl. That's all I was told. She also appeared to be known to my son, but was not a family friend.'

'So has Mrs Knightley ever been here, to your knowledge?'

'Not — to my knowledge.'

It went on painfully, painstakingly, with Waites holding nothing back. But with every answer he was clearly more disturbed.

'Thank you, Sir Arthur, for your help.'

'That's all?'

'I may need to speak with you again. Now I should like to see your son, then the two casino ushers who were present the night Chloë Knightley was brought here.'

'I'm not sure about Neil,' the doctor put in

quickly. 'His mother's death has shaken him badly, however long expected.'

'Is he sedated?'

She hesitated. So concerned for Arthur, she hadn't checked this morning on the boy. He could be hungover, stoned afresh or simply shattered. Anything she could offer him might well form a dangerous cocktail.

'I should like to be present.' Waites raised a haggard face and Mott wondered again. 'How old is he?'

'Twenty.'

'Legally of age. There is no requirement for a responsible adult to be present. So we'll see what he feels about it.'

Waites rose, uncertain what state the young man's room might be in, but afraid that interviewing him elsewhere — in alien territory — could provoke an unhelpful reaction.

'I'll see how he is,' Dr Parrish offered.

'Nancy, thank you.'

The affection in the man's voice alerted Mott's baser suspicions. Was the widower truly grieving, and would the lady doctor's death certificate be genuine? How many nasty creatures would crawl out as all the stones were turned over in this case?

Henley nick had already provided some general background: that Havelock House had been in the dead woman's family for generations. Doubtless there had been money too on that side of the alliance. In which case Waites stood to inherit.

Mott moved across and held the curtain aside to peer down into the driveway. A blue pick-up containing a number of large potted plants had just driven up and with surprise he recognised the car parked ahead of it as Beaumont's.

As he watched, the pick-up's driver, a small man, swung down and went to the rear to unload. Mott's DS stood up from crouching in front of a silver Mercedes and went jauntily to confront the man. Through the closed window Mott was unable to hear what they said.

* * *

'Mr Pimm,' Beaumont greeted the newcomer expansively. 'What an unexpected pleasure.'

'Mister Beaumont.' Irony wasn't the man's natural style and it came out bitterly. He wasn't unloading, just releasing the truck's rear gate. Ben Carter came shambling out of the house to take on the heavy stuff.

'Both of you.' Beaumont beamed. 'How very fortunate. Is Mr Piggott inside as well?

It's good to play with a full deck. I see you're into horticulture.'

'A few plants on hire to brighten up the place,' Pimm excused them.

'A celebration with potted palms? Rather unusual for a wake, I'd have thought.'

'Wake?'

'You haven't heard. There's been a death in the family.'

'Who?' demanded Pimm. Again Beaumont had the sense of the man's ears flattening against the sides of his head.

'Her Ladyship,' Ben mumbled. 'She passed away last night.'

'Never met her,' Pimm grunted, relieved.

'So Mr Piggott's little casino party may have to be postponed. Never mind. I take it you're familiar with the place. And the people. Not to mention their cars. Now why didn't you? — mention the cars, that is, and one in particular, when you knew I was interested in Mercs.'

A sly look passed over the weasely features. 'Didn't want to make no trouble, did I? Anyways, it's silver, not white.'

'Much the same to look at, in a dark lane when you're leaping for your life.'

'So you've had a dekko at it.' Pimm was probing.

'And it seems to fit the bill. It's a tad bent.

Not so much as some people I know, but enough to qualify.'

Beaumont had time to register the flash of satisfaction on the man's face before Ben broke in. 'That happened last night. Young Mr Neil ran it into a wall. I had to get him out. His head was bleeding.'

'In the driving seat, yes? But not over the radiator grill?' He watched them both and wondered if his bluff had come off. Pimm had frozen, ready prepared, but Ben had a weird expression of puzzlement, shaking his head.

'Let's go indoors,' the DS suggested, 'and I can take down your statements.'

*   *   *

Neil's 'room' was in fact a suite with sitting-room, study and bedroom connected by broad archways. As Mott entered, the young man was seated unnaturally upright in a chair facing him with the grim-browed doctor behind, a hand on his shoulder.

'My son, Neil,' Waites said flatly.

One glance at the pale flesh, sunken cheeks and haunted eyes gave Mott a fierce upsurge of excitement. This was it. Here was the reason for Waites' defensiveness and the woman's truculence. He would need to

361

proceed carefully. He shook his head at Z's questioning eyes and she put away the recorder. Not now; later, in a different place.

'Neil,' he began pleasantly, 'we're here to talk about Chloë. Do you remember where you first met her?'

He looked up. 'Saw her. In the library.'

'Here, at Havelock House?'

'He means the public library,' his father interrupted. 'I take him there sometimes. Or he goes by taxi.'

'So you don't drive a car, Neil?'

The young man stared back, uninterested.

'He lost his licence after an accident eighteen months ago,' Waites explained. 'He hasn't driven since.'

'To your knowledge.' He turned back to Neil. 'You drove your father's car last night, though.'

'Going to see her.' There was a little more life in the eyes now.

'You didn't get far. That was unfortunate. Better, perhaps, if she came to you here.'

'Chloë — ' He went quiet again, lethargic. Mott wondered if the doctor had slipped him a sedative before they met up.

'Did you go out to her house on Sunday night? In your father's car? She was walking with a friend in the dark, wasn't she?'

Again no reaction. Try another tack, Mott told himself.

'A lovely girl. Did you meet her mother? Her stepmother actually.'

Neil shook his head.

'She was lovely too,' Mott reminisced. 'Another one with red hair, but dyed, I think.'

'Dyed. She died,' Neil echoed. 'Cheat, cheat!'

Mott's eyes met Z's again. She went out into the corridor and phoned for back-up to take the young man in.

★ ★ ★

Superintendent Yeadings received the news that Leila Knightley's killer was in the building as he strove to put order and a modicum of good grammar into DC Silver's report on his computer researches. A promising technocrat the lad might be, but basic English had apparently escaped his curriculum.

Patting his pockets before remembering that pipe and tobacco were now consigned to history, Yeadings made his way down to Interview Room I.

The sight of Neil Waites shocked him. He had seen many before reduced to wrecks by concentrated use of illegal substances and he knew the lengths of amoral behaviour they were capable of. He thought he recognised here a victim-criminal.

He didn't doubt for a moment that Mott had picked the right man, but in his present state he would surely be found unfit to plead. Then, after the long delays of the law, by the time he was finally detained at Her Majesty's pleasure, something of the original man might have been rehabilitated. But the damage was done, the crime still committed and a life lost. The psychiatrists wouldn't consider that when they eventually declared him fit to be let loose again among innocents in the community.

He sat listening for only a few minutes to Mott's careful questioning with Z alongside before he left. Z intoned, 'Superintendent Yeadings is leaving the room,' for the benefit of the tape.

A middle-aged couple he took to be the parents were sitting in Reception. Almost as a penance he introduced himself and escorted them to his office, offered coffee and a willing ear.

'I can't believe it,' Waites said. 'Neil's such a gentle boy.'

The woman explained she was the family doctor, but not how she came to have neglected the young man's physical condition. 'The damage was already done at Oxford,' she said, seeing his disbelief.

'Nobody at home knew anything until after he was sent down and we heard he was living in a squat in Reading. They were a group of drug addicts, thieving to support the habit, the girls employed as prostitutes. Believe me, he is much improved from then. At least he keeps himself clean and takes a little nourishment. He is prescribed methadone as a heroin substitute, but I fear he's using other substances. Whoever is dealing to him has an eclectic taste in drugs. I suspect that person must have access to hospital supplies. I've found a positive reaction to one or two medical specialities as well as to diamorphine, which you'd know better as heroin. It makes it very difficult to treat him safely.'

'I'm surprised you didn't insist he was sent as an inpatient to a drugs rehabilitation centre.'

'There was an extra problem.'

'His mother,' Waites explained. 'My wife had been almost totally incapacitated after a car crash just before Neil went to university. I believe that was behind his sudden collapse of morale. She was making no progress in hospital and I had her moved home, with nurses in attendance. Neil and she had always

365

been particularly close, so we did all we could to keep them together. I still believe we made the right decision. Nancy — Dr Parrish — has been a tower of strength to me.'

'Your wife's nurses, could they be supplying the drugs to your son?'

Dr Parrish intervened. 'I vetted them myself and they have impeccable reputations. Also they were well aware of the dangers of contact with Neil and the need to stay above suspicion. In any case, since Lady Waites passed away yesterday evening, they will not be returning to the house once they've cleared up after their patient.'

Nor, sadly, will Neil, Yeadings thought. Which can prove nothing. 'My inspector mentioned an accident that also happened last night,' he prompted Waites, 'when your son received an injury to his forehead.'

'That happened just as we found my wife had — had slipped away. Our attention was entirely on that and we didn't notice what Neil was up to. He'd taken my keys from the hall table and driven my car straight at an outside wall. It was no accident, Superintendent. I think in his head he wanted to kill himself, in the same way that had eventually killed his mother.'

There was little more Yeadings could do for them, except take them downstairs again to wait until such time as Mott was through with the questioning. Then, he promised, they should see Neil for a few minutes.

In the hall, waiting on the same bench they'd used, was a large ungainly figure in overalls who rose at sight of them.

'Why, Ben,' Waites said, 'what are you doing here, man?'

'Young Mr Neil, sir, is he all right?' The man was distressed.

'He's with the police now, Ben. They're having to talk to him.'

'But he's done nothing wrong!'

Waites' face twisted bitterly. 'They think they have enough to charge him.'

'What with?' Ben Carter looked at Yeadings. He shook his head.

Bitterly Waites opted to list the alleged offences as he understood them. 'Abduction of a young person and murder of a woman by strangulation. The police have found a length of the woman's hair in Neil's room. Also — although it's impossible — he's suspected of attempted murder by running two other women down with my car. It's being examined now, apparently for traces of blood.'

'No,' Ben Carter exploded. 'He never did and it wasn't your car. They'll be able to tell, won't they, that the blood's not human?'

'If it isn't,' said Yeadings quietly, 'what is it?'

'A deer's. My boss went out poaching and brought back a young one to cut up. You'll find some of the venison in the fridge at Sir Arthur's.'

'Who is your boss?' Dr Parrish demanded. 'Did you know, Arthur, what was going on under your roof?'

'Not the half of it, apparently. You mean Piggott's been illegally shooting game?'

'But how did its blood get on the car?' Yeadings wondered aloud. 'Did someone run a deer down?'

'No, it was put there, so the police wouldn't look elsewhere for another Merc.'

'I think,' Yeadings decided firmly, 'this needs sorting out.'

25

Mott was confident they needed to look no farther for Leila's killer. In a written statement Neil had wretchedly agreed that a woman wearing a bird mask and 'Chloë's dress' had visited Havelock House on the night of the Venetian carnival. He was less clear what had happened to her subsequently.

A blood sample taken from him by the duty police surgeon had proved to be of the same general group as the second type found on the mask. DNA would later determine whether the two samples were identical. Neil admitted that he had somehow cut his left hand on a broken mirror that night but seemed not to understand that this had any special significance.

It remained now to find witnesses who had seen Leila in his company. For this Mott referred to the Boss, who was involved with interviewing both of Piggott's men alternately in separate rooms.

After his first outburst about the blooding of the Merc, Ben had clammed up. While he was eager to exonerate Neil, he wouldn't point the blame elsewhere. Pimm was uncooperative from the start, snapping out, 'No comment!' cockily after each question. Both had declined the offer of a brief, but Pimm had used his permitted phone call to contact Piggott, who arrived half an hour later with Paddy Mellor in tow. The lawyer pleaded non-involvement for his client and Pimm was allowed to leave.

Recognizing the solicitor as an age-honoured opponent, Mott decided to sit in on the recorded interviews.

'We haven't had a lot of assistance from your employees so far,' Yeadings greeted the bookie sweetly. 'So it is good of you to volunteer your help.' Which is how Piggott came to be requiring the brief's support for himself.

He blusteringly denied poaching deer. He had no idea how venison came to be in Sir Arthur's fridge. He had done nothing whatsoever to Sir Arthur's car, not having been near Havelock House since overseeing the tables at the previous Friday's gaming. He had a cast-iron alibi for last night. He'd attended a Rotarian dinner, arrived back at his flat at 2am and allowed a buddy to kip in a sleeping-bag on his sitting-room floor.

Reassured by so much denial, Yeadings assumed an air of innocent surprise. 'Then if you didn't interfere with the car, who did?' he asked.

Paddy Mellor requested a moment to consult with his client and the pair were left together to concoct a suggestion.

As Yeadings had expected, Piggott opted to cover himself by sacrificing another. 'Pimm borrowed my gun a week back,' he claimed. 'I didn't know what for until he dumped all this meat on me and said he'd buried the animal's head, feet and offal in the woods. And I still don't know anything about any-bloody-body's Merc except my own.'

'Which had bodywork repairs carried out during the night of this Sunday-Monday.'

The man's indignation wasn't feigned. He roared denial and accused the police of stitching him up.

'Then to prove your point, you won't object to forensic examination of the vehicle?'

Piggott, aglow with anger, was forced to concede the point.

'One down; two to go,' Z murmured as Piggott left, to be replaced by Carter. 'Not getting Pimm back, sir?' Z queried.

'We're saving him for the sweet course.'

Ben Carter was shaken at having — however briefly — seen the inside of a police cell. He knew it shouldn't happen to a law-abiding person like himself.

'That's what comes of keeping bad company,' Yeadings said sadly. 'Though it's hard to avoid when you're obliged to work together.'

Ben considered this and decided the Superintendent was referring to Walter Pimm.

'It's all right, Ben. Mr Piggott has been in with his solicitor and made a full statement. Your partner Walter Pimm will be charged later today. All we need now is your confirmation of what he's been up to.'

The big man's face lost all its puckered lines. 'That's a relief, Mr Yeadings. I wouldn't want to grass on him, but if my boss says so, I will.'

'Right. The deer's blood first then.'

'Well, we had all this meat Mr Piggott had shot, see? So he said let Sir Arthur have a load. Then last night, after young Mr Neil had run his dad's car into the wall I saw Walter smearing venison blood on it out of the fridge. Not a lot, mind. He wiped some on and then he wiped it off. Left a bit round the broken headlamp.'

'Why do you suppose he did that?'

'He wanted it found with blood on. So Neil would get into trouble. There'd been a hit-and-run Sunday night. I heard it on local news. That's when Walter had brought back

Mr Piggott's Mercedes from London. And it was away until the evening after. It came back all shiny-bright and new. I knew I hadn't polished it. I reckon Walter knew sommat about that accident.'

'What if I told you we don't think it was an accident?'

Ben shook his head in disbelief.

'Two women were the victims. A Mrs Hetty Chadwick — know her? No? And young Chloë Knightley.'

'Chloë!' The word exploded from him as if he'd been stung. 'That's young Mr Neil's friend. He'll be that upset.'

'So why should Walter Pimm deliberately want to hurt a nice girl like that?'

'So she wouldn't talk.' He seemed to have answered without thinking.

'Exactly,' Yeadings agreed, still uncertain but bluffing like mad. 'And we all know what about, don't we?'

Ben looked puzzled. 'But Mr Piggott can't have told you that. He didn't know about what Walter was doing on the side. Walter said he'd slit my gizzard if I said anything. And he would, if his job was at risk. He can be savage when his blood's up. I guess he uses as well as deals. He goes crazy sometimes. That's how I think — '

'Yes?'

' — how the other one died.'

'The other one?'

'In the mask. She was all right when Mr Neil left her to get his fix. He won't use a needle when anyone's there. Then Walter went into his room and I heard them shouting, the woman and him. She sounded a bit drunk-like, talking about some white powder her daughter had been given. I moved off a bit so I couldn't hear. Then Walter came storming out and said he wished he'd left her gagged, because when he tore the tape off her mouth she gave him an earful, threatening him. So he'd shut her up.'

'You never actually saw her?'

'Not then.'

'So when?'

'A bit later. Some guests had started to arrive for the party. Walter said we had to get rid of her before she upset everyone. So he closed the door on the gaming room and we walked her out between us. She'd passed out by then. He was going to leave her in the spinney to sober up, only then we found her car under the trees and he put her inside. He said he'd drive her home later and that's the last I saw of her.'

'When did you realise she was dead?'

'When I heard it on the news. 'The body of a woman . . . ' I started to wonder. Then yesterday, in the *Star* it said about a bird mask. So I knew for sure it was her. Poor lady, she'd had all her lovely hair cut off. Walter said Neil had done that in a temper.'

'And he couldn't let her live to tell about what he'd done to her stepdaughter? I see.'

'No! Not Mr Neil. He wouldn't kill anyone. It had to be Walter, because she'd guessed he was dealing.'

'So where was Neil when you both took the woman away?'

'He'd jumped out the window. I found him crying in the shrubbery when I came back from putting her in her car.'

'The car's still missing. A red Volvo. So will Walter have destroyed it?'

Ben thought a moment. 'No. He wouldn't waste it. He'd want to sell it on. He knows some car dealers.' Who would do a repaint job, swap licence plates and have it on the continent within hours, Yeadings appreciated.

'Thank you, Mr Carter. This young lady will take you to the canteen now for some lunch, while I get the recording typed up for you to sign. And we'll need your signature there too on the tape, with the date. And here's your copy.'

Ben stood up, still a little uneasy. He pocketed the tape. 'There won't be anybody there as I know, like? In the canteen?'

'Don't worry. Walter Pimm will be closeted with me. We'll use separate doors.'

Z enjoyed watching Ben eat. He put the food away as if a great burden was off his mind. There was only one piece of information she pursued with him between mouthfuls.

'I expect they'll have cancelled the gambling for tonight.'

'Yes. Because of Sir Arthur's wife, poor soul.'

'All those preparations for nothing. You probably enjoy dressing up for these party nights. Where do you keep your posh gear?'

'We use a gardener's room out at the back for changing, Walter and me. So we always leave our dinner jackets there and Sir Arthur has them valeted for us.'

Right, Z marked up invisibly: one item of concrete evidence to be picked up asap. The large suit would be Ben's made-to-measure. The smaller one, cut down from one of Piggott's, so probably of superior quality, would be the one which Pimm had worn when he garrotted Leila. And, almost certainly, it would also provide fibre identical to that found under her nails.

'Oh, one other thing,' she remembered to ask. 'What was Neil wearing that night, when you found him in the shrubbery?'

A flood of red travelled up Ben's neck and suffused his face. He avoided her eyes to answer. 'Nothing. He was as naked as the day he was born.'

★   ★   ★

Mott too was now on the track of evidence. Interviewing Pimm along with Beaumont, his eyes narrowed. 'Are you a religious man, Mr Pimm?'

Walter's reply was blasphemous by any standard. Then, 'Why?' reeking with suspicion.

'I thought you might be wearing a cross round your neck.'

Pimm's hand darted to the grubby cord barely discernible at the edge of his open collar.

'What, this? I carry me key there. Ben Carter and me share rooms, see? And I get to hold the key. Wouldn't trust it to a numbskull like him.'

Understandably he would want to keep control. That was the sort of him. Mott rasped a hand over his chin. 'One moment.'

Beaumont murmured for the tape, 'DI Mott is leaving the room. Interview suspended 14.40.' He switched off the recording. 'You want a mug of tea or something. No?'

Andrew Beale was custody sergeant. He nodded as Mott gave his instructions. 'Is this kosher, sir?'

'It will be, if the Super's on the right line. We'll hold Pimm until the lab has checked. If it's spot on then his stay could be more permanent.'

Beaumont ushered out a protesting Pimm wild at the idea of being 'banged up'. He emptied his pockets with a bad grace.

'Rings, watch, money, jewellery,' Beale intoned, not looking up. 'You get a receipt and can check when your stuff's returned.' He reversed the pad for Pimm to sign the form. 'What's that round your neck?'

'Me bloody key. You're not having that.'

'Believe me, Mr Pimm. We are. Let's have your shoelaces too while we're about it.'

Pimm was assigned to Cell 4 and his name chalked up on the slate outside. Then Beale returned to inspect with distaste the greasy knot he was obliged to undo. An inch of the cord would be enough for the lab, Mott had said. Then DS Beaumont was to borrow the key for a quick shufty round the man's rooms when the search warrant came through.

★ ★ ★

At a little after 4pm a trace came in on Beryl Ryder and her mother. Dublin Gardai faxed through that the two women sought as witnesses had booked into the Phoenix Park Hotel there.

'We need Beryl's angle on what happened when she handed Chloë over to Neil Waites on that first occasion,' Yeadings told Mott. 'If you suddenly turn up at her hotel when she's holidaying on Knightley's handout it could be shock enough to squeeze the truth out of her. I'll authorise your flight. You can team up with an Irish WPC at the other end.'

Which left only the Knightleys to speak with before he settled to building up the case on paper. Beaumont had relieved Z of Ben Carter's company and was taking him as witness to his search of the rooms he shared with Pimm. The hoped-for object of this was a drugs cache, but if they also turned up a length of cord identical to the sample held, and tallying with microscopic marks on Leila's neck, then that would be a bonus.

★ ★ ★

Through the drawing-room window at Knollhurst, Charles Hadfield saw Yeadings' Rover draw up, and went himself to let the detective in.

379

'Superintendent, what news?'

'We've arrested a man on suspicion of attempted murder, but he's not yet been charged.'

'Attempted? I don't understand.'

'Concerning the hit-and-run. We believe now that Chloë was the intended victim but she was nippy enough to get clear. Nearly pulled Hetty free too, brave lass.'

Hadfield looked appalled, then disappointed. 'That's splendid, but I was hoping you'd got someone for killing Leila.'

'Between ourselves, Mr Hadfield, we're hoping to press more serious charges when material evidence is substantiated. Rest assured; it's all in hand. How is Chloë now?'

'I'm all right,' said a cool voice from the doorway. 'I've had another session over the phone with the Gregorys' mother in Montreux and that's helped a lot. She's a shrink, you see.' She pulled a childish face. 'Must've cost the earth but I don't care any more about running up huge phone bills.'

'A sense of proportion,' Yeadings agreed, beaming. 'That's what a quiet life's really about. I was hoping to have a word with you if you felt up to it. There are one or two missing patches in your story that I might be able to fill in now.'

'I'd like that. The blanks have been bugging

380

me. Once it's all properly come back I want to forget it entirely this time.'

'Did you ever meet Neil Waites before that night? He said he'd seen you first in the public library.'

She shook her head. 'He used to leave messages there later. That's when I felt I was being stalked.'

'It won't happen again. He's going voluntarily into a nursing home for treatment, though it's doubtful he'll ever completely recover. The drugs have damaged his brain irreversibly.

'If he comes out, and if you wish it,' Yeadings suggested, 'he can be charged with abducting and holding you without your consent, and sexual assault. That would mean your having to give evidence in court and live through it again.'

Chloë shuddered. 'No. I want it to be over. It's enough living with what happened to Leila. I'll never get over the awful gap she's left. She was my real mother, you know; no matter who birthed me.'

Janey stayed with the girl while Hadfield saw him out. 'D'you remember,' the older man said on the doorstep, 'once calling Janey Mrs Hadfield? I've decided it's time I put that right. It'll make a better case for claiming the children. Actually Chloë's the only one underage, and it's unthinkable leaving her with her father. Then when Eddie comes back from America he'll want to share a home with his sister.

'Knightley's had a sort of breakdown; confessed to me this Beryl girl was blackmailing him to marry her. Claimed she was pregnant, but he had his doubts. He had to buy her off, on top of gambling debts. It leaves him short of cash, so I've offered to buy the house. Leila liked it and that's good enough for me. Can't go uprooting the child any more, eh?'

Yeadings grasped the man's hand. 'I wish you all the best.'

★ ★ ★

He found Beaumont and Zyczynski had taken over his office and presumed to get the coffeemaker going. 'We saw your car drive in,' Z said in excuse.

They were both grinning like monkeys. There was nothing like success to give the team an infusion of goodfellowship. Jeffrey Piggott had just been charged with illegal slaughter of a deer.

'Is Walter Pimm talking yet?'

'Silent as the grave,' Beaumont assured him. 'But we've got him on the lot: dealing;

attempted murder of Chloë; strangulation of her stepmother; and attempting to pervert the course of justice.'

Yeadings sighed. ' 'That man's silence is wonderful to listen to,' ' he quoted.

He saw Z grasped the quotation but couldn't place it.

'Under the Greenwood Tree,' he supplied. 'Hardy.'

Beaumont looked more wooden. 'That'd be a Laurel then?'

Good, Yeadings thought, watching Z wince, then smile: Beaumont's in punny form again. Team harmony's restored.

But heaven help us when Mott pulls out. That's when the sparks will really start to fly.

THE END

We do hope that you have enjoyed reading this large print book.

Did you know that all of our titles are available for purchase?

We publish a wide range of high quality large print books including:
Romances, Mysteries, Classics
General Fiction
Non Fiction and Westerns

Special interest titles available in large print are:
The Little Oxford Dictionary
Music Book
Song Book
Hymn Book
Service Book

Also available from us courtesy of Oxford University Press:
Young Readers' Dictionary
(large print edition)
Young Readers' Thesaurus
(large print edition)

For further information or a free brochure, please contact us at:
Ulverscroft Large Print Books Ltd.,
The Green, Bradgate Road, Anstey,
Leicester, LE7 7FU, England.
Tel: (00 44) 0116 236 4325
Fax: (00 44) 0116 234 0205

Other titles published by
The House of Ulverscroft:

COLD HANDS

Clare Curzon

A dead body is found on a railway line — a straightforward suicide, or something more sinister? When the dead man is identified as a customs officer investigating counterfeit currency, it seems like more than just a coincidence. Superintendent Mike Yeadings is suspicious, so he sends his undercover team, including DI Mott and DS Zyczinski, to Fraylings Court and the heart of the operation

DEATH PRONE

Clare Curzon

Bachelor recluse Hadrian Bascombe has summoned his family to announce his imminent death. They learn that his fortune is to pass to a single beneficiary whom he will choose from among them that night. However, when the company leaves he has given no more than cryptic hints of his intentions. On their way home the two youngest guests meet with a serious accident. When further violence reduces the number of potential heirs, Superintendent Mike Yeadings of the Thames Valley Police follows an intuitive line, which ends in confrontation with an embittered killer.